Shifting
Gears

D1430482

Shifting Gears by Melanie Moreland
Copyright © 2022 Moreland Books Inc.
Copyright ©1190982
ISBN Ebook 978-1-988610-85-6
Paperback 978-1-988610-92-4

MORELAND
BOOKS INC.

Edited by Lisa Hollett — Silently Correcting Your Grammar
Cover design by Karen Hulseman FeedYourDreamsDesigns.com
Photographer Eric D Battershell — O'Snap Media
Model Burton Hughes
Cover content is for illustrative purposes only and any person depicted on the
cover is a model.

Dear Reader,

Thank you for selecting Shifting Gears to read. Be sure to sign up for my newsletter for up to date information on new releases, exclusive content and sales. You can find the form here: https://bit.ly/MMorelandNewsletter

Before you sign up, add melanie@melaniemoreland.com to your contacts to make sure the email comes right to your inbox!
Always fun - never spam!

My books are available in paperback and audiobook! You can see all my books available and upcoming preorders at my website.

The Perfect Recipe For **LOVE**
xoxo,
Melanie

ALSO BY MELANIE MORELAND

The Contract Series

The Contract (Contract #1)

The Baby Clause (Contract #2)

The Amendment (Contract #3)

The Addendum Coming to Radish 2022 - Wide Release 2023

Vested Interest Series

BAM - The Beginning (Prequel)

Bentley (Vested Interest #1)

Aiden (Vested Interest #2)

Maddox (Vested Interest #3)

Reid (Vested Interest #4)

Van (Vested Interest #5)

Halton (Vested Interest #6)

Sandy (Vested Interest #7)

Vested Interest/ABC Crossover

A Merry Vested Wedding

ABC Corp Series

My Saving Grace (Vested Interest: ABC Corp #1)

Finding Ronan's Heart (Vested Interest: ABC Corp #2)

Loved By Liam (Vested Interest: ABC Corp #3)

Age of Ava (Vested Interest: ABC Corp #4)

Men of Hidden Justice

The Boss

Second-In-Command

The Commander

Reynolds Restorations

Revved to the Maxx

Breaking The Speed Limit

Shifting Gears

Insta-Spark Collection written by M Moreland

It Started with a Kiss

Christmas Sugar

An Instant Connection

An Unexpected Gift

Harvest of Love

An Unexpected Chance

Following Maggie (Coming Home series)

Mission Cove

The Summer of Us

Standalones

Into the Storm

Beneath the Scars

Over the Fence

The Image of You (former title My Image of You)

Changing Roles

Happily Ever After Collection

Heart Strings

DEDICATION

For my friends who have become my family

Thank you for being in my life.

And to Matthew

My Forever.

CHAPTER ONE

Brett

The room was dim, cool, and closed off. The cement floor and wooden shelves rudimentary. A required spot, but not decorated to please the eye. Necessary for storage—parts and supplies kept in neat order.

And right now, deserted.

The perfect spot to fuck her.

The door shut behind us, cutting off the noises from the garage out front. The darkness was welcome, needed. She liked to be fucked in the dark.

She gasped as I pushed her against the shelves, her low moan of pleasure a quiet sound in the room as I slid my hand up her neck, around her head, feeling the silkiness of her short hair whisper along my fingers. I cradled her skull as my mouth descended, feeling that grip of intense pleasure flow through me when our lips melded. Our tongues slid together, a sensuous dance we'd done before. Her mouth was hot, wet, and sweet. She wrapped her arms around my neck, rising on her toes to be closer. I dropped my hands to her perfect ass and lifted her, groaning in satisfaction as she wrapped her legs around my waist and my cock settled between her legs, the warmth of her blazing even through the material of my coveralls. I slanted my head, taking her mouth harder, the passion inside me sizzling and popping. We were a mass of touch and sensation. Our hands were everywhere, skimming, touching, pressing, pulling.

I ran my mouth over her cheek to her ear, my tongue tasting her skin. "You want me, Shutterbug? You want my cock inside you?"

"Yes," she gasped as I bit down, teasing the juncture between her neck and shoulder. "Please."

"You ask so nicely," I teased.

I slid one hand up her torso, cupping her breast, using my thumb to tease her tight nipple. As usual, she wore nothing beneath her shirt, her skin smooth under my touch.

"What else do you want?" I asked, lifting her higher, sucking her through the thin material of her tank top.

She whimpered as I took the other nipple and sucked. Slid my hand back to her thigh, delving under the loose shorts she wore and teasing the lace between her legs.

"Oh, I feel you," I whispered. "Wet and hot for me. You're aching for me, aren't you?"

"Brett," she gasped as I slipped my finger under the lace and touched her. Lightly. Teasing—letting my index finger barely stroke her.

"Tell me."

"Yes, I want you. I want you to fuck me. Ease the ache," she pleaded.

"And what do I get?"

"Me. My mouth around your dick, then buried inside me."

I grunted in approval.

She pushed on my chest, and I stepped back, setting her on her feet. The sound of the zipper being tugged down on my coveralls was a low, metallic growl in the dark. I shrugged my shoulders, letting the heavy denim material fall away, groaning as she dropped to her knees, engulfing me in her eager mouth. I let my head fall back, the feelings of her mouth and hands on me intense. The sensations were as new as they were familiar. Only she could bring forth these volcanic stirrings. Her lips moved over me, licking, stroking, teasing. She cupped my balls as she swallowed around my cock, taking me deeper. I had to turn my head to muffle my groan into my shoulder. I felt her gaze burning me in the darkness around us, watching me even in the black.

"Enough," I hissed, grabbing her shoulders, lifting her away. I bent and picked her up, pressing her against the shelves.

"Hold tight, Shutterbug. This is gonna be hard."

"Yes," she replied, lifting her arms and gripping the shelf over her head.

I didn't stop to take off her loose shorts; I pushed them and her lace aside and slammed into her, groaning low as the sensation of her surrounded me.

She gasped and pushed closer. I pulled back and thrust again. I wrapped one arm securely around her waist and buried my other hand into her silky hair, covering her mouth with mine. I could taste the sharpness of myself on her tongue. The underlying cinnamon and sweetness that was all her. I moved hard and fast, exactly the way I promised.

She gripped me, her fingers tightening on my damp shoulders. I kissed her as if I was angry. Deep and claiming. Because I was. I was always angry when we fucked.

I sped up, feeling her beginning to come around my cock, her muscles fluttering, her moans constant. I swallowed all her noises, keeping them just for me. They were all I was allowed to keep.

She stiffened, locking down and shaking. Whimpering as she drenched me. I thrust again, orgasming at the intensity of the moment. Coming inside her, some small piece of me acknowledging the fact that I liked it. She would be marked by me, even if she refused to admit it.

We stilled—for one moment at complete peace and in accord.

She pushed at my shoulders, and I set her feet on the floor.

She didn't say a word as she headed toward the door.

"No," I begged. "Not this time. Come back."

She didn't even look my way. She opened the door and left me.

Again.

I stared at the door in the darkness. Waiting.

I was always waiting.

And then someone knocked on the door.

"Brett, you in there, buddy?"

The knock sounded again, louder. "Brett?"

I woke up, shaking and alone in my bed.

I was a mess. Covered in sweat, my hand around my weeping dick.

I wasn't in the storeroom, and she wasn't here.

The knock sounded impatient this time. Louder. The locked door handle rattled.

"Brett?"

"Yeah, hold up," I called out.

I swung my legs over the mattress, drawing in a long breath and grabbing my sweats, yanking them on.

I opened the door, sticking my head through the space. "What's up?"

Chase frowned. "You were yelling."

"Oh, sorry. Nightmare, I guess," I lied. "I shouldn't have eaten that pizza so late."

He didn't look convinced, but he let it go.

"It's eight. I'm heading to pick up the ice and the ribs Stefano ordered and dropping them off before I go to the garage. You wanna come with?"

I scrubbed my hand over my face. "No, I'll meet you at the garage later."

"Okay." He paused. "You sure you're okay?"

"I'm good."

I shut the door and returned to the bed, sitting down on the mattress, feeling exhausted.

Another dream of her. Of us.

Always the same.

Us together, in perfect synchronization, our bodies saying everything our mouths couldn't or weren't allowed to say.

And her, leaving.

She always left.

I thought I was used to it.

Until last time.

That was when she left forever.

I sighed, whispering her name.

"Kelly."

CHAPTER TWO

Brett

I wiped my hands on a towel, surveying the engine I had just finished tuning up. I had Chase start the car, and I listened in satisfaction. It purred like a kitten—or, in this case, growled like a lion. The client liked the loud roar of the super-powerful turbo this rebuilt Mustang had. He had done a lot of work himself, but we had fine-tuned the engine, and Stefano had done the complex paint job. It was spectacular, the color constantly changing in the light. It looked black until the sun hit it. Then it was like a kaleidoscope of color—green, purple, red, pink, gold, silver—the list was endless. It drew stares everywhere it went, which was great for the shop when the client was asked where it was done.

I waved my hand in a slashing motion, and Chase cut the engine. He slid from the driver's seat.

"Sounds good."

I nodded as I shut the hood. "It just needed tweaking."

Chase grinned. "I'll tell Jack. He's been pacing outside like you were working on his firstborn in here."

I laughed. "To him, this is as important. Go tell him his baby is all good and he can take her home. I'll write it up."

I headed to the office, surprised to find Charly there. She looked up, a frown marring her pretty face. Her red hair was wild today, and she looked anxious.

"Hey, Charly," I greeted her, dropping a kiss to her head. "You're not supposed to be here today."

"Yeah, the stroll from the house was long and arduous," she said flippantly.

I chuckled. "Chase and I have this covered. It's a quiet day."

"I know. I, ah, needed to talk to you."

Her nerves were obvious. Charly had lots of tells. She fidgeted when upset, her fingers in constant motion. They were moving continuously right now. Obviously, something was bothering her.

I sat down, curious. "Something wrong?"

I tried not to be amused when I noticed her toes wiggling in her sandals. Whatever this was had to be big.

"Maxx send you here to fire me?" I asked lightly.

She slapped my arm. "Holy moly, don't even kid about that."

I chuckled. "Spill, Red," I said, using Maxx's nickname for her.

She blew out a long breath. "Kelly showed up late last night."

I stilled in the chair. "Oh?" I managed to get out through my tight lips.

"I was shocked to see her. She never told me she was coming."

I didn't say anything.

"I-I wanted you to know."

"Where is she now?" I asked quietly.

"Asleep. She looked exhausted when she showed up."

"Ah."

"And drained."

"Hmm."

"As if she'd been through something."

I shook my head. "If you think I might know something, I don't, Charly. I haven't heard a word from her since she left last year. I have no idea what's going on with her or her life." I stood. "I don't care to either."

"You're still angry with her."

I scrubbed my face. "No. I'm ambivalent," I lied. "She made it clear there was no future for us, nothing permanent, and she left. End of." The words were out of my mouth before I could stop them. "You understand me? *She* left, Charly. Not me. She ended whatever was happening between us without a word. She walked away and left me. If she's had a hard time and came for a visit, well, I'm happy for her that you're around. But I'm not getting involved this time. I can't." I paused, swallowing the constricted feeling in my throat. "I can't go through that again."

She grabbed my hand. "I know," she said simply. "I just wanted to tell you. I didn't want you walking into the house unprepared."

I sighed, rubbing the back of my neck. "I'll avoid the house, and I am sure she'll avoid the garage for the few days she's around. If we bump into each other, I'll be polite. She will be too. It's fine."

She shook her head, her wide eyes round in her face.

"She told me she's here indefinitely, Brett. She quit her job with Carl."

I stared at her.

I wasn't expecting that.

I sat outside in my car, staring at Stefano's house. I'd been there a hundred times. Felt the genuine welcome of my friend and his wife. The excitement from Theo for being there. I always enjoyed coming here. And get-togethers were usually no exception. The house would be full of people I knew and cared about. Friends and adopted family I liked spending time with.

But today, the house would have an extra person in it. Before leaving me in the office earlier, Charly had told me she was bringing Kelly as long as I was okay with it. I had paused before giving my answer, unsure how to feel about it. Uncertain what to say.

"As I said before, we're adults, Charly. I think we can behave accordingly."

But now, knowing she might be somewhere inside those walls, I wasn't sure. There was a good chance Charly had invited her and she'd stayed behind. She might have decided she didn't want to see me. She was the one who left, after all. It had been her decision.

But I knew there was a chance she was here now.

It was odd; it was as if I'd sensed her close the day before.

I thought back to the sudden reoccurrence of the dream last night. The replay of the last time we were together. Alone. Locked in the storeroom. The only difference was the end of the dream. I always woke up before she left, but in reality, once we'd finished, she'd slipped away. I saw her only briefly one more time, and she was gone without an explanation.

Why had the dream returned?

Had I somehow sensed her return even then?

I shook my head to clear it. What a stupid idea.

I sighed and scrubbed my face. I needed to make a decision. Call Stefano with an excuse, drive away, and find a bar to drown my sorrows in, or man up and go inside. Greet Kelly like the adult I insisted I was and ignore her.

There would be lots of other people in attendance. She'd probably hang with Charly, Gabby, and the kids most of the time. She usually did if we were in a group anyway.

I shook my head and got out of the car.

I could do this.

I paused at the corner of the house, feeling like a stalker as I peered around the lilac bush. I scanned the backyard, not seeing Kelly. I listened but didn't pick up her voice. I huffed out a sigh of relief, knowing my first instinct was correct and she hadn't come. Straightening my shoulders, I walked forward, holding out my arms.

"Okay, people, I have arrived! Let's get this party started!"

I was met with laughter and catcalls. I stopped to hand Gabby the flowers I picked up for her, dropping a kiss to her head and peering down at Luna, who was asleep in her mother's arms. She had crazy curls like her mother and a stubborn set to her jaw like her dad. She was gonna be a handful, and I was going to enjoy watching Stefano deal with it.

Gabby smiled at me. "Thanks, Brett."

Charly pouted, and I chuckled, pulling a chocolate bar from my pocket and handing it to her. "My dad got this in for you."

Her eyes widened and she grabbed it, looking around to make sure no one noticed. She loved a certain English chocolate bar, and I made sure to get my dad to order some in every so often as a treat. It was one thing she refused to share—even with Maxx or her kids. I knew she'd find a corner to eat it in later.

"Just the one?" she asked.

I winked. "Nope. I know where there's an entire box. You behave, I might let you in on the secret."

She sniffed. "*Behave?* I'll just ask Chase. He knows all your hiding spots." She winked back at me, looking mischievous. "It's far more fun to misbehave."

I was laughing as I headed toward Stefano, Maxx, and Chase, manning the barbecue and smoker. The scent of roasting meat filled the air. My stomach growled at the smell, reminding me I hadn't eaten all day.

I grabbed a beer, leaning on the deck rail. "Boys," I greeted them. "Smells awesome."

Stefano chuckled. "Ready in about half an hour. Mama and Vince should be here soon."

"Just two of them?" I asked, shocked.

"Vince is bringing her so I can look at his car. We'll see the rest of them tomorrow. But Mama was missing Luna and Theo."

I laughed. Rosa took every opportunity to see Stefano and his little family.

"She's, ah, bringing pasta, right?" I asked hopefully.

Theo ran out the door, looking excited. "Ziti!" he exclaimed, jumping off the deck, letting me catch him.

"Oomph," I groaned. "You're getting too big to do that anymore. Far too much ziti in you already."

He laughed in delight. "That's what Dad says too!"

I saw the look of happiness on Stefano's face. He still smiled every time Theo called him Dad.

Theo leaned closer. "I can't stop growing no matter what I do. I tried."

I set him on his feet and ruffled his hair. "You can't stop nature, bud. It's just the way it is. You can't control it."

He nodded. "Dad said that to Mom this morning."

"Oh yeah?"

He looked confused. "Not sure why. He was hugging her, and Mom slapped his arm and told him to stop it. He said he had no control over it." He scratched his ear. "Maybe he was growing too?"

I had to look away. Stefano bit back his grin, and Maxx covered his mouth. Chase broke into laughter and turned his back. Theo looked at me. "What?"

"I think your mom meant something else."

"Like what?"

Stefano met my gaze, his amused. He wasn't going to help with this one.

"He was probably tickling her." I bent and grabbed him under the arms. "Like this!" I wiggled my fingers, laughing as he squirmed and squealed, trying to get away. It did the trick, and he pushed me away and ran, laughing, to his mom.

I picked up my beer and grinned at Stefano. "One of these days, he is gonna know what was growing."

Stefano clinked his beer with mine. "God help us then."

The backyard was warm, the sun bright in the late afternoon. Stefano's mama was in her glory, surrounded by everyone. She was adored by each person here, and with good reason. Mary had joined us, and the two of them got on like a house on fire, constantly talking, playing with the kids, overseeing the food. It was loud, fun, with the laughter never-ending. We fixed the loose belt on Vince's car, but Stefano wanted to give the engine an overhaul. He scolded his brother, telling him to bring it to the shop.

Vince lifted one shoulder. "I barely have enough time to sleep these days, never mind take a day to bring the car out."

Stefano shook his head. "I'll have Chase drive you a loaner. He'll bring this to me. You only have to tell me."

Vince shook his head. "I hate bothering you, little bro. You're busy enough."

Stefano gripped his shoulder. "Never for family," he said firmly. "It'll happen this week."

Vince nodded, looking grateful. I knew how important family was to them. Given the fact that I had only my father, it was nice to see the siblings care for each other.

Gabby slipped inside to feed their daughter, and I noticed Stefano disappear after a few moments. I knew he was crazy about them both and liked helping Gabby with the feedings. I distracted Theo, playing soccer with him, Maxx, and Chase, and keeping an eye on Thomas as he toddled over. Maxx's daughter, Vivvy, was too little and far more interested in the stuffed animals spread around her than the boisterous game we had going on. Charly sat on a blanket with her, tenderly stroking her red hair and smiling. Rosa watched over them, looking content. She loved all the kids and the women who had become part of her life. Mary sipped wine and chatted to them, sitting on the blanket with Charly.

I hadn't asked about Kelly, but at one point when I met Charly's gaze, she had lifted a shoulder, shaking her head, and I knew she was telling me Kelly wasn't there. I felt a swell of relief at her assurance, and I squashed the fleeting disappointment at the knowledge I wouldn't see her. No doubt she'd avoid me at all costs.

It was for the best.

Stefano and Gabby returned, Gabby sitting with the other women and Stefano joining us.

After another few moments, I held up my hand, catching the ball with my foot. "I need a break and a drink." I kicked the ball to Stefano and walked to the cooler, deciding I needed water instead of beer.

I headed inside, filling a glass with ice and adding cold water from the fridge. I drained the glass and refilled it.

I watched from the window, smiling as Stefano lifted Theo after he scored, putting him on his shoulders and celebrating.

I felt an odd pulling in my chest as the thought that I might never experience that hit me. It happened a lot these days seeing my friends so happy, but somehow, I had no desire to try to change my life. Something held me back from doing so.

I heard a sound, and the base of my neck prickled with sudden heat. I felt the pull of a different source tug at me.

I turned and met the light-blue gaze I knew so well, had missed so much, and had hoped never to see again.

"Hello, Kelly."

CHAPTER THREE

Kelly

God, he looked good. I watched Brett drink his water in long pulls, the tendons in his throat contracting as he swallowed. He was shirtless, his torso covered in a sheen of sweat. His back was a road map of muscles, his arms solid. I knew how his broad shoulders felt under my fingers, how his biceps felt as they swelled and moved. His longer, wavy hair was gone, the cut shorter at the back now, the front longer and brushed up high away from his face.

I had tried to stay away. I knew he didn't want to see me—not that I could blame him. But the silence at Charly's place was too much to take. The painful recent memories burned hot, playing over and over again in my mind until I couldn't handle it anymore. I had borrowed Charly's old bike and peddled my way to Stefano's.

Gabby was outside on the porch rocking Luna when I arrived, and she welcomed me.

"Come to the back!" she exclaimed. "I just finished feeding and changing Luna. Stefano just headed there."

"Can I use your washroom first?" I asked. "Little sweaty after the ride."

"Of course. See you there. I won't say anything, so it'll be a surprise. Everyone will be so happy to see you."

I hadn't expected to bump into Brett as soon as I stepped out of the washroom, feeling fresher now that I had washed my face and wiped off my arms and legs with a cool cloth.

But somehow I wasn't surprised. I was never very good at avoiding the man.

Something alerted him to my presence, and he turned, our eyes locking across the room. He didn't seem shocked to see me as our gazes connected, his clear blue calm and steady.

"Hello, Kelly," he said, his tone polite and distant, as if greeting a stranger.

"Brett," I replied, after swallowing the thickness in my throat. I tried not to stare at his bare torso, not to remember how his muscles rippled as he moved inside me, the way he would groan when I would suck his nipples into my mouth and nip them playfully with my teeth. How his chest would rumble in pleasure as I kissed my way down his torso, ghosting my lips over his tight abs.

The crack of his glass slamming down on the counter brought me out of my lust-induced haze. I lifted my eyes, meeting his narrowed stare.

"You done?" he asked.

"Sorry, I lost my train of thought," I murmured.

He stepped closer, his gaze like ice. "I know exactly where your train of thought went, Kelly. And let me tell you, the station is closed. That—*us*—is never happening again." He bent, his breath hot on my face as he spoke, fury dripping from his voice. "You fucked me over once too often. Not interested. Understand? You got me?"

His heat surrounded me. His strength was palpable and his anger raw.

"Yes," I whispered, sorrow filling my chest. I had anticipated his anger, but I was still disappointed.

I expected him to push past me. Walk away. But he remained close for a moment, the feel of him tempting. I wanted to move in closer, to feel his arms around me. His hand twitched as if he felt the draw between us.

Then with a muttered curse, he spun on his heel and stalked toward the door.

"Stay the fuck away from me," he demanded, slamming out of the house.

I had to stay in place, trying not to shake as I closed my eyes. For a moment, I had felt it. That odd, intense connection we always had between us had blossomed and grown, filling the air around us like a balloon filling with helium. Light and buoyant, only to fizzle and fall as reality set in.

But I had felt something else when he was close. His desire. The hardening of his cock when he was in front of me. Close enough to touch. He had felt that draw too.

Only this time, he walked away.

I sighed. It was for the best. I wasn't good for him, and I couldn't give him what he needed.

As always, I ignored that little voice in my head that whispered that maybe he could give me what I needed.

I sat down at the table for a few moments to calm my nerves. I shouldn't have come, but I couldn't leave now. Gabby knew I was here. So did Brett. If I left, he would know why.

I sighed, running a hand over my hair with a frown. I needed a haircut. The last couple of locations we'd been at, we were too busy to take the time out for something as trivial as a haircut, and it was too long, brushing the collar of my T-shirt. I would have to find a place in town and get it trimmed.

I blew out a long breath and attempted to center myself. I shut my eyes and tried to concentrate on my breathing.

Except all I could see when I closed them was Brett. His glistening torso. All the times I saw it as he was over me, fucking me. How incredible we had been together.

I sighed, recalling the first time I had met him.

Charly had called me to tell me she was getting married. I had a break coming up, so I flew home to be part of her day and take her wedding photographs. The event itself was laid-back and casual, and the night before, there was a get-together at their place. I arrived the day before the wedding, and I helped out in the kitchen, enjoying the camaraderie with Mary and Charly. Outside, the men were setting up tables and chairs, instructing the florist, who was constructing the arbor where they would exchange their vows. I took out a tray of lemonade and handed out the drinks to Maxx, Stefano, and Brett. Stefano was tall, handsome, and intense, his dark hair and eyes giving away his Italian heritage. Brett was the exact opposite. Golden-brown hair, blue eyes, with an easygoing smile and a friendly disposition. Both were in their early thirties and single. Whereas Stefano was denser with muscles, Brett was leaner but cut and defined. They all wore muscle shirts, and I found my eyes drawn to Brett over and again. How he moved. His wide smile. The way he teased and laughed. His frank stare when our eyes would meet.

It was the same later that night as we sat around a fire Maxx built. Our gazes kept meeting across the dancing flames, and something in Brett's stare ignited a different fire within me.

At one point, I went into the house to get some more marshmallows. Brett was leaning on the counter, sipping a glass of water. Our eyes locked, and he watched as I opened the cupboard, reaching up to grab the marshmallows. They were just out of reach, and before I could ask, he was behind me, his body pressed against mine, the heat of him soaking into my back. His scent was clean and masculine, laced with woodsmoke from the fire.

"I'll get those," he murmured, stretching his arm over my head, pushing into me more. He was hard and firm behind me. Every part of him. A small whimper escaped my mouth as he grabbed the bag and lowered it to the counter.

He stayed behind me, his arms caging me in. He lowered his head, his breath hot on my neck.

"You are one sexy woman, you know that?"

"I am?" I responded.

"I see you eyeballing me," he whispered.

"You're doing the same thing," I retorted.

"I like looking at you," he said, his lips ghosting my earlobe. "Imagining doing more than looking."

I turned, and our lips met in a violent rush. He speared his tongue inside my mouth, his taste exploding. He slanted his head, going deeper. It was hot, wet, and passionate. He was everything I thought he would be as he yanked me tight to his chest, kissing me as if he needed the oxygen from my lungs to survive. I groaned as he lifted me to the counter, standing between my legs. I could feel every hard inch of him, and I wrapped my legs around his waist, drowning in his kiss. His taste. The sheer strength of him. He gripped my hip, pulling me tighter, and I was lost to him.

Until we heard footsteps and he broke away, heading toward the hall. I jumped down, grabbing the bag of marshmallows, and walked toward the door. Mary stepped inside as I got there.

"I thought maybe you couldn't find them," she said, indicating the bag in my hands.

"Nope, got them. I had to, ah, use the bathroom," I ad-libbed.

"Ah," was all she said, but I couldn't meet her eyes. I brushed past her, heading for the fire pit, hoping no one would notice my swollen lips and how quickly I was breathing.

Luckily, everyone was too busy and was happy there were more marshmallows.

Mary followed, sitting down next to me again.

A few moments later, Brett strolled back to the fire, sitting down. He balanced a glass on his bent knee, the amber liquid glinting in the firelight.

Our eyes met, his filled with a silent promise.

To be continued.

I shook my head to clear it. Then I stood, knowing I had to face the group of people waiting in the backyard.

I never should have come.

BRETT

Kelly walked into the backyard, smiling and looking pleased to see everyone. I observed her from my chair, lifting a hand to wave at her in greeting, knowing without a doubt we were being scrutinized by the entire group.

"Kelly," I said, acting as if we hadn't already had a moment in the kitchen. "I heard you were back."

She nodded and sat across from me beside Charly. "A bit of a break," she said.

I pursed my lips, saying nothing. Theo broke the tension, pulling on Stefano's hand. "Dad, you said you'd push me on the swing. Bring Luna."

Stefano gathered his daughter against his chest, walking toward the play set we had built. Theo loved the slide and the monkey bars. He liked to go high in the swing, and as long as one of us was there to watch him, he was allowed. The baby swing for Luna was swung with far more care, acting as a soothing motion for her. I stood and joined him, unable to be so close to Kelly at the moment.

I strolled over and took over pushing Theo, smiling at his shrieks of delight. Luna gurgled and kicked her feet, grabbing one foot and lifting it to her mouth. Stefano chuckled, tickling the tiny toes. "To be that flexible," he muttered.

"No kidding."

With his focus on his daughter, he spoke again. "You okay?"

"I'm good."

"Gabby said she was in the house. I assume you saw her, given your brilliant performance of nonchalance over there," he said.

"Yeah, I did."

Theo decided it was slide time, so I helped him slow down, chuckling as he jumped off the swing, rolling in the grass and bounding to his feet, running to the slide.

"If only I recovered that quickly," I observed, moving over to where Luna was cooing and still grasping for her toes.

"You sure you're okay?"

I met Stefano's concerned gaze.

"I'm fine. Given she is Charly's best friend, we were bound to run into each other again. It's all good."

"You know she's staying."

I snorted. "She says that, but it never happens. She'll make up with Carl and be off soon enough."

"Charly thinks it's different this time."

I heard his warning. His worry. I met his gaze with a curt nod. "It's fine. The bottom line is I no longer care."

"You sure about that?"

"Yes."

He lifted Luna, cradling her against his chest. "You might want to tell your fists that. If they were curled any tighter, you'd snap your bones. Never mind the tension in your shoulders. You're gonna have one hell of a headache later, my friend."

He walked away toward the group, leaving me alone with my thoughts.

We ate the feast Stefano and Gabby laid out, including the delicious ziti and meatballs Rosa brought with her. Theo ate two plates of it, making Rosa beam at him, pinching his cheeks and calling him her favorite bambino. He grinned in delight.

A short time later, Rosa and Vince left. She patted my cheek, telling me to come with Stefano and Gabby for lunch soon. I kissed her cheek, promising I would do that. I walked the property, gathering up some sticks for kindling, knowing we'd have a fire soon. Gabby and Charly loved evening fires, and it was a tradition for us.

I wasn't sure how I was going to sit across from Kelly with a fire going. It always seemed to spark something intense. As if the glow from the burning wood lit the silent flame that existed between us.

The first time we'd kissed was the night of a bonfire at Maxx's place. I'd fucked her for the first time later that night.

In the barn.

I was still living at Maxx's place, in the apartment behind the garage. Chase wasn't part of our circle then, and Stefano was living at Mary's. After the fire broke up, I headed toward the garage when I noticed the barn door was partially open. I peered in, surprised to see Kelly sitting on the workout bench. She was doing something with her hands, concentrating in the little pool of light of her phone.

I stepped in, meeting her gaze.

"What are you doing?" I asked.

She looked up. "Waiting for Charly and Maxx to wear themselves out."

I chuckled, walking toward her. "You might wait a while."

She shook her head. "They just need to move out of the kitchen area. I figured I'd give them fifteen and head on in. They should have headed upstairs by then. Pre-wedding celebrations and all."

I stopped in front of her. "What are you doing there?" I indicated the straw in her hand.

"Oh, just weaving a silly thing to pass the time."

She met my eyes, falling silent. The heat from earlier flared and grew again. I shifted on my feet as all the blood pooled from my body into my cock while I thought about kissing her before. How she felt pressed against me. She was small and slender, with perky, high breasts, and a tiny waist that flared to softer hips. Her legs and arms were well muscled and taut from the work she did carrying equipment all the time. She was incredibly sexy, and I found it hard to keep my eyes off her.

"Something about that kitchen, I guess," I murmured, my gaze on her mouth.

"I suppose so," she replied.

I wasn't sure who moved first, but suddenly she was flush against me, and my mouth was on hers. We kissed frantically. Licking, sucking, and biting. I bent, cupping her ass and lifting her. She wrapped her legs around me, the heat of her evident even through the material that separated us. I sat down on the bench with her straddling me. I pulled my mouth from hers, dragging it over her cheek, down her neck, licking, and kissing at her soft, fragrant skin. I slid one hand up her thigh, dipping under her shorts, cupping her ass again. She undulated over me, whimpering. I grasped the back of her neck, meeting her wide gaze in the light glowing from her phone, which had ended up on the floor somewhere.

"We're not going to be interrupted this time, Kelly. So you either need to climb off my lap and head into the house—" I leaned close, my mouth almost touching hers "—or know that I'm going to have you right here. Right now."

"You gonna fuck me?" she responded, snaking her hand between us and wrapping her fingers around my hard dick. "You gonna use this big cock and fuck me?" Her eyes gleamed in delight as she spoke.

I grinned. She liked dirty talk? I could accommodate.

"You gonna get on your knees and suck my big cock?"

Nothing prepared me for how quickly she did exactly that. Her mouth around my cock was heaven and hell all rolled into one. Her tongue did things to me that I was certain were illegal in parts of this country. She rolled my balls and sucked the head, tonguing the slit and humming around it. I shook with the force of the desire pulsating through my veins. I slid my hands into her silky hair that hugged her head like a helmet, groaning her name. Every nerve in my body was on fire. I tugged at her head. "Enough, Kelly. Stop."

I pulled her onto the bench, yanking off her shorts. I tugged her sexy legs apart, burying my face between them, grinning at her muffled gasp. She was sweet and musky on my tongue. Wet and ready. I planned on making her wetter. I licked and teased at her clit. Slid in one finger, then another, listening to her pleas and gasps of pleasure. Felt her orgasm growing, her legs tightening.

"Give it to me," I demanded, adding a third finger and feeling her pulsating around me. She cried out, her head back, the tendons in her neck taut as she orgasmed. I stood, grabbing a condom from my back pocket, rolling it on as my pants dropped to the floor. I pulled her to the edge of the bench and slid into her, the feel of her around me tight and hot. She was still trembling from her orgasm as I began to move. I bent over her, grasping her hips and thrusting. Her breasts bounced as I drove into her, and she stared at me, wide-eyed and pleading.

"Play with them. Let me see."

She plucked at her stiff nipples, rolling them between her fingers. She moaned as I lifted her higher, changing the angle. Sweat beaded on my head and the back of my neck.

"You need to come again soon," I grunted. "You feel too good."

"Oh God," she moaned. "Not a problem."

"Touch yourself. Show me."

She slipped her hand between us, her fingers on either side of my dick. The sensation was too great, and I came. Moaning her name, thrusting harder, seeing stars as I shut my eyes, the sensation overpowering. She locked down, tightening around me, milking my cock and sighing my name.

When I came back to my senses, I bent over her and kissed her. We tasted like us.

"Is this how you welcome all the female visitors?" she teased quietly.

I kissed her again. "Only the sexy Shutterbugs that show up for weddings."

"I feel special, then."

"Good," I replied. "You are."

She frowned. "Don't get attached, Brett. I'm not that sort of girl."

"Good thing I'm not looking for an attachment," I replied. "Just this."

"Then we understand each other."

"We do."

The truth was, I never understood a single thing until it was too late.

CHAPTER FOUR

Brett

I returned to the present and the fire currently blazing, pushing my chair back farther into the shadows. I laughed as Theo insisted on toasting me a marshmallow, and despite its blackened exterior, I ate it, assuring him he had done a great job. I teased Gabby and made Stefano frown as I took Luna, cradling her in my arms.

"Perks of being favorite uncle, you know," I informed him.

"Hey," Maxx and Chase both objected.

"Give it up, boys. We know I'm her fave," I said with a smirk, looking down at her little face. She was adorable with her plump cheeks and wild curls. She wrapped her fist around my finger, making her little noises and squirming until she was comfortable. Being an only child, I had zero experience with babies, but I enjoyed spending time with Maxx's children and now Stefano's. I was an adopted uncle to all of Stefano's nieces and nephews, although they were all big kids when I met them. Being around the babies as they grew up was a cool thing.

I rocked her in my arms, liking how she snuggled into me. It was a nice feeling.

Someone had put on some music, and I relaxed back in my chair, enjoying the peacefulness of the moment. Through my half-opened eyelids, I peered around at the group. Stefano sat with his arm around Gabby, nuzzling her head. Maxx had Charly tucked beside him, the two of them watching their kids, who were playing in front of them. Chase was talking to Mary and laughing.

And despite my best efforts, my gaze took in Kelly. Like me, she was off on her own. I studied her, noting how thin she looked. Weary and worn. Kelly was always smiling, filled with life. She seemed downtrodden. She stared at the flames, her expression blank, none of her usual sassiness evident.

What had happened that brought her back?

I hadn't been sure she would ever return to Littleburn—except to see Charly. I knew she gave up her apartment in Toronto last year when the owner sold the house. Maxx and Charly had gone in and brought back her things, storing them in the back of the barn. There were only some boxes, no furniture. I had helped Maxx empty his truck, and he explained that the small place Kelly had been living in was furnished when she moved in, so there were no big pieces to move. I had only nodded, realizing how little I truly knew of the life Kelly led.

Kelly wiped her cheeks, sliding back in her chair, lifting her face to the sky. I glanced up, seeing how bright the stars were tonight. She had always liked to look at them, pointing out the constellations and getting excited over a shooting star. I knew she would be finding her favorites right now and studying them.

I had to pull my gaze away.

What she was looking at, how she was feeling, was no longer any of my business.

It never really had been.

KELLY

I woke up, stretching and curling back up in the comfortable bed. It was early—I knew that before I even opened my eyes. There were no signs of life from upstairs or in the kitchen. Slowly I shifted, lifting my eyelids. The sun was just coming up, the rays still dim and soft. Soon, the room would be bright and filled with sun. The diffused light made me itch to get my camera, so I slid from the bed, pulling on a hoodie over my sleep pants and T-shirt I liked to wear at night, slipped on my sneakers, and padded outside.

The morning air was crisp and refreshing. I glanced at the barn, mesmerized by the way the light hit the structure, turning the faded red wood to a beautiful hue. I snapped some pictures, then headed toward the fields of tall grasses around the house. The sun was changing them a brilliant golden color, and my lens captured the beauty of it all. I tracked the sun in my viewfinder, click after click of the shutter showing its ascent higher in the sky. I caught the trees varying from dusky gray to a rich green as the sun kissed them.

There was so much beauty here. And peace. It surrounded me.

How had I never seen all the beauty that was right here until now?

I shook my head as the answer became obvious.

I wasn't looking. I wasn't in the moment. I was always waiting to leave. Looking ahead. Comparing the what-ifs to the now. Worried about missing something, when, in fact, I missed everything.

I sighed as I sat on the porch, enjoying the quiet. The rocking chairs Charly had put out here were comfortable and inviting.

I was surprised when the door opened and Charly came out, carrying two cups of coffee.

"Finished taking pics?" she asked, handing me a cup.

"For now. The light was so beautiful, I couldn't resist."

"I know. It's stunning here."

I nodded, taking a sip of the strong coffee. "It is." I frowned. "Why are you here?"

"I live here," she deadpanned.

"I mean why aren't you inside with your husband and babies?"

A soft smile lit her face. "Maxx has Vivvy, and he is feeding her, then he's going to give her a bath. He loves doing that in the morning. Thomas is still asleep. When he wakes up, the two of them will fuss over Vivvy for a while. I often sit out here in the early morning on the weekends." She lifted one shoulder. "The weekdays are so busy I don't have much me time. Maxx tries to give me some on the weekends. Gives him a chance to be with the kids on his own too, you know?"

"You're really happy, aren't you?" I asked.

"I am. Maxx makes me happy. So do my kids. And the garage. I love all of it." She sipped her coffee, observing me over the rim. "I don't think I can say the same about you, Kelly. What's going on? Why are you here?" Her gaze was direct and frank, her tone patient.

I looked away, hating the quiver in my voice. "I can't, Charly. Not yet, okay?"

She leaned forward, clasping my hand. "It was Carl, wasn't it?"

"Yes," I whispered.

"Did he touch you? Hurt you?" she demanded.

I shook my head.

"Are you sure? Maxx will go and teach him a lesson. He'll take Brett and Stefano. The man will never walk properly again, and his dick will always remain at half-mast."

I blinked at her words, then chuckled.

"He didn't hit me," I assured her.

"You can hurt in other ways than your fists," she stated wisely.

I could only nod, my throat tight.

"He needs to be held accountable."

"I don't care about that. Besides, I don't think Maxx or Stefano would leave to go fight my battles." I swallowed. "And Brett doesn't give a damn."

"I wouldn't be too sure of that."

I shook my head, unable to speak. He loathed me now. I could feel it.

For a moment, she was quiet—which was unusual for Charly. Then she huffed a sigh. "What are your plans, then?"

"I'm going to apply for some jobs."

"Where?"

I frowned. "Toronto, Charly. Where else?"

"But you don't have a place to live."

"I'll find one."

Setting down her coffee, she crossed her arms, using her feet to push the rocking chair.

"Pardon me, but with what? I know you had to get home using your own funds. No job, no money—do you have any idea what the going rent in Toronto is now?"

"I'll find a room, then." I ran a hand through my hair. "I know I had lucked out with my little place before. It's a shame Sal decided to sell the house and they changed it to a single-family dwelling. But I'll find something. I don't need a lot of room."

"The apartment over the garage is empty. And as soon as the damage from the leaking pipe is fixed, you could move in there."

"What?"

"I need help in the garage. With the baby and Theo in school, Gabby isn't ready to come back yet."

I gaped at her. "Do you have any idea how bad an idea that is?" I shook my head. "No thanks."

"Because of Brett?"

I leaned over, serious. "This is Brett's turf. I will not make him uncomfortable. He doesn't deserve that."

She pursed her lips. "The offer is open. I spoke to Maxx, and we would talk to Brett first. But you are welcome to stay in the house as long as you need."

I stood, bending down to kiss her cheek. "You're the best, Charly. I'm lucky to have you in my life. But I can't do that. I'll find something and be out of your hair soon. I'm going to go take a shower and get ready for the day. I think I'll wander a bit so you guys have your house to yourself."

"You don't—"

I cut her off. "Yeah, I do."

I paused at the door. "Thanks, Charly. For caring. For being there for me."

"The offer is open."

I smiled. "I wish I could accept, but it would be too hard on everyone."

I headed to my room to get ready for the day.

It would be far too difficult.

And the reason for it was all my fault.

A week later, I was ready to admit defeat. I had gone into Toronto every day looking for a job and a place to live. I scoured the internet, put in my resume, answered ads—nothing. Not even a nibble. Maxx had insisted on coming with me to see a couple of apartments, and both times, he took my arm, escorting me back to the truck with one firm word.

"No."

"I need a place, Maxx," I said after the second instance. "Those were the two cheapest places." I barked a humorless laugh. "I could barely afford them."

"Not there. Charly would never forgive me."

"I'm a big girl, and I can look after myself."

He shook his head. "Never said you couldn't. But places like that? Nope."

I huffed a long breath and looked out the window, silently grateful for his vehemence. Both apartments were basically small rooms in basements of houses that would probably give me nightmares. The rent alone would keep me broke, even if I found a job.

"Well, one good thing I got out of this week is a wedding shoot next week for a couple who had their photographer bail on them," I said. "The money will help. And maybe it will lead to other jobs."

"Great. In the meantime, you're welcome to stay with us. Charly likes having you around."

I laid my hand on his arm. "Thanks, Maxx. You're a good guy."

He grunted and threw me a wink. "Don't spread that around. I like my grumpy rep."

"Okay, then."

I hadn't picked up any more jobs yet. And had only one phone interview. The money they were offering wouldn't even pay for rent for two weeks—even in the horrid little places I had seen with Maxx. Or bus fare in and out of Littleburn if I stayed there. I racked my brain. I had to come up with a plan; I was going stir-crazy. I tried to stay clear of Brett and the garage. Give Charly and Maxx their privacy. Mary already had a lodger, so I couldn't go there. So for the moment, this was where I had to stay. The repair in the apartment over the garage wasn't complete, so I couldn't stay there until the damage the leaking pipe had caused was fixed.

Every day, I got up early, went for walks, took a lot of pictures. I helped Charly with the kids and otherwise stayed in my room. I hated the feeling of being cooped up, but for a while, it was what I had to do.

I simply wasn't sure how much longer I could do it.

That afternoon, I took Charly's bike and pedaled to the local general store. It was run by Brett's dad, Mack Conner. He owned the hardware store next door as well, the two businesses joined by an opening in the middle. I had only ever met him a few times, and simply as a friend of Charly's. I entered the store, looking around in fascination. It was old-fashioned, with thick shelves, the wooden floors dusty and worn under my feet. There was an old drink cooler, filled with ice-cold water and bottles of soda. Two overhead fans that moved the air slowly. A candy shelf. A row of odds and ends. A small meat counter. The other side was filled with tools and home renovation items and decorated in the same manner. You could find some screws, pick up screening to repair a window, and grab a pound of ground beef with a tub of ice cream for dinner, all in the same place. A real throwback.

A younger man waved to me as I peeked through the cased opening in curiosity. He was busy stocking shelves, and I waved back.

Sitting behind the counter of the grocery side was Brett's dad. He was reading the paper, glancing up as I walked in.

"Afternoon," he grunted.

"Mr. Conner," I greeted him.

With the sunlight behind him, his white hair glowed. He was a tall, lean man, his face surprisingly clear of wrinkles, with his hair slicked back and his shoulders still straight. He was dressed in a cardigan, his shirt buttoned, and when he came out from around the counter, his shoes were shiny.

"You're Charly's friend," he mused. "Kathy?"

I smiled, extending my hand. "Close. Kelly."

"You take pictures."

"I did," I said, feeling the frisson of sadness go through me.

"Did? Break your arm or something?" he asked, leaning on the counter.

"No. Lost my job."

He nodded slowly. "Lots of that these days."

"Yes."

"What are you looking for?"

"Oh, um, Charly needs some of your double-smoked bacon."

He nodded. "She likes that."

"And a few other things," I added, holding up my list.

"You get what you need. I'll slice the bacon. She likes it thick."

I picked up a small basket and grabbed the few things on the list. Unable to resist, I took one of the cold sodas and a bag of chips. I paid for the items then went outside and sat in one of the old rocking chairs, enjoying the sunshine. I sipped the sweet beverage, the bottle ice-cold on my palm. I opened the bag and munched on the chips, marveling at the quiet around me. Mr. Conner came outside, carrying a bottle, and sat beside me in the other rocker. We shared a smile and clinked the necks, but neither of us spoke for a moment. I was acutely aware of how much Brett looked like his dad, with the same blue eyes and body structure. Finally, he spoke.

"My boy behaving?"

I almost choked on the liquid.

"Pardon me?"

"At the garage," he added mildly.

"Oh. I don't think Maxx has any complaints." I felt the sudden need to defend Brett. He always complained his dad treated him as if he was still sixteen and constantly criticized him. "He's not a boy, you know. He is highly thought of by everyone. He runs the whole place, and his staff thinks the world of him. So do Maxx and Charly. Stefano too," I added.

He grunted. "He will always be a boy to me, Kelly. He's my son."

"You should be proud of him."

He turned, narrowing his eyes. "What makes you think I'm not? I know what he does, how hard he works. How people feel about him. I'm very proud of him." He turned away, dropping his voice. "His mother would be too."

"Have you ever told him that?" I asked.

He paused. "I'm not so good with that."

"You should try. It would mean the world to him."

"It sounds as if you know my son well."

I paused, taking a drink of the cold liquid. "We were friends."

"Were?"

"We argued. I think he's mad at me." It was the only explanation I could offer.

He chuckled. "He's been mad at me for years. He's still my son."

"Maybe you need to change that. Him being mad," I said. "Talk to him man-to-man, not father-to-teenager."

He huffed a dry laugh. "He *has* been talking to you."

"Maybe at one point."

He drained his bottle and stood.

"John Hicks at the local paper is looking for someone to take pictures. Go see him, and tell him I sent you."

I sat up straighter. "Oh, thank you."

He held out his hand, and I gave him my empty bottle. He paused before he walked back into the store.

"And maybe take your own advice, young lady. Talk to him. Don't make my mistakes. Life is too short."

Our eyes met, and I saw the sadness in his. I nodded in silence. He pursed his lips. "I like you. Come see me again. Next time, I'll buy you a soda."

Then he went inside, shutting the old wooden door behind him.

I put the small bag in the basket and turned the bike in the direction of downtown. I had a man to see about some pictures.

CHAPTER FIVE

Brett

I looked over the schedule, shaking my head. We were booked solid. We'd already expanded the garage, extended our hours, and still, we were barely able to keep up. Maxx didn't want to extend Saturday hours past noon since that was his family time, and Sundays were the only day most of us got off. I rubbed the back of my neck, thinking about the idea I'd had. I needed to discuss it with Maxx and see what he thought.

Another expansion. Two more bays, at least two more mechanics. I'd been running numbers, and the profit would be worth the outlay.

Charly came in, perching herself up on the stool beside me. She peeked over my shoulder. "Holy moly. What is all that?"

"An idea," I said dryly.

She stopped me from closing the file, flipping through the papers. "You think it's a good idea?"

I sat back, crossing my arms over my head. "I think it's the only option. Unless Maxx agrees to six-to-nine daily, including Saturdays. Have you seen the appointments?"

"I know. It's crazy. I can barely keep up with the paperwork or inventory."

I shot her a look. "You need to get some help."

Her toes started wiggling, and I held in my groan. "What?" I asked.

"I do need some help. Gabby is so busy with the baby and Theo, she can't do as much. I'm busy too and, frankly, I'm tired. Maxx is insisting on it."

"Then get some help. We can put an ad in the paper. I can ask around at other shops."

Her fingers joined in the wiggling. "I, ah, kinda had an idea. I talked to Maxx, and he said I had to talk to you."

I sat back, crossing my ankle over my knee. "Spill it, Charly."

She met my eyes, her wide mossy-green gaze worried. "Kelly," was all she said.

"What about her?" I asked, then realization sank in. "What? Her work here? *No.*" It was hard enough with the glimpses I caught of her coming and going. Overhearing Maxx and Stefano talk about her looking for work in Toronto. The awful places she was looking at living in. I had to stay out of it. But her working *here*? Unthinkable.

She grabbed my hand. "Please listen, Brett."

I withheld the string of curse words I wanted to yell and flicked my fingers, indicating she could talk.

"She can't find a job in Toronto. Or a decent place to live. Maxx offered her the apartment here. Now that the leak is fixed, she can move in and settle. She found a part-time thing with the local paper, and she has a couple of photo shoots scheduled. She could help me with inventory and ordering. Booking appointments, keeping the place running."

I gaped at her. "You want me to work with her in this office every fucking day? Are you crazy, Charly?"

She shook her head. "I've been working from the house, and Kelly could take over. It's not full time, so she can do her other work, but it's enough it will give me more time with my babies." Her gaze became pleading. "I want more time with them."

I hung my head, knowing I wouldn't be able to refuse her. She so rarely asked anyone for anything.

"Charly——" I began, but she interrupted me.

"You would have the barest of contact. I'll deal with her. So will Maxx. She won't invade your space."

"She'll be living here," I pointed out, knowing I was going to lose this battle.

"It's not forever," she said.

I barked out a dry laugh. "It never is with her."

Charly frowned. "If you say no, I'll drop it. I'll figure out another way to help her."

"What does she say?"

"The one time I brought it up, she said no. But I think she might be more open to the idea now. I haven't spoken to her again. I wanted to talk to you first."

"Where is she?"

"In the barn, working."

I stood. "I'm going to talk to her."

She stood as well, crossing her arms, looking like the little spitfire we all loved. "Are you going to be nice, or are you just going to chap her ass and the two of you fight?"

I rested my hands on her shoulders and bent, kissing her forehead. "I'll be nice. But we need to clear the air and set boundaries if this ludicrous idea of yours has any chance of working."

"Okay."

"And I expect you to support me with my plans when I go to Maxx."

"You are such a bad negotiator. I already planned to."

I swatted her butt as she moved past me.

"Whatever, Charly. You are going to owe me for this."

She sniffed. "I think you are going to owe me."

And with those cryptic words, she walked out.

I paused in the barn door, watching Kelly. Maxx had set her up a desk by the workout area, and she had two laptops on it. She was studying something on the screen, her brow furrowed, and she was muttering to herself. The T-shirt she wore was loose, hanging off her frame. She still looked tired and too thin, and before I could stop myself, I began to worry, wondering how she was sleeping. Was she eating enough? I racked my brain, recalling the small plate of food she'd consumed at the barbecue at Stefano's. She always had a healthy appetite before.

Was she sick?

Why did she quit her job?

Why was she back?

How long was she going to stay?

I shook my head to clear my thoughts and rapped on the wood. Kelly looked up, shocked to see me.

"Um, hi." She stood. "Oh, if you're here to work out, I'll go. I'll just push the desk back to the corner. I needed the light over here," she rambled, tapping on the screen and beginning to shut down her laptops.

I held up my hand. "Not here to work out. You don't have to put your stuff away."

"Oh." She stilled, her nerves evident. "What do you need?"

"I want to talk to you."

Her eyes got wider. "Okay."

I began to walk in, but memories assaulted me. Her naked with me on the bench. The two of us playing hide-and-seek in the dark corners of the barn. The time we made love up in the rafters while it rained—when I was hopeful our *"for now"* was turning into our *"forever."* She'd left shortly after that.

"Not here," I said, sounding curt.

She looked puzzled, then realization dawned, and she stood. "Of course."

I turned and she followed. I headed up the stairs at the side of the building and, using my key, entered the apartment over the garage. It was furnished and homey, although a little stuffy and dusty from the repairs being done. Charly would have the place cleaned once it was finished, but it had been shut up and unused for a while now. I opened the window and indicated the small table in the kitchen. We sat across from each other, not saying anything for a moment.

Finally, she cleared her throat. "You wanted to talk to me?"

"Charly came to see me. She wants you to take over some of her hours at the garage."

Her light-blue eyes flew open wide, and color stained her cheeks. The tips of her ears grew red. I could tell she was as taken aback by the news as I had been.

She shook her head. "I'll tell her no, Brett. I had no idea she was thinking about it again and planned on talking to you. I'm sorry."

She began to stand. "I have no desire to hurt you more than I did. If I had anywhere else I could be, I would go there. I'm sorry," she said again. "So very sorry."

Before I could think, I stood, grabbing her arm to stop her leaving. "Why are you apologizing? For this, or for something else?"

I was shocked to see the tears in her eyes. Kelly never cried.

"I'm sorry for so many things," she murmured. "But right now, I'm sorry Charly put you in this position. I know you don't believe me, but I had nothing to do with it. I'll make sure she understands not to ask you again."

She turned and hurried to the door. Anger and frustration exploded from me, obliterating any common sense I had. I raced after her, stopping her from opening the door.

"Stop running," I snapped.

She shook her head, pulling harder on the door.

I grabbed her arm and spun her around.

"Stop," I commanded. "Why the fuck do you always run?"

She met my eyes, the tears and heartbreak in them cracking open something inside me.

"Because I don't know how to stop," she wailed, then burst into tears, covering her face.

There was no thought. No careful consideration. No reminders of the turmoil she had caused me. All I saw, all I felt, was her pain. Her need.

I dragged her into my arms, feeling her fall against me, her hot tears soaking my shirt.

I held her close.

"No more," I murmured. "It stops now."

KELLY

Being back in Brett's embrace was like coming home. He held me tight in his arms, and he stroked my head gently, his voice a soft hum in my ear as I cried. His scent surrounded me, the unique blend of his soap suiting him so well. It was like a warm summer day, which Brett always reminded me of.

I had missed him so much.

And I was so tired.

He led us to the sofa, and we sat down, me still in his arms. When I was finally cried out, he pressed some tissues into my hand and let me compose myself. He left the room, returning with a glass of water that I sipped. I cleared my throat.

"Sorry about that," I whispered, my voice rough.

"It's fine."

I shook my head, looking down. "No, it's far from fine," I whispered again.

I was shocked to feel him stroke his hand over my head again. "Your hair is longer."

"I need to get it cut."

His hand fell away. "I kinda like it."

"You lost your curls," I replied.

He ran his hand through the longer top of his hair. "I wanted a different look."

"I liked them."

He shifted, not saying anything. Those few words were the most personal we had gotten since I came back.

I wiped my eyes and nose and met his gaze. For the first time since coming back, it wasn't filled with anger or dislike. It was compassionate and patient. It made me want to weep again.

"Talk to me, Kelly. Tell me what's going on."

"I'm sorry Charly—"

He shook his head, interrupting me. "This doesn't have anything to do with Charly asking me about you working in the garage. What brought you back here?"

I sighed and chose my words carefully. "You were right about Carl. He wasn't the person I thought he was."

"Did he hurt you?" he asked, his hands tightening on his thighs. I thought about what Charly said the other day.

"There are lots of ways to hurt a person." I cleared my throat. "He stole some of my work and claimed it as his."

"*What?* That fucking *bastard,*" he snarled.

"You were right, Brett. He was using me. Holding me back. When I discovered it, we argued. It got ugly—very ugly. I quit, and he didn't take it well. Told me I owed him. That I was nothing and he was everything. The name, the star." I shook my head. "He was right, of course. I was just the assistant."

"What happened?" he asked.

"I, ah, got sick and ended up in the hospital. He packed up and left. Just deserted me in Costa Rica. I had to pay the medical bills and get myself home. It ate up a lot of my savings." I met his eyes. "I had nowhere else to go, Brett. My apartment was gone, I couldn't afford to stay in a hotel for long. I had to come to Charly." A tear ran down my cheek. "I wasn't even sure if she'd let me stay after the way I left. But she was my only hope."

"She's your friend. Of course she'd be there for you."

"She's your friend too. She's very fond of you." I swallowed. "I'm sorry she put you in this position. I'll talk to her."

He shook his head, impatient. "We'll talk about that after. Is that why you are so thin and tired-looking? You were ill?" He took my hand. "Are you okay?"

I was shocked at his words. He'd noticed more than I thought he had.

"I will be." I squeezed his hand. "I just need some more time."

"Good." He huffed out a breath. "You're in the right place. You need your friends around you. You need a place to recover."

"Are we?" I asked.

"Are we what?"

"Friends?"

He was quiet for a moment, stroking his chin.

"Kelly, we have a lot of history. You showing up, us hooking up, you leaving. Last time, I thought we'd moved past that, but you left again. I don't understand. I have never understood why you left the way you did."

"I know." I got up and walked the room, stopping at the window. I stared outside. "I'm sorry about that too."

"I don't know what we are, but I care about you. I hate seeing you like this," he admitted.

I turned. "Like this?"

"Withdrawn, not yourself. I miss the spunk."

I sighed. "I'm trying. I'm s—"

He held up his hand. "I don't want another apology." He studied me for a moment. "I don't know the whole story of why you came back. I know you're editing. And I don't know what made you run in the first place. Both figure strongly in the person you are and our past relationship."

I knew what he wanted. To know everything. But I couldn't. Not now. The reality was I didn't know if I'd ever be ready. He deserved to know the truth, but the words were too ugly to say, capable of causing even more damage than they already had.

"I can't," I whispered. "Not yet."

He scrubbed his face. "I'll leave it. It's not really my business anymore anyway."

My heart sank at his words.

"Come sit down, and we can discuss the garage."

I sat across from him, too afraid to sit beside him. All I wanted was to lean into him again. To feel his arms around me and let his strength surround me. But he didn't want that, and I was afraid if I tried, he would reject me—or, worse, I would break and tell him everything. I wasn't ready for that yet.

"Charly needs help," he stated. "She wants more time with the kids. Gabby is busy with her own family. Charly doesn't want to hire a stranger. You've helped in the garage before, so as much as I dislike the idea, it makes sense."

"I can work in Charly's house."

"She offered that, but then it defeats the purpose. If she wants more time with the kids and less worrying about the garage, having you work there won't solve the issue. You know what she's like. She'll be micromanaging everything."

I had to laugh. "True. Charly can't help herself."

He caught on to the levity of the moment and grinned, his adoration of her clear. "One of her best traits. She needs it to handle Maxx."

"She handles him well."

Brett groaned. "Too well at times. The things I've witnessed..." He trailed off, meeting my eyes. We shared a moment of joint laughter, then I returned to the subject.

"What do you propose?"

"Work in the office beside mine, like Charly did. It's not full time, and we're adults."

I nodded, wondering how it would feel to see him all the time.

"You think that would work?"

"I'm willing to give it a try." He paused. "Charly says you got some sort of gig with the paper?"

"Oh yes," I said, feeling excited. "Your dad mentioned they were looking for someone to take pictures for them when I was at the store last week. I went and saw the editor. His son, Rob, has joined him and wants to bring some new life into the paper. They want pictures of festivals and things going on around town and the area. I suggested a couple other things they could do to help readership, and they liked my ideas."

"My dad did that?"

"Yeah, he did. He remembered I took pictures."

"Huh," he muttered.

"You're very much like him."

He barked a laugh. "I don't think so, although it might be better if I were."

I frowned, unsure what he meant.

"He's very proud of you."

Brett's eyebrows shot up. "Is that a fact?"

"He told me so."

"He's never mentioned it to me."

"Maybe you need to sit down and talk to him."

He narrowed his eyes. "I don't think you're the right person to be offering relationship advice, Kelly."

"Sorry. He just seemed…lonely when I was talking to him."

"He made his bed," Brett muttered.

I wasn't sure what that meant, but before I could ask, he changed the subject.

"What were they?" he asked, curious. "Your ideas, I mean?"

"I suggested featuring local businesses. Pictures of their wares and the people running the place. Like your dad. Maxx. Zeke's Bar. The lady who sells the homemade jams and syrups people love so much. A buy local sort of thing. It's so popular now. And include the other towns the paper encompasses. It services more than Littleburn."

Brett nodded.

"I also suggested they do an article on a different citizen every week. Not just the well-known ones like Maxx or the president of the bank. The local high school coach who spends his time working at the food bank. The retired principal who tutors kids in need. The lifeguard who works overtime so special needs kids can swim after hours in a safe environment. Everyday heroes. I can take their pictures, and he can run the stories."

"Sounds like you'll be busy."

I shrugged. "Not more than a couple days a week. And they only pay for the pictures I sell to them. But it's a way to keep taking pictures and get my name out there. Maybe help me score more wedding gigs. Those pay well. I can start saving again."

"What about your other photos? I saw your work. Can't you sell some of those?"

I felt the color drain from my face as I struggled to answer him without having to give him more information.

"I am keeping my eyes open for places to submit," I managed to get out between tight lips.

"Okay." He nodded. "Okay, that's good."

He lowered his head, rubbing his chin. He always did that when he was thinking.

"All right. I'll tell Charly we can try this. But there are rules."

"Okay."

"I'll be polite. But there is nothing between us. Our past is exactly that—the past. I'll work with you because it helps Charly and Maxx."

"Not even friends?" I asked, pushing the words out through my thick throat. The gentleness from earlier had melted. Brett wasn't as cold as he had been since I got back, but he wasn't going to forgive me. Not yet, not easily, and I had to come to terms with the fact that that may be…never.

"You have to have trust to be a friend. You broke that, Kelly. Not me. My mistake was letting you know how much you meant. And you walked away from that. *From me.* I can't forget that, and I won't make the same mistake again."

"I know."

"You work in the garage, you live up here until you have the money you need to move on. We both know you hate small towns and being in one for long, so I'm sure it won't take you much time to get on your feet again."

It was on the tip of my tongue to tell him I had been wrong about that too, but I kept it to myself.

"Keep me up-to-date on your schedule. I realize things might come up at the last minute, and that's fine. We'll work it through."

"I appreciate that."

"That's all I can give you. I'll treat you with courtesy and respect, and I expect the same from you. We're coworkers. Acquaintances. That's it." He met my gaze, his steady and distant. "I'm sure there'll be barbecues and suppers with staff and friends, and I'm fine for you to be there. I don't expect you to hide up here. But that's all we are. Are you clear?"

"Yes."

He stood. "Fine. I'll go tell Maxx and Charly."

He turned to leave, and I stood as well. "Brett?"

He turned and looked over his shoulder. "Thanks for this. And earlier—when I was crying. I'm sorry I overreacted."

He shook his head. "I wouldn't call that overreacting, Kelly. I'd call that being real with me. I think that was the most honest emotion I have ever seen from you." He paused, his hand on the door handle. "Too bad it happened too late for us."

And he walked out.

CHAPTER SIX

Brett

Her sobs, her words, echoed in my head all night.

Because I don't know how to stop.

I had the feeling Kelly had been on the run her entire life. Searching for something. Trying to escape memories.

The memory of how she felt in my arms stayed with me. I swore I could still smell her fragrance on my skin. I couldn't shake the feeling that it was as if that was where she belonged. I couldn't stop the thoughts.

Her tears had gutted me. I had seen Kelly happy, teasing, angry, and defensive. Sexy and alluring. Sleepy and quiet.

I had never seen her cry. Never witnessed her so vulnerable.

There was more to her being here than a fight with Carl. She'd held him on a pedestal so high it was unreachable. Her friend. Her mentor. I had met him once in Toronto and disliked him intensely. He'd had a last-minute shoot and called Kelly to assist him. I had gone in with her out of curiosity, wanting to see her in action. When I mentioned going, she seemed surprised but pleased.

Carl didn't look overly happy to see me. His handshake was brief, and he ignored my presence except to snap that I needed to stay out of the way. I stood in the corner, watching and silent. He barked orders at her and another assistant. He pointed and demanded. Kelly was patient, often talking quietly, pointing out an angle or making a suggestion. He rolled his eyes, yet I noticed he often used her advice. But he was an asshole about it, somehow turning it into his own idea. He came across as arrogant, selfish, and narcissistic, and I told Kelly so.

"He takes credit for your ideas," I insisted.

"He has to roll them around in his mind. That's how he works. He interprets and makes them his own."

I barely withheld my snort.

"He's an egotistical jerk."

Kelly laughed and told me he was artistic and broody. I hated the way he talked to her, ordered her around like a lackey. She shook her head.

"He's my boss, and he expects me to do my job."

"Maxx doesn't expect me to mop his brow and cut up his fruit," I snapped. "Or is so lazy he can't get a piece of equipment from a table five feet away."

"It's my job to make his life simple. He can concentrate on taking pictures, capturing the beauty he sees through his lens, and I do the rest."

"You're far more talented," I argued. "Your suggestions were dead-on every time."

She had smiled and kissed me. "You're biased. I'm still learning."

I'd had the feeling if Carl had his way, she'd be learning for a lot of years to come.

She thought the world of him and his talent. She idolized him.

Why would he steal her work, and what had made her ill?

Was she really okay?

Why did I feel so much anxiety from her now?

Those questions plagued me.

And considering how it felt when I held her, how right it felt to have her in my arms again, the biggest question of all was—how I was going to handle seeing her in the office beside mine? Hearing her voice? Her laughter? Knowing that I had to stay away from her?

My head felt as if it was going to explode.

She shouldn't still affect me this way, but she did. As much as I denied it, nothing had changed for me.

I sighed, leaning my head back on the chair. I sipped the bottle of beer, barely tasting it. My thoughts were never-ending, focused on the upcoming week.

I knew she had moved in to the apartment after I left. I saw Maxx carrying some boxes up the steps when I was leaving. Chase was coming out of the barn with others. I didn't offer to help. Charly would help her unpack and settle.

I couldn't stop wondering how long she would stay for this time. I scrubbed my face as memories, ones I didn't like to think about, hit.

Stefano's wedding day had dawned bright and clear. I had arrived at his place early, helping him set up. Maxx and Chase were there, as well as Stefano's brothers. We had everything ready in short order. The entire day was filled with laughter. Kelly was everywhere, snapping pictures, taking candid shots, setting up more formal pictures to please Rosa. From my seat, I had a clear view of her as she slipped around, taking pictures of the brief ceremony. She looked beautiful, her dark hair gleaming in the sun, a bright smile on her face. Our eyes met time and time again during the day. Glances that held and smoldered. Beckoned and promised. The emotion of the day was heightened, strumming in my veins. Every chance I got, I touched her. She sought me out to do the same. Fast kisses when no one was looking, longer, lingering ones in the kitchen, the hall, and one intense set of foreplay locked in the bathroom had me anxious for the day to be done. How it had happened, I didn't know, but every time she came back, I felt more. Her visits became more frequent, our time together more intimate. Our goodbyes longer, the pain of her departing more intense. But I let her go every time, knowing that was what she needed. Or at least, it used to be.

She came home with me. In my room, I watched her as I locked the door behind me, my frantic need morphing into something else. Something more tender, more intense, and deeper. Fabric whispered as it fell to the floor. We kissed endlessly, each touch of our lips a silent conversation. Our caresses were soft, exploring. Her whispered pleas were music to my ears. Her body said what her mouth couldn't.

I heard every word.

After, we lay wrapped together, a newer, powerful intimacy between us. Another shift had happened in our relationship. One more permanent and strong. We both felt it.

The next few days only solidified that. We were barely able to be apart. She found excuses to show up in the garage. I found reasons to be wherever she was. Sex became...more. One look or touch from her and I was ready. We were together every chance we got. In the barn, behind the garage, rolling together in the fields behind the house.

The storeroom was a personal favorite.

Until the day it came to an abrupt end.

I hadn't seen her all morning, which was a rare occurrence now. After I closed the garage at noon, I headed to the house. Maxx and Charly had gone to Mary's, but I knew Kelly was in the house. I headed upstairs, stopping in the doorway, freezing at the sight in front of me. The bags on the bed, Kelly busy loading up her camera equipment.

"What the hell?"

She spun at my voice.

"What are you doing?"

"Carl has an assignment. I have to get back to work."

"When are you leaving?"

"In a couple of hours."

"Hours?" I questioned. "When the hell were you going to tell me?"

She didn't meet my eyes. "I was going to call from the airport."

I grabbed her arm, spinning her to face me. "Call? You were going to call?"

"Yes."

"And say what? Thanks for the great sex, but I'm off?"

She shook off my hold. "You know the rules, Brett."

"Fuck the rules, Kelly. You know those changed. We both know those changed."

She shook her head. "What did you expect? That I'd stay, and we'd play the happy couple?"

"There's no playing, Kelly. We are happy."

She zipped her bag shut. "I don't know what you want from me."

"I want you to talk to me."

"I have nothing to say. I have a job, and I have to leave. You knew it would happen."

"When will you be back?"

She shook her head, turning away. "I don't know."

Her words felt like a bomb going off in my chest.

"Will you be back?"

Her silence said it all.

"So, that's it—nothing's changed for you? All I am is a good fuck in between assignments?" I sneered. "You're telling me I imagined what was growing between us? I'm the only one who felt it?"

"I never promised you anything."

"Not in words. But you were right there with me. Things changed. We changed. And you're scared," I accused.

"Scared of what?"

"Of the fact that you're falling in love with me."

She shook her head. "No."

I stepped closer. "You are. You're lying to yourself. You keep coming back. Staying longer. We're together every time." I paused. "There's no one else but you."

"I haven't been with anyone else either. But that doesn't mean—"

I cut her off. "Yes, it does. That's why you're leaving. You feel something for me, and you're afraid."

Silence hung between us.

"I love you," I said, laying it on the line.

She shook her head wildly. "I never asked you to."

"But it happened. For both of us."

She shook her head again, refusing to admit it.

"I never took you for a coward, Kelly."

"I'm sorry," she whispered.

Our eyes locked, her expression sad but determined.

"Don't," I pleaded. "Stay. Or promise me you'll come back."

"I can't do that. Not this time."

"So, all this—all the time, the hours we've spent together, have meant nothing? I'm just what—a fill-in?"

She turned, reaching for a piece of clothing that she folded and put in the bag.

"If you do this, that's it, Kelly. I'm not waiting. We're done," I threatened.

She turned and looked at me. The next moment, she was in my arms, kissing me. I tasted her tears, her regret, my pain, her torment. She stepped back, looking determined, shaking off my hold.

"We already are."

The front door opened, and Chase strolled in, pizza box in hand, interrupting my dark thoughts.

"Hey, Brett. You eat yet?"

I shook my head to banish the memories. "Nope."

"Great." He slid the pizza box on the coffee table and went to the kitchen, returning with a beer, two bottles of water, and a pile of napkins. He handed me a water. "Ronnie was working, and she looked pretty heavy-handed with the hot peppers."

"Great." I opened the lid, the spicy aroma hitting my nose. I took a piece and some napkins. We rarely bothered with plates. We ate in silence, the only sounds our chewing, some low mutterings over the spicy toppings, and the swallows of the cold water or beer. After a couple of slices, I sat back, taking a break.

"She was pretty damn generous with the hot sausage as well."

He chuckled. "I told her I like it spicy. The same way I like my women."

I burst out laughing. "Kid, you need to up your game."

He snorted, draining his beer. "Says the guy sitting at home eating pizza with me on a Friday night." He held up his phone. "I got her number and a date for Tuesday, so I think my game is better than yours, old man."

I had to join in his amusement. "You got me there."

He got us each another cold beer and sat back, relaxing into the cushions. "I heard we have a new staff member on Monday."

"Yeah."

He was quiet for a moment, picking at the label of his bottle. "You okay with that? I know you have history."

I shrugged. "I'll handle it."

"I helped take her stuff up to the apartment." He took a pull on his bottle. "She didn't have much."

"She traveled so much she kept her life pretty light," I agreed.

"She seemed...sad."

"I don't think her life is the way she expected it to be at the moment."

"I suppose." He sat forward, resting his elbows on his knees. "Mine is better than I thought it would be."

"Really?"

He nodded. "When I was in jail, I had no idea what life would be like when I got out. The first time I came out to the garage, I only wanted to apologize to Charly and Maxx. My therapist thought it would help me. I had zero idea Charly would insist Maxx hire me. And I never expected to become part of their family."

I nodded in understanding. "Charly was determined. And she is pretty hard to resist when she's made up her mind."

"She is. She's like a sister, a mother, and a friend, all rolled into one. I wouldn't be here if it weren't for her. I'll always be grateful to her for sticking up for me to Maxx and giving me a chance."

"You've earned your spot, Chase. Your past is just that now. Past. You don't have to prove yourself anymore. To any of us."

"Charly says that too. Sometimes it's still hard to believe, though, you know?" He stared into space. "Sometimes the pain you caused another person is harder to forgive yourself for."

"You can't change the past. You have to go forward."

He met my gaze. "Exactly."

I rolled my eyes. "Nice one. I will be polite to Kelly. Respectful. But I won't put myself in the position to be hurt again."

"Sometimes you have to take that chance."

"And other times, you know when not to. I've been burned too often by that flame."

"And what if I asked Kelly out on a date?"

The words were out before I could think. "I don't fucking think so," I practically growled.

He stood, chuckling, taking the pizza box. "That's what I thought."

"I just meant we don't need more drama in the garage," I insisted.

"Yep. Sure. I'm going to go have a shower while you sit there and insist denial is just a river in Egypt. There's a game on later, right?" His amused voice faded down the hallway. "We can watch that and pretend everything is normal."

I glared at his retreating back. Little fucker.

He had no idea what he was talking about.

CHAPTER SEVEN

Brett

Monday, I was at the garage early. Not long afterward, Kelly showed up with Charly, heading straight to the little kitchen.

"Always make coffee first," Charly said with a laugh. "The boys make tar, and you'll be stuck drinking it."

Then she sat with Kelly, showing her the system and going through the basics.

I concentrated on the schedule, sipping the coffee Charly kindly brought me, half listening to their conversation. I tried not to notice the way the jeans Kelly wore hugged her rounded ass, or how her T-shirt stretched tightly over her pert breasts.

I failed.

She'd had her hair cut, the short cap hugging her head once again, dark and gleaming in the bright lights. It suited her, setting off the row of freckles across the bridge of her nose and her unusual light-blue eyes. They were almost silver in this light. She was still too thin, but I found her incredibly sexy, regardless. She moved with an innate sense of grace, and I enjoyed watching her. I had always enjoyed it, especially when she was naked.

I shook my head to clear it. Those days were past, and now we were simply forced coworkers.

I headed to the office and rapped on the door. "Everything good, ladies?"

They glanced up, and Charly smiled. "Kelly remembers most of it. I'm just showing her the new banking and payment processing stuff."

"Great. If you need anything, I'm either in the office or on the floor. I don't leave without letting someone know."

Kelly offered me a tight smile. "Okay."

"Anyone gives you a problem, get me."

"You expect that to happen?" Kelly asked.

"No. Just saying." I shrugged. "New, pretty face... Sometimes the customers push the envelope."

Charly looked away, a grin tugging on her lips. She muttered something that sounded strangely like *"Holy moly, here we go."*

"What was that, Charly?" I asked, folding my arms across my chest.

"Nothing," she lied, her eyes dancing. "Just our customers are usually pretty nice. Kelly will figure out everything. Easy peasy. I wouldn't have asked her if I didn't think so."

"Of course not. Anyway, I'll leave you to it. If you need me..." I trailed off.

"I'll find you," Kelly finished.

I walked away, refusing to turn around when I heard Charly's low laughter. She said something to Kelly, who made a strange noise, but I kept walking. I knew whatever Charly said was about me, and I wanted no part of it.

I managed to maintain my polite, dismissive veneer the entire week. Kelly kept her word, and our interactions were professional and brief. She was a hard worker, her few questions intelligent and easily answered. She got along well with the other mechanics and customers. I chose to ignore the few who lingered longer than necessary at her desk, although some may have felt my glare and left quicker than they planned. I made a point of keeping the door between the two offices open most of the time. Kelly never questioned it, although Charly chortled a few times when she came in and noticed it. I ignored her.

Friday afternoon, Kelly disappeared to head to the bank. I finished the engine rebuild I had been working on, then headed to the office to check the payroll and other items that needed my approval before going to Maxx for final confirmation.

Once I was done, I sat with Maxx, who checked everything quickly, signing off on it all. When he was done, he tapped the file I'd given him earlier in the week.

"Big undertaking."

"Necessary. Unless you want a second location or to start turning business away."

He frowned. "I don't like either of the last two options."

"The build will be fast, Maxx. We'll add it to the left, blow out the side for access, and be in business. Most of the work can happen without disturbing this part of the garage. It doesn't affect the paint bays or the production area. Just two simple stalls. Two more mechanics. Or we can do four part-timers if you want."

He ran a hand over his head. "Our custom work is getting busier all the time."

"So we add another artist to the works too."

He chuckled. "If my dad could see this place now, he'd be blown away."

"All thanks to the vision Charly had."

He smiled, his eyes straying to a picture that hung on the wall. Charly and his kids, all dressed in garage uniforms, sitting on his prized Indian motorcycle, smiling at the camera. "My Red is a force," he said quietly.

"One for good," I acknowledged.

"She changed my life."

I had to chuckle. "Holy moly, Maxx. That's an understatement."

He threw back his head in laughter. "You got that right." He tapped the folder. "Okay, let's do this. I assume we'll use Crayton's again?"

"Yep. He gave me the best quote, and he did a great job on the other expansion. Stuck to the timeline and came in on budget." I smirked. "Having Charly ride his ass helped. I'll put her in charge again."

"You do that. She can oversee it and let Kelly work in here." He paused. "That working okay for you?"

"It's fine. She sticks to her side. I stick to mine. We're polite, and I have to give it to her. She works hard and takes a lot off my plate."

"Good." He paused. "Where is she?"

"At the bank and a couple of errands." I frowned as I glanced at my watch. "I thought she'd be back by now, actually."

"I'm sure she will be back soon." He stood. "Okay. Let's move ahead with the project, and I like the idea of us all switching Saturdays again. Gives us all time with our families. But I don't expect you and Chase to cover every second one."

I shrugged. "I don't mind. I like working with the kid. He's become a really good mechanic."

"Maybe we should hire a new runner. Make him one of the team permanently."

"He'd like that. He deserves it too."

He nodded. "I'll talk to him."

He left, and a short while later, Kelly walked in, putting the bank books on the desk and bringing me the petty cash I'd requested.

I frowned as I looked at her. "Why is your shirt wet?"

She glanced down with a laugh. "Oh, I stopped to get some more bacon from your dad for Charly, and when we were having a drink on the front step, he told me he was having trouble with his soda machine. I was trying to help him, and I dropped a wrench in the water and it splashed all over me."

"A drink on the front step?"

"Yeah. We sit and chat a little. Like I said last week, I think he's lonely. He asked about the paper and the garage, and it was nice to talk to him."

The thought of Kelly and my dad sitting, sharing some time together, somehow made me unsettled yet pleased. It was an odd sensation.

"What kind of trouble?"

"It's not keeping the bottles cold. I think it needs a new compressor."

"Why didn't he call me?"

She lifted one shoulder, studying me. When she spoke, her voice was gentle. "I don't think he wants to bother you, Brett."

"He's my father—he's not a bother."

"Maybe you need to tell him that. In fact, I think the two of you need to talk and, for a change, really listen to each other." She set down the envelope and headed to her office. "I'll see you on Monday."

"You aren't going to Rosa's on Sunday?" I asked before I could think about it.

She shook her head. "You're stuck with me during the week. I won't interfere with your downtime too. Stefano is your friend, that is *your* circle. Not mine."

Then she walked away.

For some reason, those words bothered me the rest of the day.

The next day, I closed the garage at noon, packed up some tools and parts, and headed to the store. My dad was inside, adding a few items to the shelves. His radio was set to an oldies station, and the sound was staticky and muffled. He needed a new one, and I wondered how much resistance he would put up if I tried to give him one. I studied him from the open door. He was dressed as usual, his shirt crisp and white. A dark cardigan was pulled over top, and his tie matched. His hair gleamed in the light, and his shoulders were still broad under his sweater. His shoes shone. But I noticed the lines around his eyes were deeper, and he looked almost forlorn.

I felt a flash of guilt. Kelly was right. I needed to see more of him. He wasn't getting any younger, and we needed to move past this impasse we seemed to have been locked in for years. I knew Charly checked in on him regularly. Brought the kids to see him. She had him to dinner on occasion, always making sure to invite me. I always declined, letting her have a relationship with him that didn't include me. I only dropped in on occasion, and my visits were always brief and usually fraught with tension. Maybe I needed to do something about that.

I rapped on the wood as I walked into the store.

"Hey, Pops."

He looked up, surprise on his face. "Brett. What are you doing here?"

"Can't I come see my old man?"

"You can, but you rarely do."

I bit back my usual retort of saying he never asked me to. "Well, here I am."

He set down the can he was holding. "Here you are." A glimmer of a smile crossed his face. "I like surprises."

"I hear you're having a problem with the soda refrigerator."

He scratched his head. "It doesn't seem to be working so well. Like a lot of things in the store, it's getting old."

"Old isn't bad, Pops. But maybe it needs some work. Want me to have a look?"

"You have time?" he asked, once again looking shocked.

"Absolutely."

"It's not a car," he pointed out.

"The parts are similar," I said. "I can look anyway."

"Sure."

He sighed. "I hope it doesn't die. Those new ones don't keep the soda as cold."

"And they aren't as cool. We'll fix it."

He smiled. "Great."

Half an hour later, I wiped my hands. "That should do it. One of the coils was blocked. I'll have Stefano come check out another part I think needs some work. But it should help. Chase is great at finding parts. I'll have him hunt down a compressor we can rebuild and tweak so we can keep it going." I patted the lid. "I always liked this old girl."

"I can already hear it humming."

"Me too."

"Grab a soda, and we'll sit outside a spell." Dad hesitated. "If you have time."

"Add in some chips, and you got yourself a deal."

I sat down in one of the rockers, taking a long pull on the orange soda and smacking my lips. "I always loved this one."

He chuckled. "You were forever getting me in trouble with your mother, sneaking those. And the KitKat bars. You were the reason I had to get a locking candy display for the longest time." He paused. "Until you learned to pick the lock."

I laughed, remembering when he caught me. "You were so mad."

"You were eating my profits, son."

I chuckled. "Mom was pretty mad too."

He sighed. "She was. I had to hold her back from grounding you."

The bottle paused partway to my mouth. "You did?"

He took a sip of his soda. "Yep." He met my confused glance. "She was the one who decided on the punishments, not me. She said I went too easy on you all the time." He shrugged. "You were my boy," he added, sounding self-conscious.

I shook my head. "I had no idea."

"You weren't supposed to."

"You never said anything."

"There's a lot of things I never said," he admitted, looking out over the road to the field beyond. "And sometimes I said too much."

I thought of what Kelly had talked about. Of all the silence that lingered between us. My dad had always treated me like a kid. Second-guessed my decisions. Argued with me over my thoughts until I stopped expressing them—especially after my mom died. Until all that was left between us was silence.

"Maybe we both have a lot of things we need to say," I offered.

"Hard to do that when I never see you."

I leaned forward, resting my elbows on my thighs, staring straight ahead the way he did.

"Maybe we could change that."

"I'd like that."

I knew somehow I had to make the bigger effort. Bridge this gap between us.

I pulled out my phone and sent off a message, which was answered right away. I slid my phone back into my pocket.

"What are you doing tomorrow, Pops?"

He frowned. "It's Sunday."

I sat back and drained the orange soda, setting down the bottle. "I'm aware."

"Church in the morning. Lunch at the diner."

"Nope. Tomorrow, you're coming with me after church."

"Where?"

"Stefano's mother's place for lunch. It's a weekly thing for her, and I join them on occasion. Stefano says you're welcome."

"I can't do that. That's her family."

75

"Yes, you can. And you are. To Rosa, everyone is family. Me included."

He looked at me. "Is Kelly included in the invitation?"

I paused.

"She's a nice girl."

I sighed. "Yeah, Pops, she is. But she's more Charly's friend."

He emitted a low snort, shaking his head.

"What?"

"I'm old, not senile, blind, or deaf, Brett. I saw you two last summer in Lomand, holding hands, walking down the street. I saw how withdrawn you became when she left. I think she's more than a friend of Charly's."

"Leave it, Pops. It's ancient history now."

He leaned back, finishing his soda, placing his empty bottle beside mine. "Your mom and I had our problems," he said. "We even broke up before we were married."

I looked at him, surprised at his words. "Oh?"

He nodded. "I was twenty-six when I met your mother. I was crazy about her, but I didn't want to settle down. I wanted to see the world. She wanted a family."

"Obviously, something changed." I turned to look at him. "Jesus, she wasn't pregnant with me, and you stayed. Is that it?"

Was that why he resented me?

He shook his head. "Math was never your strong suit, was it, son? We were married for four years before you came along."

76

"Oh, right." I chuckled sheepishly.

"I had been working and saving for years. Planning a three-year trip. I was going to see the world. I realized as I was working out the details of my time away that I wasn't excited. I didn't want to go anymore. My dreams had changed, and it took losing your mother for me to realize it."

"What did you do?"

"Put my pride in my pocket and went to your mother. Told her how I was feeling. We compromised. We were married a month later and spent a year traveling together. Then we came home, and I opened the store with the rest of the money I hadn't spent. We did well. I bought the building, and we moved upstairs. A few years later, you came along. My life was pretty complete."

"Until Mom died."

He nodded, not speaking for a moment. "I had her by my side for a long time. Over twenty years. A lifetime would have been better, but those years were the best of my life." He rocked his chair a little, the motion slow and methodical.

"You were so angry over losing your mother. Then you became angry at me. I felt as if I lost you both."

I sighed. "I was lost, Pops. Mom was always the go-between for us. I didn't know how to talk to you. Express what I was feeling. You always treated me as if I was an idiot who didn't know his own mind."

He chuckled. "When you were younger, you didn't. I guess I got in the habit of second-guessing you. Your mom always said we struck sparks because we were so alike." He sighed. "I didn't mean to push you away."

I was quiet for a moment, trying to process everything. His truth. Mine. Two people running opposite of each other instead of parallel. Away instead of together.

"Perhaps we can meet in the middle. Two grown men with something in common," I offered.

"Which is?" he asked, sounding wary.

I met his gaze. "Family." I paused. "Our family."

His eyes became misty, and he glanced away, clearing his throat. "I like the sound of that."

"Okay, then. Lunch tomorrow with Stefano's family? I'll pick you up about eleven thirty?"

"I'll be waiting."

I stood. "Okay. I have to get going."

He held out his hand. "Thanks for stopping by, son."

I accepted his handshake, suddenly feeling odd. Stefano's family hugged. Joked. Laughed. Expressed their feelings for one another freely.

I wanted to get to that stage with my dad.

I walked down the steps, thinking.

"Brett."

I turned.

"Remember, we all make mistakes. Sometimes we regret them for the rest of our life. Sometimes we correct them. Think about that."

I left, mulling over his words, still blown away by the fact that we had actually talked. There had been no yelling or accusations. No him talking over me. None of my usual sarcasm I always had ready to throw at him. We simply talked.

It felt good.

And of all the people in the world I had to thank, it was Kelly.

That was the oddest sensation of them all.

CHAPTER EIGHT

Brett

K elly's face was shocked when she opened her door and found me on the other side of it.

"Brett?" she asked, looking confused. "Is everything okay?"

"Yeah," I assured her. "Could I have a moment of your time?"

She frowned, looking worried.

"Nothing bad," I said. "Just a private word with you."

She stepped back and let me in. The apartment already looked different. When Chase lived here, it was rudimentary. The furniture Charly had bought was all he had. No knickknacks or pictures—nothing personal. For him, it had been a place to live, and that was about it.

Kelly had added a couple of bookshelves, and they held a collection of things I assumed she picked up from her travels. On the walls, she had hung some pictures I knew she had taken. She watched me look around and shrugged self-consciously.

"Charly insisted I unpack my stuff and make it feel like home," she said. "We ordered the bookshelves and spent an evening putting them together." She laughed lightly. "Thank God for Mary, or they might still be in the boxes."

I chuckled.

"Did you want something to drink?" she asked, sounding hesitant.

"Sure. Water would be good."

She went to the kitchen and came back with a tall glass, the cold frosting the sides. "Lots of ice the way you like," she said, offering it to me.

I smiled and sat down. She sat across from me, crossing her legs underneath her. Her hair was damp, and she was dressed in a loose shirt and yoga pants that hugged her slim legs. She had on no makeup or shoes, looking relaxed and still so beautiful it made my throat tight looking at her.

And my cock twitch.

I shook my head. "I came to tell you that it's okay for you to come to lunch tomorrow." I drew in a deep breath. "In fact, you *should* come to lunch tomorrow. Rosa would be pleased, and so would Charly."

"I don't want to make you uncomfortable."

"You won't. I also came to thank you."

"Thank me?" she repeated, sounding incredulous.

"I went and saw my dad today and looked at the soda machine. We shared a drink after." I paused. "We talked. Not argued, not yelled. Talked."

"How did that feel?"

"Good. Really good. He shared a few things with me, and I promised to see more of him. In fact, he is coming to Rosa's with me tomorrow. I would like it if you came as well." I paused. "He likes you."

"I—"

I cut her off. "Please just come. It's lunch, and there are lots of people. But my dad would be more comfortable with as many friendly faces as possible."

"So, you want me to come for your dad?"

"Yes." Then I grinned. "Plus, you know, the lasagna."

"I do remember that it's pretty awesome."

"Best in the country. And she always makes ziti and meatballs for her Theo. Those aren't too shabby either."

"And it wouldn't bother you?"

"No." I took a sip of water. "Despite our past, Kelly, I do care. There is no reason for you to be alone here when you could be part of a nice afternoon. I don't want to be the reason you're on your own. Charly will be unhappy. Rosa won't be pleased. My dad wouldn't like it either. So, come."

She was quiet for a moment, then nodded. "Okay, I'll think about it. I appreciate it, Brett."

"I appreciate you encouraging me to talk to my dad."

She smiled. "The two of you are so alike."

"My mom used to say that."

"How did your mom die?" she asked quietly.

"Cancer," I said shortly. "I was sixteen. My dad and I were already at loggerheads. Once she wasn't there to referee anymore, it got worse. We stopped talking. All we did was yell and accuse. We lived in the same place, but it was as if there were walls around us. When I moved to Toronto to be a mechanic, I rarely saw him. He didn't approve of my choice of career. I went to school and busted my butt to learn. He thought I was thumbing my nose at his life. I wasn't, but I didn't want to be stuck in a grocery store. That wasn't my calling. I always loved cars and taking them apart. Engines. That was what I wanted to do. I put myself through school and lived in a horrible little place until I could get something better. And I did it all on my own, with no help from him." I rubbed my eyes, suddenly tired. "When I lost my job and came home for a brief while, I hoped things would get better, but we seemed to be stuck in a rut. He disapproved of everything I did. I felt as if I were sixteen again, working in the store, being told what to do constantly, second-guessed about everything. Any suggestion to upgrade the store or the apartment was met with resistance. The day Charly breezed into the store changed my life. She told me where she worked, and I told her I was a trained mechanic. After that, she would pop in all the time. Chat to my dad. Talk to me. Then she asked me to come see Maxx, and the rest is history. My life changed again—this time for the better. But I stagnated with my dad. Today was the first time we connected in a really long time."

I met her gaze. "And I have you to thank for it."

She smiled, the movement lighting up her pretty face. "I'm glad," she murmured.

"That's the most personal thing you have ever asked me," I said, sipping my water, studying her.

"I never felt as if I had the right to ask you anything," she admitted.

"Can I ask *you* something?"

"Um, sure?"

"What about your parents? Your childhood. You never talk about it."

"Oh, ah…" She trailed off.

"Too personal?" I questioned.

"No, I suppose not." She shifted, looking uncomfortable. I was about to tell her it was okay when she spoke, her voice soft. "I was never sure why my parents had me. I always felt like an afterthought. A shadow in their lives." A pained look passed over her face. "I often heard my mother talk about 'the mistake.' I didn't figure it out until I was a teenager. *I* was that mistake."

Jesus. I felt her pain behind those words. The need to reach out and comfort her was strong, but I could tell from her body language my touch wouldn't be welcome.

"I'm sorry," I offered quietly.

She shrugged, shifting and pulling her legs to her chest, wrapping her arms around her knees.

"My parents only had eyes for each other. My dad was controlling, and my mom loved it. He handled everything. The house, the bills, the decisions. She cooked his favorite meals and made sure to look beautiful for him when he got home. I ate at the kitchen table and was sent to my room by seven."

I frowned. "So basically, they ignored you."

"Inside the house, yes. Outside, people thought we were a normal family. Church every Sunday. All the local events. I wasn't given any choice, and I was expected to behave. We lived in a small town—smaller than here, even—and everyone knew everyone." She sighed. "Yet somehow, to the town, I was invisible too. Everyone knew my parents, but I was always on the edge, sort of looking in."

"That must have been lonely."

"It was. And yet, I felt trapped all the time. I hated it."

"Why?" I asked.

"If I misbehaved at school, someone told my parents. If I got into a disagreement on the playground, they found out. Once, I was riding my bike, and I ignored a stop sign and kept peddling. It wasn't a big deal—most of the kids did it too. Nothing happened except someone saw me and told my dad. My bike was taken away, and I had to walk everywhere. Plus, I was grounded. I hated that. Nothing was private. I was ignored yet spied on all the time. It was a fine line to walk."

"That would be difficult being a kid."

"The only real freedom I had was going to the library. I read travel books and dreamed of the places I would go and things I would see. I longed to get out of that town. Away from my parents. Go somewhere where I would be seen."

"And?" I prompted, knowing there was more to the story.

"My dad had a heart attack when I was fifteen. Dropped dead at the office he worked in. My mom was left floundering. She had built her entire world around him, and she was lost. She had no idea how to do the banking or pay the bills. What had to be done for insurance or to keep the house going. And again, everyone in the town knew. It was embarrassing to hear them talk. Poor Doris. Lost without Ed. What will happen to her?" she mimicked. "No one seemed worried about me."

I waited.

"My mother sank into a depression. I had no choice but to learn. I figured out the banking. How to pay the bills. Grocery shop. Even cook."

"And no one helped you? Usually small-town folk gather together," I questioned.

"That was the thing. My mom and dad were so close, they had very few friends. And they were other couples, and suddenly my mom was left on the fringes. Not that she cared. She refused any help. I struggled to learn everything with no one to ask for help from—no other adults I trusted. The only one who helped me was the librarian. She showed me what things to read so I could learn more. I even took her the bills so she could help me understand them and pay them on time. She helped me fill in the paperwork for the insurance so we got his death benefit."

"A lot of responsibility for a teenager."

"It was. I was a kid to everyone, but at home, I was the adult. At school, I was invisible. At home, I was alone. The only thing that saved me was when I used an old camera that belonged to my dad for a school project, and I got hooked on photography. After that, I read photography books and travel books. Dreamed of combining the two. As soon as I graduated, I was out of that town and away from my mother. By then, she'd decided she hated me. I was the cause of all her misfortune. Because of me, my father had to work so hard it ended his life. She was alone with no one." A glimmer of tears appeared in her eyes, and she wiped at them furiously. "That was what did it. She had never really wanted me. The town didn't want me. No one did. I left, and I never looked back."

"Where is your mother now?"

"She died a year after I left. She got sick and refused any sort of treatment. She told me she had nothing to live for." Kelly drew in a deep breath. "After she died, I went back and cleaned out the house, sold it and everything inside, and walked away." She huffed a humorless laugh. "The only person who came to see me was Mrs. Cameron, the old librarian. Again, I was invisible. But by then, I no longer cared."

It was on the tip of my tongue to tell her she did care, which was why it hurt so much, but I remained silent.

"How did you end up as Carl's assistant?"

"I worked a bunch of part-time jobs and lived in that little basement apartment. I studied photography. Volunteered with places just to get experience. I got some paying gigs, but not enough to earn a reputation or open my own place. I heard one photographer I was helping talking about a job he'd heard about for an assistant. He saw me listening and asked if I was interested. He warned me Carl was high-maintenance and traveled a lot. He said I'd have to go somewhere at the drop of a hat." She shook her head. "I was all in, and he helped me get an interview." She lifted her hands. "And the rest is history. Carl was as demanding as I had been warned. But I learned a lot, and I felt as if I mattered for the first time, if that makes any sense."

Listening to her words, I suddenly understood her better. Her refusal to get close to many people. Why she hated to be tied down. Her fear of love. Her acceptance of the way Carl treated her. He saw her, but for all the wrong reasons.

"What happened with Carl?" I asked.

Her shutters came down, and she sat up straighter, scrubbing her face.

"I told you. We had a disagreement."

"You've had them before," I pointed out.

"Not like this. I'm done being kicked around by him."

"I like hearing that."

We were quiet for a moment, then Kelly looked up, meeting my eyes.

"Why did you come here tonight, Brett?"

"To ask you to come to lunch tomorrow."

"Why are we sharing our stories?"

I shrugged. "I have no idea. Maybe if we'd talked more, understood each other a little better, we wouldn't be in this position."

"You mean you hating me?"

"I don't hate you, Kelly. I hate how we ended. But I think I understand a little more now." I stood. "Thanks for the water and the talk." I paused. "Will you come tomorrow?"

"I'll think about it."

I nodded. That was all I could ask.

I headed to the door, stepping outside. Kelly followed, laying her hand on my arm. "Thanks," she murmured.

"For what?"

"For making me feel seen. Talking to me. Inviting me."

I looked down at her. "I've always seen you, Kelly. The moment I met you, my eyes were glued to you."

I laid my hand on hers. "And I want you to come tomorrow."

"Okay."

I smiled. "Great."

Our eyes locked and held. Around us, the air grew warm, pulsating with a steady beat that grew the longer we stared. My pulse picked up, and Kelly's breathing deepened. I dropped my gaze to her mouth, memories assaulting me. Her warmth. The feel of her soft lips underneath mine. How she tasted. I felt the pull I always experienced when we were alone and this close. All I had to do was drop my head, and our lips would mold together. Our bodies would connect. Chances were, in a few moments, we'd be in her room, naked and joined in a passionate coupling that would leave us breathless and sated.

And completely ruined.

I stepped back before I could act on my impulse.

"Goodnight."

She blinked, stepping back. "Goodnight."

This time, it was me who ran.

CHAPTER NINE

Brett

I picked up Dad in the morning, smiling as he came out the door. Dressed in a sport coat, a dress shirt, and dark slacks, he looked well-groomed and put together. He carried a bunch of flowers, setting them on the back seat as he climbed in beside me.

"You look very dapper," I said as I eased out of the driveway.

He shook his head. "I think you're pulling my leg."

"No, honest, Pops. You look good."

"I feel a bit overdressed now I see you," he confessed.

"Rosa is used to my T-shirts and jeans. I dress better if it's dinner. The flowers are a nice touch," I added. "She'll love them."

"You always bring a lady some flowers when she invites you to dine at her home."

"Noted," I said, hiding my smile.

"She host this often?"

I checked my shoulder and merged onto the highway. "She has her family every Sunday. At least once a month, she extends the invite to me, Chase, Maxx, and his family. Mary. She feeds us all and sends home leftovers."

"That's kind."

I chuckled. "Rosa is a phenomenal cook, Pops. Her lasagna is kissed by the angels, I swear."

He hummed. "I haven't had a good lasagna in ages."

Guilt hit me, and I shifted in my seat. "Ah…"

He waved me off. "Nope. We're not going down that road." He pointed out the windshield. "We're headed forward. Toward the lasagna."

I laughed. "Toward the lasagna, then."

He nodded. "I hope there's meatballs."

"Pretty certain you won't be disappointed."

"Excellent," he murmured. "Well worth upgrading the flowers."

Despite his nerves, Pops did well. He was welcomed by Stefano's family and all my friends warmly. He accepted a glass of wine from Rosa, made me smile widely as he presented her with the large bouquet of flowers he'd brought, thanking her sincerely for her gracious invitation and friendly welcome.

"He good boy," she insisted, indicating me. "Should have brought you sooner, though," she scolded gently.

"I'm here now, that is all that matters."

"Such beautiful flowers," she murmured. "I no get those much."

"You should," he insisted. "Lovely flowers for a lovely lady."

I coughed into my hand, but he ignored me.

It was a large and boisterous bunch that sat down for lunch. Rosa served the food in the kitchen, but we all found places to sit outside in the sun. There was a large glass-topped table and a couple of smaller picnic tables, as well as chairs to sit in. I sat with Stefano and Gabby, Charly, Maxx, and Kelly. I noticed she took the seat farthest from me, not doubt to give me space. I wasn't sure I liked it. Chase joined us, and we watched as Rosa and my dad laughed and shared stories at the table. Grandkids ran around, babies were held, and siblings teased and enjoyed the sun.

"Shame Mary couldn't come," I said. "She'd love this."

Charly nodded. "Her hip is really bad. She couldn't do the drive today. Rosa is going to send her leftovers."

I chuckled as I watched my father accept more lasagna. "If Pops leaves any," I said. "I haven't seen him eat like this in a long time."

"He's enjoying himself," she said. "It's nice to see him here." She nudged me with her elbow. "He should have come before now."

I glanced at her. "I'm trying, Charly."

She smiled. "I know. It's good to see. Should I ask what prompted this reconciliation?"

My gaze drifted to Kelly, who was sitting next to Gabby. She was in a pretty dress, her legs bare and pale in the sun. She held her hand over her eyes as she spoke to Gabby, shielding them from the brightness. Her dark hair gleamed in the light, and I recalled how soft it was under my fingers. I had to pull my eyes away, but Charly noticed.

"Ah," she hummed with a small smirk.

"Don't read anything into it," I growled quietly. "I listened to her advice, is all."

"Wouldn't dream of it."

I rolled my eyes and stood, going to get another plate of food. I paused by the table, smiling at my dad and Rosa, who were talking. "Doing okay, Pops?"

"I'm great," he replied. "Best food I have eaten in years. My poor attempts at cooking will seem even worse now."

Rosa patted his hand. "I send food. You be okay."

I laughed as I went inside and filled my plate. I stayed for a few moments, enjoying the cool. It had gotten warm outside. After a bit, Kelly came in, setting down her half-eaten meal.

"Is that all you're going to eat?" I asked. Kelly had always had a good appetite.

"I just needed a break. I, ah, felt a little off."

I set down my plate and hurried toward her. "What is it? What's wrong?" I gripped her shoulders. "Are you ill? You're pale."

She shook her head. "Just a little too much sun, Brett. Since I got sick, I've been a little more sensitive."

I laid my hand on her head, feeling the heat of her skin. I pulled out a chair, tugging her into it. I went to the freezer, taking out one of the ice packs Rosa always kept on hand, and wrapped it in a towel, returning to Kelly and resting it on the back of her neck. She yelped quietly when the cold hit her, then sighed in relief.

"That's nice," she whispered.

I crouched beside her. "Do I need to take you home? To the hospital?"

"No," she replied. "A few minutes of cool will help."

"You need to move to the shade."

"I-I didn't want to intrude."

I shut my eyes at her words. I was sitting in the shade. She didn't want to bother me.

I slipped my fingers under her chin, forcing her to meet my eyes. "You sit beside me when we go back out. And if you don't feel well, you tell me, you understand?"

She furrowed her brow. "Okay."

There was no thought to my actions. I leaned close and pressed a kiss to her forehead. "Promise?" I asked against her skin.

"Yes," she breathed out.

I kissed her again. "Okay."

She let her head fall forward onto my shoulder, and we sat in silence as the ice cooled her down and I felt the slight tremor in her shoulders ease away.

"Ready to go back?"

She lifted her head. "Yes."

I stood and held out my hand. "Okay. Let's go."

No one commented on us returning together. Or that I pulled another chair over beside mine and sat her next to Charly.

"Too much sun over there," I grunted as Charly lifted one eyebrow in silence.

"Ah," was all she hummed.

I ate, keeping one eye on Kelly and glancing at my dad on occasion. Rosa said something to him I missed, and he followed her to the kitchen. Beside me, Charly and Kelly chuckled. Gabby clapped her hands.

"Go Mama Rosa."

I frowned. "Go Mama Rosa what?"

"She's got Daddy Mack following her."

"They are so cute together," Charly mused.

"Mama Rosa still got some moves," Kelly added.

Stefano and I exchanged confused glances.

"What?" I asked.

"The flirting. They are so cute," Kelly said patiently.

I gaped. "Pops isn't flirting. He's being friendly."

Stefano shook his head. "Not my mother. She is being a good hostess."

The girls all laughed.

Charly snorted. "She just asked him to help her open a jar."

"And that's considered flirting?" Stefano scowled. "I don't think so, Charly."

Charly sat back, shaking her head. "Rosa Borelli can open any jar in that kitchen of hers. She's stronger than you are, mister. She just wants Daddy Mack's attention."

"Shut up," I said. "That is *not* true." I met Stefano's shocked eyes. "Is it?"

The door opened, and Rosa and my dad came out, laughing and talking. I zeroed in on the fact that his hand rested on the small of her back. They sat down, and I blinked as she lifted a piece of cake to his mouth and he took it, shaking his head and saying how delicious it was.

Stefano and I shared another look.

"Well, I didn't fucking expect this," I muttered.

"Maybe you and Stefano will be stepbrothers," Gabby said gleefully. "Can you imagine?"

Stefano leaned forward. "Not happening. Fix this, Brett."

"What do you want me to do? Ground them? Send them to their rooms?"

"Oh, I bet Rosa would like that," Charly purred. "Look at them."

I turned in my chair, staring at Pops and Rosa. Was she touching his arm? And where the hell was his hand under the table?

"Fuck," I muttered.

Stefano stood. "I'm going to stop this."

Gabby pulled him down. "No, you're not."

"*Tesoro*, that is my mother," he hissed.

"And she is loving the attention of a male who is not related to her. Let her enjoy it. And he is having a wonderful time. A little harmless flirtation is good for both of them."

"As long as they keep it harmless," both Stefano and I said at the same time.

The girls all laughed, even Maxx joining in on their amusement. I glanced at Kelly, who was watching me, a small smile on her face. "They do look as if they are having a good time," she said quietly. "I think they're allowed some happiness too."

She was right. I hated to admit it, but she was right.

Then I leaned over, grinning at Stefano. "Does this mean I can borrow your bike, bro?"

He blinked, then narrowed his eyes. "No."

"Ah, come on. We're family now."

His eyebrows shot up, and he glared. My lips quirked, and I began to laugh. Gabby said something to him, and he relaxed and joined in my amusement.

I looked over at Rosa and my dad again. Drinking coffee, eating cake, and smiling. Enjoying themselves. Kelly was right. They deserved happiness, and if they enjoyed each other's company? There was nothing wrong with that.

Right?

In the car later, I turned to my dad. "Enjoyed yourself?"

"Tremendously. You were right. Angels sang while I ate that lasagna. All of it, actually." He glanced out the window. "Quite the woman, that Rosa Borelli. Raised all those kids on her own after her husband died. Strong. Fierce."

"Uh-huh."

"Reminded me of your mother. She was always a force to be reckoned with. I like that in a woman." He paused and chuckled. "You take after me that way."

"What are you talking about?"

"The women around you, son. Charly, Gabby, Mary. Your Kelly. All strong, independent women."

I huffed out a breath in annoyance.

"What?"

"You're right about the women around me, but she's not '*my Kelly,*'" I replied.

"I saw how you watched her."

"She wasn't feeling well. I was simply concerned. She's Charly's friend."

He laughed. "You keep telling yourself that. Every time I looked over at you, you were watching her."

"And every time I looked over at you, you were making goo-goo eyes at Rosa."

"She's a lovely woman. I enjoyed looking at her."

"She is Stefano's mother."

"I know. I enjoyed meeting her and making a new friend. We have a lot in common, and I liked talking to her. I loved her cooking. My God, Brett, I'm over sixty. I'm not looking for some passionate affair. But a new friend is always welcome."

"Oh," I said, somewhat relieved.

"But that doesn't mean I have no intention of calling Rosa Borelli and asking her to dinner."

"Oh," I said again.

"Lots of levels of friendship out there. Yours with Charly. Or Gabby. Maxx." He paused. "Kelly. All different."

"Jesus, Pops. Stop it."

He chuckled. "Let me live my life, Brett, and I'll let you live yours. I'll give you one piece of advice, though."

"Which is?" I asked, checking the lane beside me and easing the car onto the highway.

"Don't let the past dictate your future. Things change. People change."

"Pops," I groaned, knowing where he was going with this. "Kelly and I have history. It's not that easy."

"It's never easy. That's all I'm saying. I saw how you looked at her, son. You can tell yourself anything you want, but I'm telling you what I saw."

I concentrated on the road, not responding. Then I spoke.

"I have some advice for you too."

"Go for it."

"Rosa Borelli has three sons. One of whom is Stefano. They know where to hide bodies, and I can't stop him. Watch it with their mother."

He burst out laughing, holding his stomach as he shook with amusement.

"Good advice. I'll remember that."

I wound up on Kelly's doorstep again later that night. I couldn't stop thinking about her. Worrying and wondering if she was okay. What had caused her to feel ill. Finally, I gave in and went to see her.

She answered my quiet knock, once again looking surprised to see me.

"Brett," she greeted me.

"How are you feeling?" I asked, studying her. She still looked paler than usual and tired.

"I'm fine."

"I brought ice cream. And ginger ale. An ice pack in case you didn't have one."

"You didn't have to do that."

I held out the bag. "I wanted to."

She accepted the bag with a small frown.

"Get some rest."

"You're not coming in?"

"I just wanted to check on you because, well, because I was worried. And I wanted to bring you some stuff. I don't want to intrude."

"I can't eat ice cream alone. It's not right."

"Oh."

She opened the door wider, and I stepped in. Following her to the kitchen, I watched as she reached up, grabbing a couple of bowls. Her shirt rode up, and I saw her stomach, the sliver of skin enticing. I also noticed how loose her pants looked.

"How sick were you, Kelly?" I asked.

She turned. "Sorry?"

"You're too thin. You're not eating." I walked toward her, standing in front of her. I leaned forward, resting my hands on the counter, meeting her nervous eyes. "How sick were you?" I repeated.

For a moment, she didn't respond. "How sick *are* you?" I asked, my throat constricted as fear set in.

"No," she said firmly. "I am not sick. I mean, I was, but it was a temporary thing. I caught a bug in the islands and it did a number on me, and I'm still recovering. But it's not life-threatening, Brett."

"You promise?" I asked. "I need you to be okay," I murmured.

She cupped my face in her hands, bringing my head lower. She pressed her lips to my forehead, imitating my gesture from earlier. "Promise," she whispered against my skin. "I promise I'm okay."

Of their own volition, my arms went around her, gathering her close. She slipped her arms around my neck, and we stood together, both of us finding what we needed for the moment with each other. No anger. No past coming between us. It was simply us.

And dammit, it felt good.

Her face buried in my shoulder was warm. I felt her tears on my shirt, how she gripped my neck. I tightened my embrace, holding her as close as I could.

"Why are you here?" she asked.

"I couldn't stay away," I confessed. "I was too worried."

"You don't hate me?"

I held her tighter, letting the truth out. "I don't hate you, Kelly. I could never hate you."

"What does this mean?"

"I don't know," I replied honestly.

She looked up, her lovely eyes wet with tears. "This is enough," she whispered.

I shut my eyes, feeling her head fall back to my shoulder. It felt right, holding her again. She was accepting the comfort I wanted to give her—something new for us.

"For now," I said quietly. "It's enough for now."

CHAPTER TEN

Kelly

I woke up, warm and cozy. Too warm. When had my blankets become so heavy? I opened my eyes, blinking in the semilight. Instead of the window that was on the wall across from the foot of the bed, I stared at the torso of another person.

Confused, I lifted my head, feeling my eyes widen at the sight of Brett's sleeping face inches from mine.

Desperately, I tried to recall what had happened the night before. Brett had held me, offering me his comfort and strength. For the first time ever, I accepted it, burrowing into him. After I calmed, we dished up ice cream and sat on the sofa, eating the sweet, creamy treat he had brought with him. I asked him about his dad and how the drive home had been earlier, smiling at his rendition of the conversation he'd had with his dad in the car.

"Would it be so bad if they formed an attachment?" I asked.

"No, unless it didn't work out. Then Stefano and I would be caught in the middle." He frowned. "I want Pops happy, but I don't want to lose my friend."

"Maybe they simply want that too. A friend. Someone to have a meal or go to the movies with who isn't one of their kids or grandkids. Rosa is still a woman. It's nice to have the attention of a man for her... Well, just for her. Same for your dad. I think he's really lonely."

"You're probably right. Besides," he sighed, "I can't do anything. He's a grown-ass man."

"Just be supportive. Both you and Stefano."

He nodded, staring into space for a moment. Then he turned to me. "What kind of bug do you think you caught in the islands?"

He wasn't going to let this go. I couldn't lie to him. I couldn't tell him the whole truth either.

"I ingested something."

"Like food poisoning, you mean?"

I drew in a deep breath. "No, like drugs."

He drew back, horrified. "You were doing drugs, Kelly?"

"No."

Understanding dawned, and he became furious. His mouth pulled into a tight line, and his shoulders went back. His hands curled into fists. "Someone gave you drugs? Someone—" He stopped, fighting back his anger. "Someone drugged you?"

"Yes." I swallowed. "And I had a bad reaction."

"And that fucker Carl abandoned you, leaving you alone as you recovered."

I could only nod, afraid to say anything more.

"That selfish bastard," he snarled.

He stood and paced, the lighter mood from earlier vanishing. He yanked on his hair, muttering. He cursed and walked to the window, looking out into the darkening sky. I waited as he got his anger under control. He returned to the sofa and sat beside me. He took my hand, holding it tight, not meeting my eyes. His voice was low, fury dripping from his words. "Did anything else happen?"

"No."

He lifted his eyes to mine, searching them for the truth.

I shook my head. "No," I repeated. "Not what you think."

"Thank God." He hauled me to his chest. His heart was racing, his hold tight. "I can't even think—Jesus, Kelly. I can't."

"I'm fine."

He pulled back, cupping my face. "You're still suffering."

"I-I have trouble sleeping at times," I confessed. "And my appetite is off. But it's getting better."

I was shocked when he pressed his mouth to mine, his lips soft against me. "Kelly," he murmured.

I covered his wrists with my hands. "Brett," I breathed. "I'm fine. Promise."

He kissed me. Just a light brushing of his mouth to mine. A press of gentleness to my skin. Then he sat back, taking me with him. He wrapped his arm around me, letting me rest my head on his shoulder.

"Will you tell me?" he asked.

"When I can."

He nodded, threading our fingers together and holding my hand on his chest. "I'll listen anytime."

I only nodded.

I must have fallen asleep. Brett must have as well. And somehow, we ended up entangled on the sofa, me trapped between the back of it and Brett's hard body.

I wasn't sure what to do.

Then his eyes fluttered open, his sea blue meeting my gaze. He frowned, looked down between us, then around the room.

"I fell asleep," I offered.

"Apparently, so did I."

"What time is it?" I asked.

He glanced at his watch. "Six." Then he sat up, getting off the sofa quickly. "I need to go grab a shower downstairs and change before the staff comes in." He groaned. "Before Charly walks in and figures out I was here all night."

"Okay."

He bent and kissed me. Another soft press of his mouth. "Thank you for trusting me. Telling me. Promise me you'll take care of yourself."

"I am."

"Does Charly know?"

"No."

"Tell her," he demanded. "Tell her as much as you can. You need to tell someone." He paused. "Are you seeing a doctor?"

"No."

"Charly has a good one. You tell her, and you go see him. You understand?"

I blinked at the worried, insistent tone of his voice. "Okay."

"Today."

"Okay."

"I'll see you in the garage in a while. Take your time."

Then he was gone.

I touched my mouth, feeling the pressure of his lips. It had been brief and soft, yet I felt branded.

I sighed, sitting up carefully. I still got dizzy at times.

Brett was right. I should see a doctor. I needed to tell Charly.

I wasn't sure how she would react, though.

BRETT

"Come on, Tom. You can do better than that price," I insisted. "You have a shit-ton of those kicking around the junkyard. I saw them myself last time I was there."

"I gotta make a living, Brett," he replied, his gravelly voice even rougher-sounding over the phone than in person.

"And I'm trying to help a customer." I waited a beat. "And I'm pretty certain Reynolds & Co. Restoration is *your* best customer, and you want to keep us happy."

He chuckled. "Jesus, you're worse than Maxx. Fine. Two fifty."

"Two twenty-five."

He cursed. "Send Chase. I'll get it brought to the front." He hung up.

I smirked. I would have paid the two fifty. The part was worth it.

But the customer would be happy. And Maxx would be happy with the markup. A win-win situation.

I glanced at my watch. It had been three hours since I left Kelly. Woken with her in my arms. It had been a strange sensation— something that had been rare in our relationship. At first, it was simply hookups. Each of us scratching an itch when she was in town. Except the visits became more frequent. The itch became stronger. When she came for Stefano's wedding, she had stayed longer than ever, and we had spent some nights together. I liked waking up with her nestled into my side, her head on my chest. At one point, I thought it was the start of a more permanent stage in our relationship.

I had been wrong.

I shook my head to clear it. I had seen her walking across the grass, heading to the house. That had been well over an hour ago.

I couldn't get over what she had told me. She had been drugged. The drugs made her ill, and she was still recovering. And that bastard Carl had left her to fend for herself. He stole her work. He was every bit the asshole I thought him to be.

And now she was here. I was still unsure what it meant. For her. For us. Would she strike out on her own? Take off again once she recovered and the wanderlust hit her, leaving me alone yet again? Did I dare put myself out there with her?

My thoughts were interrupted as Charly burst in the side door, heading straight over to Maxx. He straightened as she stormed over, bending his head to listen to whatever she was saying, his hands stroking her arms in long passes. He frowned, anger passing over his face. He lifted his gaze, meeting mine, then dropped it again to concentrate on Charly. I was out of my chair and heading toward them before I realized what I was doing. As I got close, I heard Charly's furious voice whispering.

"…with my bare hands, Maxx. I'll kill him myself."

"Okay, Red. Calm down," he directed, tugging her into his arms. "Let's handle this one step at a time, okay?"

"What's going on?" I asked.

Charly pulled back from Maxx. Her red-rimmed, furious eyes met mine. "You have to do without Kelly or me today."

"Okay. Is she all right?"

"I'm taking her to the doctor's. Gabby is bringing Theo and Luna here."

"Is this precautionary, or did something happen?" I asked, my throat suddenly feeling constricted.

"Precautionary."

"Because she was drugged and had a reaction," I said bluntly since it was obvious Charly now knew the story. Probably more than I did.

Fury crossed her face again. "Yes."

"Okay. You take her. We'll manage."

Maxx released her from his arms. "Are you okay to drive, Red? You want me to take you? Or Chase?"

"No, I'm fine. I just—" She flung herself into Maxx's arms, dissolving into tears. He held her close, bending low to whisper to her. She muttered words between her sobs I couldn't hear. I turned and headed back to the office to give them a few moments of privacy, grateful Kelly had someone like Charly to care for her.

It took everything in me not to detour and go to the house. Make sure Kelly was all right. Hold her the way Maxx was holding Charly. It wasn't my place.

And I hated that more than anything.

That afternoon, I came back from the storeroom, shocked to see Kelly sitting at the desk. She had the phone braced between her shoulder and ear, talking as she typed into the computer. I headed over to Chase, handing him the part.

"You okay to keep going?"

He glanced toward the office and nodded. "Is Kelly okay?" he asked, keeping his voice low. "Charly looked pretty upset this morning."

"I think she's fine. I just want to check."

He took the part. "I got this. You can check my work after."

I clapped him on the back. "I have every confidence."

I went to my office, shutting the door, then walked into Kelly's. I closed the door leading to the garage and waited until she hung up. She finished typing, then turned in her chair, facing me. She looked worn but calm.

I sat in the visitor's chair, pulling it close. "How are you?"

She offered me a smile. "I'm okay."

"What did the doctor say?"

"He checked me out, took some blood. I had copies of the medical records from Costa Rica, and he went through them. Apparently my reaction to the drug is not uncommon, but it seems to be lingering for me. I have to make sure to keep my fluid intake up, rest, eat, and no operating heavy machinery." She lifted one shoulder, trying to be funny. "No forklifts in my future."

I reached for her hand. "Will this fade?"

"Yes. The headaches are already going away. The lethargy and dizziness should start to pass. Charly plans on fattening me up."

"She was pretty upset this morning."

Kelly grimaced. "She was mad at me for not telling her sooner."

"You told her everything?"

"Yes."

"Will you tell me?" I asked.

She shut her eyes, her shoulders drooping. "The doctor is going to hook me up with a counselor. I would rather burden them."

"You're not a burden."

"Not today, Brett," she pleaded. "I can't…" She trailed off.

I could hear the weariness in her voice. The slight tremor that underscored her unusual vulnerability.

"Okay," I agreed. "What can I do?"

"You're already doing it," she whispered, opening her eyes and meeting mine. "You're sitting here with me, not hating me." She smiled. "Being my friend."

I squeezed her hand. "Why don't you take the rest of the day off? Get some rest."

"I would rather stay here." Her gaze skittered over my shoulder. "Sometimes the quiet in the apartment is too loud."

"All right." I stood. I felt better having her here where I could see her anyway. "No lifting heavy stuff in the storeroom. Ask one of us to help."

"Okay, boss."

It took everything in me not to bend over and kiss her. Instead, I winked and returned to Chase and the car we were working on. I glanced over my shoulder, meeting Kelly's eyes. I winked again, adding a grin, which made her smile.

Oddly enough, I felt ten feet tall doing so.

I watched Kelly closely for the next few days. She seemed better. She had a little more color in her cheeks, and she appeared to be more relaxed. It made me grin when Charly would appear every day, carrying lunch for Kelly and insisting she eat with them every night. At least I knew she was being fed. It helped knowing she had confided in Charly. I wanted the whole story, but I had to respect Kelly's decision to speak to a professional. I had to admit it bothered me, the odd need to know her story, to be the one she trusted enough to share, but we weren't at that point. I wasn't sure we ever would be.

Friday afternoon, she left for the bank, returning faster than I expected.

"No sodas on the porch with my dad?" I teased when she brought me the bank deposit book to look over.

"Um, Daddy Mack was too busy today. Lyle was behind the counter." He was the same young man who had waved at Kelly the first day she went to the store. She had asked, and I'd told her that he'd been working with my dad since I had started at the garage.

"He's trying to get my dad into the twenty-first century. Not sure it'll ever happen, but he works hard, and my dad likes him. He's young, newly married, and he's a nice guy. Lives in Littleburn and likes working there, so it's all good," I had told her. "I think he hopes to buy the place from my dad when he retires."

"How do you feel about that?"

I shrugged. "I have no interest in it, so I'm fine. The town needs it, and I think with Lyle's more forward-thinking, he can make a go of it."

"Pops was busy?" I asked. "Doing what? Is there a run on canned goods? A sale on bulk nails?"

"No, he was washing his car." She paused. "For his date tonight."

I blinked. "What?"

She grinned, her light-blue eyes dancing brightly under the lights. "His date—with Rosa."

I blinked again.

"He bought a new shirt and tie for the occasion."

"Does Stefano—" I was interrupted when the man himself walked in.

"Brett, your father—"

"I know. With your mother."

Kelly looked between us, trying not to laugh.

"It's just dinner, boys. No one is breaking any laws."

I shook my head. "You don't understand, Kelly. My father never goes into Toronto. I can't remember the last time he drove in by himself."

"And my mother goes to dinner with us. Not a man," Stefano grumbled.

"Well, tonight, *your* father—" she pointed at me "—is driving into Toronto in his new shirt and tie to pick up *your* mother—" her finger moved in Stefano's direction "—and she is going to eat dinner with another grown-up. A lovely man and a sweet woman are going to enjoy themselves." Then she waved her finger at us both. "And you two idiots are going to let them."

I frowned, and Stefano glowered at her. She rolled her eyes.

"They aren't going to elope or anything. You two need to relax. Good God, Daddy Mack and Mama Rosa are lonely. Don't you get it?" She threw up her hands. "Your dad sits in an empty apartment night after night. Your mom rattles around her house, waiting for someone to come by and visit. Both of you are living your lives, but they are alone. Tonight, they don't have to be. They can sit and talk. Laugh. Share their life experiences—some of which you cannot even comprehend. They're on an equal playing field because they have lived it." She shook her head. "Loneliness is a horrible thing. Don't ruin this for them."

She walked out, leaving Stefano and me staring at each other.

"Wow, she's pretty damn good at this guilt stuff."

"She's been taking lessons from Charly," he muttered.

I sighed. "She's right. Two people having dinner. We need to relax."

Stefano huffed a long sigh. "So, I should cancel the table I had booked beside them so we could chaperone?"

I met his gaze, and we began to laugh.

"Ah, fuck. Your dad is a great guy, and my mom thinks he's a gentleman. She is thrilled to be going out. Kelly's right."

"Yeah, she is." I shook my head. "It frightens me how often she is right these days. She sees things others miss. I never realized how intuitive she was before."

"Maybe you weren't looking."

I nodded grudgingly. "Maybe you're right."

CHAPTER ELEVEN

Brett

I knocked on her door around seven. She opened it, leaning on the frame. "This is becoming a habit."

"A good one?" I asked with a smile.

"Depends what you have in that bag."

"Noodles. Spicy chicken."

Her eyes lit up. "Spring rolls?"

"With extra spicy plum sauce."

"Then definitely good."

I grinned. I knew she wasn't eating at Charly's tonight. I also knew she liked to eat later, so I had taken the chance she hadn't had her evening meal. I followed her inside and unpacked the bag as she grabbed plates and utensils.

She sat down, almost bouncing in excitement. "I was craving Chinese all day. How did you know?"

I shrugged, smiling in satisfaction at the amount she put on her plate. "I know you."

She paused then reached for a spring roll, dipping it in the spicy plum sauce and crunching into it with a satisfied sigh.

"I don't know what that means."

I chuckled. "I heard you telling Chase how much you'd missed China Palace."

"Oh, I have. No one makes noodles like these."

We ate for a few moments in silence.

"I went and saw Pops."

"Oh?" She frowned. "You didn't give him a hard time, did you?"

"No. I checked out the car, making sure it ran okay. It's been a while since it was on the highway. Pops walks most places. It was a little rough, but I gave it a few tweaks, and it was good. He's going to bring it in next week, and we'll give it a good once-over."

"I'm sure Stefano was grateful."

I grinned. "He came with me."

"Oh God. Your poor dad!"

Laughing, I bit into a spring roll, enjoying the crisp wrapper and crunchy fillings. The plum sauce was spicier than usual, and my eyes watered a little. I took a sip of water.

"He was fine. Pops took it all in stride. Told him he thought Rosa was an incredible woman he would be proud to call his friend. Stefano relaxed a little. Helped me check the car. Had a bottle of root beer and told him to have his mother home at a decent hour."

"What did Daddy Mack say?"

I rolled my eyes. "Stop calling him that. You make him sound like some sort of sex god."

A mischievous look crossed her face. "Well, I've had sex with his son. You must get the talent from somewhere."

I choked around a mouthful of noodles. She patted my back, trying to hold in her laughter.

I wiped my mouth. "I cannot even begin to tell you how many things were wrong with that statement. Jesus, that is my dad! I can't think about him having sex—now or ever."

"Obviously since you're here, he did."

"Stop it!" I began to laugh. "We are not having this conversation anymore."

"But what did he say?"

"He said that was his plan. Then Pops walked away, looking over his shoulder, and told Stefano everyone had different ideas on a 'decent hour.' I thought Stefano was going to burst a blood vessel in his head from the color on his face."

She laughed with me.

"I convinced him Pops was pulling his leg, and we finished the car and left. Stefano saw a corsage Pops got Rosa for her wrist sitting on the counter when we went in to tell him we were leaving. He sorta caved right there."

"Ah, Daddy Mack still has moves."

I shook my head, finishing what was on my plate, pleased to see she did the same.

"Your appetite is coming back."

"Yeah. I'm sleeping a little better too."

I frowned. "What?"

She sighed. "I kept having nightmares. But since the night you stayed, they've gotten better."

"Oh, ah… Well, glad I could help."

We finished eating and cleared the table. There was little in the way of leftovers, but she assured me she would eat them for lunch. She brought us bowls of ice cream, and we sat on the sofa, eating the cold dessert.

"You want to watch a movie or something?" she asked, looking unsure. "Unless you, ah, have to go?"

"No. A movie sounds good."

She gave me the remote and took the bowls to the kitchen. I chose a newer release and took the water she gave me before sitting back on the sofa. After a while, she shifted, rolling her neck. I patted the seat beside me. "Slide over."

She hesitated, then did as I asked, moaning low in her throat as I rubbed her shoulders.

"You always carry your tension here."

"I know. One masseuse I went to called them cement," she replied.

We turned our attention back to the screen. After I rubbed her shoulders a little more, I pulled her back to my side, draping my arm around her. It felt natural to sit here with her, doing something as mundane as watching a movie. We hadn't done many of the usual things other couples did when they were dating. Mostly because we never dated. I was never sure what to call our relationship except one long string of booty calls. Until it changed. And she left.

I shook my head to clear it, focusing on the screen. The couple in the movie was heating it up, her pushed against the wall while he ravished her mouth. The angle of the shot was perfect, cutting away to his hand drifting up her body. It reminded me of the times in the storeroom. The barn. The dim light that would surround us as Kelly and I gave in to the never-ending passion that seemed to burn between us. My cock twitched in remembrance. Beside me, Kelly shifted, her breathing becoming deeper. She tilted her head, our eyes locking. My deeper blue met her silvery gaze, flickers of fire winding down my spine.

Who moved first, I had no idea. But one moment, she was beside me, the next, she was on my lap, her legs straddling mine. Her mouth was pure heat. Sweet from the ice cream, her tongue tangling with mine, both of us fighting for dominance. She wound her arms around my neck, pulling on my hair, gripping at my neck. I thrust my hands under her loose shirt, cupping her bare breasts. I always loved the fact that she rarely wore a bra. Her nipples were hard peaks under my fingers, and she whimpered as I pinched and tugged on them. She ground against me, my cock straining to get closer to her. The past, the pain, everything between us fell away. Nothing mattered except this moment. The constant push and pull between us. I broke from her mouth, running my lips down her neck, biting at the sweet juncture where head met shoulder. She tugged on my shirt, and I helped her pull it over my head. Her shirt disappeared somewhere behind me. Our chests rubbed together as I yanked her tight to me, slanting my mouth over hers once again and kissing her until she was breathless. Until all I tasted, felt, and knew was her.

I groaned as she slipped her hand under my waistband and her fingers touched my hard cock. She wrapped her hand around me, and I bucked into her touch. She stroked me, exactly the way she knew I liked it.

Exactly the way she had in the past. She knew how to please me. What to do to make me lose control.

I knew I would have regrets. But right now, I didn't give a damn. Maybe if I fucked her again, already knowing the outcome, I would get her out of my system.

I pulled back, our eyes locking. I saw a glimmer of uncertainty I had never seen before in her eyes. Another small glimpse into a hidden vulnerability that was new to me. Her words from before whispered in my brain. *"I was drugged."*

"Can we do this? Are you all right?" I asked, wanting to be sure.

She blinked at my question. "We can," she assured me, kissing my neck, still stroking me. "I'm okay, Brett." She smiled, cupping my face. "I'm safe with you."

"Always," I growled before covering her mouth with mine again. I kissed her with everything in me. All the passion I felt for her. The longing that had been building since she left. The unspoken words between us. I stood, carrying her to the bedroom, lowering her to the bed, never letting go. We kissed and teased, tasted, and explored, pushing aside the last of our clothes. We were everywhere on the bed. I rediscovered all the spots I loved. The odd smattering of freckles under her left breast. The ticklish spot by her right hip. The way she sighed as I touched her, opening her legs and letting me explore every inch of her. She stroked my rock-hard dick. Licked and sucked on my nipples. Bit at my skin with playful nips. Cupped my balls, running her feet down the backs of my legs. Whimpered and moaned, her sounds turning me on even more.

"Jesus, you're so wet," I whispered, sliding my fingers over her, gently teasing her clit the way she liked.

She gasped, arching closer, my name falling from her mouth.

"You like me touching you, Shutterbug, don't you?" Her nickname came out before I could stop it.

"Yes, oh God, yes."

I covered her mouth again, my tongue and fingers in tandem, until she stiffened, her orgasm racing through her.

"Protection," I groaned.

"Still on birth control. No one since you," she replied, pulling me down to her. "Please, Brett," she begged prettily. "Please."

Her assurances of only me did something inside my chest. Our eyes locked and held as I slid inside her. Inch by inch, her heat wrapped around me, her body drawing me in, surrounding me until we were flush, my cock inside her so deep, I couldn't tell where I ended and she began. I held myself still, the enormity of the moment crashing around me. I had never expected to be with her again. To feel this way.

"Please," she whispered, "Please."

I began to move, drawing back, thrusting forward, over and over. Faster. Deeper. Harder. She met my movements, her whimpers and cries spurring me on. The bed creaked, the mattress shifted, and I knocked a pillow off the bed as I gripped the headboard.

She used her feet to keep me as close to her as possible. Her nails scored the flesh of my back. Our mouths fused together, muffled groans, grunts, and pleas locked between us.

I felt her orgasm around me. Tightening, clenching, holding my cock in the sweetest of grips. My release tore through my body like a wildfire, burning and ravaging everything in its path. Hitting me with ecstasy so great, all I could do was ride it out until I collapsed, boneless and sated on top of her.

Kelly held me tight, her arms gripping me. I pressed kisses to her neck and chest, then rolled, tucking her beside me. I was pleased when she nestled close, her head on my shoulder, resting her hand on my chest. I tugged a blanket over us when I felt her shiver. The light from the hall was the only glow in the room, and I peered down at her quizzically.

"Okay, Shutterbug?"

She nuzzled my skin. "I'm great."

I traced a finger down her cheek. "Yeah, you are."

She sighed, the sound soft in the room.

"Did you want me to leave?" I asked.

"No."

I tucked my arm under my head. "Good. I like it here."

"Me too."

I couldn't stop my smile. All of this was unexpected. I had no idea what it meant, and I refused to ask. Not right now. Not when for the first time in months, I felt complete and at ease. I enjoyed the silence and the feeling of her nestled against me.

"Have you—" She hesitated. "Have you been seeing anyone?"

I laughed low in my chest. "I tried, Shutterbug."

"You tried?" she repeated, squinting up at me.

I sighed. "Stefano nicknamed me the relationship healer. Every woman I dated went back to her ex."

"Oh."

"I kept picking people like me," I confessed. "Women who hadn't gotten over their previous partner."

"Brett," she murmured, her voice sad.

"It's fine, Kelly. I met some nice women."

"How many?" she asked, her voice now a little sharper.

"Relax." I smirked. "Three. One I really liked. I thought she would be the one to help me get over you. She was funny, sweet, and really lovely." I huffed a humorless laugh. "And every time I kissed her, we both felt uncomfortable. She got married a couple of weeks ago."

"Were you upset?"

"I danced at her wedding with a big smile on my face. She wasn't for me."

"But you are," I added silently. "And I'm not sure how to get over you."

"I'm sorry," she whispered.

"I know."

I felt her drift into sleep, her body relaxing into mine, her breathing becoming steady and even. I thought about leaving—Kelly was never big on overnight guests—but I didn't want to. Instead, I tucked her closer and let sleep take me away.

I'd deal with the aftermath in the morning.

KELLY

I woke up once again in the safety of Brett's arms. He was solid and warm beside me, wrapped around me tightly.

I nuzzled his chest, the scent of his skin tickling my nose. He never wore cologne, but his soap was scented with cardamon and juniper. A heady, clean, masculine smell that suited him.

Last night—the past few days—were unexpected. His softening toward me. His worry when I told him about being drugged. Showing up two nights in a row with food. I had never told him the only person I ever ate China Palace with was him. The only person aside from Charly who knew about my past. The only male I trusted completely. The only person I had ever spent the night with. All of them Brett.

I hated that I'd hurt him. That my fears had made me run. That because of me he had been in pain. That he would be again when I left. Because I would leave. It was inevitable. I didn't know how to stay. I had been on the run from that small town, the life I'd left behind so long ago, I didn't know how to do anything else. I had no idea how to put down roots and stay.

And as frightening as it was to leave, staying was even more terrifying. Being locked down to one place. Allowing someone else's needs and desires to override my own. Becoming a shadow again. I had witnessed it all my life, been excluded all my life. It was never happening to me.

I pushed down that little voice that whispered it could be different with Brett. That he was different. We were opposites. He was content in this small town. Loved his job. I still wanted to travel and see the world. Take as many pictures as I could and show people the beauty of this marvelous planet we lived on.

I hated hearing he had tried dating. The horrible, selfish part of me rejoiced that none of the women he took out did anything for him. Even though I'd walked away, the thought of him with someone else ate me up inside. I felt conflicted. Jealous. Annoyed that it should bother me.

And after last night, slightly territorial.

I shifted and Brett grunted.

"Where are you going?"

I glanced at the clock. "It's almost seven. The garage opens in an hour, and it's booked solid."

He sat up, the blanket falling away, revealing his chest and abs. A love bite was next to his right nipple. Another one higher on his shoulder. I bit back my grin, knowing I no doubt had a couple on my skin as well. Brett liked to use his teeth and loved it when I reciprocated. My body reacted the way it always did when I saw him naked. Or clothed—I just pictured him naked then. An ache began between my legs, a low throbbing ache only he could ease. My nipples tightened as he looked at me, and the wetness began to gather. For him. It was always for him. Only Brett affected me this way.

"Don't eyeball me like that," he growled.

I tried to look away, but he was simply delicious in my bed, his hair everywhere, morning scruff shadowing his jaw, and looking so fine. The blanket was tented and growing as I watched him.

"Kelly," he protested. "We don't have time."

I slipped my hand under the blanket, wrapping it around his cock. Hot, thick, and hard, it was like stroking velvet over steel.

"What about a quick one?" I asked. I did enjoy it when he took me hard and fast.

In seconds, I was under him, my hands held over my head as he devoured my mouth. I opened my legs, and he settled between them, groaning.

"Fuck," he swore. "So ready. You are always so ready."

Then his phone rang out. We stared at each other.

"Ignore it," he muttered.

It rang again, and with another curse, he flung himself off the bed and grabbed his pants, taking his cell phone from his pocket.

"Brett Conner," he snapped into the phone.

"What? Okay, okay, calm down. Where are you?" He listened for a moment. "Okay. I'll get the tow truck and be there in twenty."

He hung up, bending forward at the waist with a groan. "I gotta go. Mrs. Geoffrey was in a fender bender in the middle of the intersection in Lomand."

"That's gonna cause major backup," I said sarcastically. "Especially at rush hour."

He chuckled, pulling on his pants, tucking in his still-erect dick carefully. He leaned over me, kissing me hard. "Listen to you, all frustrated because you're denied my dick this morning."

"Whatever, stud."

I grabbed my robe, following him to the door. He turned, eyeing me up and down. "Is that supposed to encourage me to leave?" he rasped, staring at the short, silky robe that showed off my legs. "Jesus, Kelly."

"Think about what you're missing," I teased, loving this lighter side to our relationship.

He opened the door, then spun, dragging me into his arms. He yanked me close, wrapping his leg around me so I felt his still-hard-for-me erection. He kissed me until I was breathless, gripping his shoulders to keep from falling down. Then he stood back.

"Think about what *you're* missing, Shutterbug." He winked. "See you at the garage."

He paused before going down the steps. "Don't touch yourself," he demanded, keeping his voice low. "I'll know."

Gaping, I followed him with my gaze as he hurried down the steps and disappeared. I was still standing there when the tow truck backed out, and he rolled down the window.

"I'll know," he called. "I won't like it."

Then he drove off.

I tried not to smile at his bossiness.

I failed.

I was keyed up all morning. Edgy. Why I listened to him and obeyed, I had no idea. I could have used my trusty vibrator and gotten off in about thirty seconds, I was so ready. But instead, I showered and headed into the garage. The place was bustling all morning. Brett, Chase, Ward, plus Stefano were all there, and everyone was busy. I was back and forth to the storeroom several times, trying to help. The phone was nonstop, and I hoped they would be breaking ground soon on the expansion. They needed the manpower and the space.

Even though the garage was to close at noon, it was past three when Brett rolled down the main door, wiping his hands on a rag. "Great job, guys," he called out. "We got everyone done, including the two emergencies. Lunch on me Monday."

Ward grinned. "Excellent."

Chase smiled, but I noticed he didn't seem as enthused. Brett walked over, saying something to him. Chase shook his head, clapping Brett on the shoulder and offering him a smile. Brett frowned, but Chase seemed to wave him off and kept tidying up his area. Stefano said something to both of them, frowning at Chase's reply, but I heard him tell him if he changed his mind, there would be plenty of food. Stefano left with a wave, heading toward the house. I knew we were having a barbecue later, so I was sure he was reminding Chase about dinner. It would be odd if he didn't show up, but maybe he had a date. Ward left, and I headed to the storeroom to straighten it up. After such a busy day, it was a mess, and Charly liked it organized.

I pulled the small stool over so I could reach the upper shelves, and I tidied the cans, bottles, and parts back into some semblance of order. I cursed as one of the overhead lights flickered then died. I would have to ask Brett or Stefano to change it—the ceiling, even with the stool, was too high for me. A moment later, Brett walked in, leaning on the doorframe.

"Ah, good," I said. "I have a lightbulb that needs changing."

"Do you?" he asked.

I looked over my shoulder. He had pulled off his coveralls to his waist, leaving him in a muscle shirt that was tight to his chest and showed off his abs. His hair was high in the front, the blond catching the light from the hallway. I had to stop myself from staring at how sexy he looked. He narrowed his eyes, studying me. I swallowed hard.

"Um, yeah."

He walked in, shutting the door, the light now even dimmer. He walked over, his eyes never straying from me.

"Anything else need changing?"

I tightly gripped the hose I had been putting back in the box. "Um, no," I said, shocked to hear the squeak in my voice.

Brett took the hose from my hands, studying it, then easily reaching over my head to drop it into the box. "No?" he asked quietly, stepping right behind me, trapping me between his chest and the shelves.

"Ah—"

He pressed forward, letting me feel him. All of him. His arousal was a hard bulge at my lower back, his breath hot on my skin. "What about your panties, Kelly? Are they still wet from this morning?" he rasped, darting out his tongue to touch my neck.

I gripped the shelf, closing my eyes and feeling his hands sliding up my legs. "Not wearing any," I confessed.

"Jesus," he muttered. "Is my Shutterbug eager?" He bit down on my lobe. "Is this what you were hoping, Kelly? I would come find you—come fuck you here like I used to? The way you liked it?

130

Hard and fast? Covering your mouth so no one heard your screams but me as I took you deep with my cock?"

I whimpered. It was all I could do.

"You know," he growled. "I used to laugh at Maxx and his lack of self-control around Charly." He gripped my waistband, yanking down my yoga pants. "Then I saw you today. Sashaying around the garage, bending to pick something up, showing me your tits in this little tank top of yours." He lifted me, pushing the stool out of the way and placing my feet on the floor. He kicked my legs open, and I heard his coveralls hit the floor behind me.

"And I got it. I really got it. And now, you're gonna get it. I've been fucking solid for you all goddamn day, and now I'm going to have you exactly like that. Hard." He closed his hands over mine, his breath hot on my neck, his voice a low growl in my ear. "Hold tight, Shutterbug."

His dirty words, his whispered filthy promises, made me shiver with anticipation. I pushed back against him, feeling his cock between my legs, hot, heavy, sliding through my wetness.

"Wider," he ordered.

His arm felt like a band of steel around my waist, and he lifted me, so my toes barely touched the floor. He bent at the knees and slid inside me—one sharp snap of his hips and he was deep. Thick. Throbbing.

He pulled out, surging back inside. Over. Again. He cupped my breasts, pulling on my nipples, playing with the hard nubs. He slid one hand down, teasing my clit, thrusting faster. I held on to the shelves with every bit of waning strength I had. He was possessed. He licked and bit at my neck. Cursed and praised.

So fucking perfect.

So tight around me.

Take it, Kelly, take it all and give me what I want.

Come on me.

My head fell back as I succumbed, no longer sure which way was up, where I was, or how I was going to survive Storm Brett. He was a Category Five hurricane destroying everything in its path, leaving nothing but dust behind. I screamed my release into his hand that covered my mouth. Shook with the aftershocks. Wailed loudly as another orgasm rushed through me as he tipped over the edge, grunting and groaning.

Until we stopped. Until the world began to rotate on its axis again.

We were pressed together, our sweat-soaked skin hot and sensitive. My legs burned, my pussy ached, and my shoulders screamed.

And I was oh-so satisfied.

And judging from the heavy breathing and the way he was leaning into me, Brett was pretty satisfied too.

He rested his head on my shoulder, pressing a kiss to my skin, his voice now a gentle hum in the room. "Tell me you're okay."

"I'm good. I'll be a bit stiff later, but I'm perfectly fine."

"You're pretty bloody perfect. That I agree on."

He stepped back, easing himself from me. I already missed feeling him inside. He pulled up my yoga pants, carefully sliding them over my butt. I heard him pick up his coveralls.

"A shower," he murmured. "We need a shower."

"Fresh clothes," I added.

"We're expected across the way for dinner," he said, turning me in his arms. "You up for that?" He smoothed my hair away from my forehead.

"Yes."

"Good. Let's sneak around back and up the stairs before we're caught. I thought Theo had seen me this morning, but I was lucky."

"Theo?"

"He spent the night with Charly and Maxx."

"Ah."

He stepped back, holding my arm as I swayed. "Shit, I was too rough, wasn't I?"

"No. I just need to get my balance. I think you fucked it right out of me."

He laughed. "That's what you do to me, Shutterbug. I'm off-balance all the time around you."

"And you hate that."

He kissed my forehead, his lips lingering. "I decided to stop fighting it. Whatever I can get from you, for however long I can get it, I'll take it."

He took my hand and led me upstairs. I followed, thinking over his words.

Somehow they bothered me.

I just had to figure out why.

CHAPTER TWELVE

Brett

We shared another first—showering together. The stall wasn't huge in the apartment, but we fit well enough. We were both too satisfied to start anything, although Kelly looked as sexy as hell with the water dripping down her shoulders and back. Her hair became ebony when wet, the darkness such a contrast to her creamy skin. She had some red patches where my scruff had rubbed her neck, and a few purple kisses to her skin where I had marked her. When I looked in the mirror, I was sporting a few myself. Thank goodness for T-shirts to cover up the evidence.

I dug through my bag I had brought to work with me, pulling on fresh jeans. Kelly appeared in a pair of long shorts with a sleeveless blouse. She looked pretty and fresh, her eyes dancing and a smile on her face.

Watching her, I knew I was in trouble. The feelings I'd had for her were still there. Bubbling and simmering under the surface. But I was keeping them locked down. I refused to let them out.

She had made the rules when whatever this was between us first started, and I had broken them. Lesson learned.

This time, I told myself, I knew what to expect. I knew she would leave, and I would be ready. Knowing the rules, I could be prepared. This time, when I was alone, I would be able to handle it. In the meantime, sex with Kelly was epic. I enjoyed spending time with her. And without the inevitable call from Carl telling her to pack up, we were actually getting to know each other on a different level.

Still, I knew it wasn't forever. She didn't work that way. I tamped down the churning feeling in my gut and stroked her cheek when she frowned at me.

"What's wrong?"

"Nothing," I lied. "You look pretty."

"Should we go over separately?" she asked, anxious.

"Whatever you prefer. You head over, I'll slip down to the garage and come out by the other side door," I offered.

She hesitated then shook her head. "No, I'm being silly. Let's go."

When we came around the building, Maxx, Stefano, and Theo were playing football. I jogged over to join them, and Kelly headed toward the gazebo. I heard laughter and chatter as she approached. Stefano looked at me, one eyebrow raised, and I met his gaze steadily. Then to throw him off, I grinned.

"How's your mama? Or should I call my dad and ask?"

He tackled me to the ground, and we wrestled, laughing as Theo jumped on us. I spied Thomas waddling over, and I sat up, holding out my arms. "Come play with the big boys, Thomas," I encouraged, lifting him high when he got close. He was another great kid. From the gazebo, Vivvy watched us, safe on her mother's lap, her dress a frilly bunch of material around her. She had zero interest in tussling with us in the dirt. Luna was still a bundle in Gabby's arms, so it was just us boys. We wrestled a while, Thomas shrieking in delight as we tossed him around gently. Finally, we set him on his feet, and he headed back to the gazebo. Mary swooped him up, giving him a sippy cup he eagerly took. We headed to the barbecue, grabbing a cold drink from the cooler. I sipped it gratefully.

"Chase not here?" I asked.

Stefano shook his head. "He said he had plans."

"He's been quiet the last couple days," I said. "I asked him yesterday and today, but he says he's fine."

Charly came out of the house, carrying a platter loaded with chicken. I hurried over, taking it from her and giving it to Maxx to put on the grill. She joined us. "This is a tough time for Chase."

I exchanged a glance with Stefano. "Oh?" I asked. "Have I missed something?"

She sighed. "Since it's the first year you're living with him, I guess you've never noticed. He never talks about it. It's the anniversary of Wes's death. His dad died a year later, but only a few days apart. He still carries guilt over it."

"Ah, shit," I muttered. "Poor kid. Why didn't he tell me?"

She shook her head. "Because he thinks he shouldn't talk about them. Because of what Wes did. All the things his dad covered up. I can't make him understand that they were still his family. He has the right to mourn them. And as his friends, we would understand that."

"Dammit. I'll call him and tell him to get over here," Stefano said, reaching for his phone. "He shouldn't be alone today." He held the phone to his ear, frowning. "No answer. Voice mail is full. What the hell?"

"Leave him. You should take him out tomorrow and talk to him." She fixed her gaze on Maxx. "You too, big guy. He shouldn't feel he needs to hide his emotions from us."

Maxx slid his arm around Charly, pressing a kiss to her head. "Okay, Red. We'll take him for breakfast and talk to him."

"Good. Now, don't burn the chicken." She turned and walked away.

"You heard her, big guy. Don't burn the chicken," I mimicked.

"I heard that!" Charly shouted, turning and flipping us the bird.

We all laughed then became serious again.

"I'll talk to Chase in the morning," I said.

"Good plan. Charly's right. He doesn't have to hide away because of his family. I get it," Maxx said. "I miss my parents. Despite everything that happened, Wes and his dad were Chase's family."

Stefano nodded. "We'll make sure he gets that."

Maxx opened the lid on the grill. "Good."

We sat in the gazebo eating grilled chicken, potato salad, and lots of other things Charly and Mary had made. I was starving. Between how busy we were in the garage and my extracurricular activities with Kelly, I hadn't eaten. My tank was empty. I was pleased to notice her tucking in, eating everything on her plate. I slid another piece of chicken onto her plate when she was talking to Charly, and although she frowned, she ate it. I wasn't the only one depleted.

"Kelly, are you feeling better now?" Theo asked, licking his fingers.

"Use your fork," Gabby admonished.

"It tastes better with my fingers, Mom."

She sighed.

Stefano chuckled and took Theo's plate, cutting the chicken into bite-size pieces. "It's a casual meal, *Tesoro*. It's okay for today only." He directed his response to Theo. "Only today, okay, little man?"

Theo nodded happily, then looked at Kelly again. "Are you okay?"

She smiled at him, puzzled. "I'm fine, Theo."

"Oh."

"Why do you think I'm not?" she asked.

"I saw Brett with his leg wrapped around you, like Dad does to Mom sometimes. Dad says it is so he can make her feel good. Mom always laughs, so it must work. I thought maybe you were sick and Brett was helping you."

My fork froze partway to my mouth. Stefano met my panicked gaze. Gabby turned pink. Kelly made an odd noise in the back of her throat.

Charly sat back in her chair, clearly enjoying this. "When did you see this, Theo?"

He picked up another piece of chicken, chewing slowly. "This morning."

I shut my eyes. The kid *had* seen me. Dammit.

He kept talking.

"I came to find you to ask, but no one was in the garage." He turned to Maxx. "I think it's haunted."

Maxx frowned. "Why would you say that?"

"I heard some weird noises but didn't see anyone."

Stefano sat back, draping his arm over Gabby's shoulders, a smirk on his mouth.

"Weird noises?"

Theo nodded around a mouthful of chicken. "Maybe it was a bear. You guys have donuts in the office." His eyes grew round. "It could still be there! If I stayed, it would have eaten me!"

"I don't think that's what was being eaten," Maxx muttered, blowing out a sharp breath when Charly elbowed him.

"Not a bear, little man," Stefano said, now grinning widely.

"Maybe a raccoon," Theo mused. "I don't know what kind of noises they make."

Stefano looked at me, smiling. "Do you know what kind of noises raccoons make, Brett? You hear anything funny in the garage today?"

Kelly covered her mouth with her napkin, clearly distressed. Charly was laughing so hard, tears were coming from her eyes. Gabby had to turn her head to hide her amusement. Mary was laughing with Charly, clearly enjoying herself. I felt everyone's stares.

"Nope," I said firmly. "Didn't hear a thing."

"Maybe it is haunted, then," Theo said.

Maxx patted his shoulder, a wide grin on his face. "Not haunted. I had a piece of machinery running. It makes some, ah, odd noises at times. Sounds like people grunting." He made a noise that made Kelly shake her head in embarrassment. It sounded far too familiar.

"Like that," he finished.

Theo nodded. "Yes! Whew. I'm glad. I don't want to work in a garage that's haunted."

"Nope," Maxx said. "Or with wild animals doing God knows what in my garage." Then he started laughing.

Mary covered her mouth, looking down. Then Stefano started guffawing. And suddenly, we were all laughing. Even Kelly. Theo, who had no idea why, joined in the merriment, his little-boy laughter high and amused.

Maxx wiped his eyes.

"If my dad only knew what his garage would become," he said.

"Maybe we should rename it the passion pit," Charly deadpanned.

That set off another round of laughter.

It felt good.

We ate and sat around, laughing more and talking. The girls set up the croquet set and played a game with Theo. Maxx built a fire, and we relaxed, talking about the garage and the upcoming expansion. My phone rang with an unknown number, and although I usually ignored those, I answered.

"Brett Conner."

"Mr. Conner, this is Officer Gallagher of the Lomand police department," a feminine voice said. "Do you know a Chase Donner?"

My gut clenched. "Yes. Is he okay?"

"He's drunk. I found him trying to get into his vehicle in the parking lot of a bar."

"Jesus, he was going to drive?"

Her voice was amused. "No, he was trying to unlock the back door so he could go to sleep."

"The back door doesn't have an outside lock."

"I pointed that out to him. Look, I can haul him to the drunk tank, or you can come pick him up." Her voice lowered. "I have the feeling he's had a bad day."

"Yeah, he has. I'll come get him. Which bar?"

"O'Shea's."

"I'm on my way."

I stood, everyone looking at me. "Chase is drunk and was trying to break in to his own vehicle to take a nap. I'm going to go get him and take him home."

Stefano stood. "I'll come with you."

I waved him off. "No, take your family home. I'll handle it."

"You need me?" Maxx offered.

"No, I got this."

I walked away, stopping at the sound of feet running behind me. I turned to find Kelly there.

She reached out, touching my arm. "I can help."

I felt the stares of our friends, knowing we were under their scrutiny. The smart thing to do was to say no. Take Stefano or Maxx.

But I held out my hand. "Yes, please."

We pulled into the parking lot at O'Shea's. Chase's truck was at the back. He was sitting on the tailgate, speaking animatedly to a female police officer. She was leaning on the tailgate, her hip perched so she was angled toward him. Her head was tilted as if she was paying close attention to his words.

"Oh boy," I muttered as we got out of the truck.

The officer looked up, standing as we approached. Chase turned his head, his glassy stare focusing on me. He slipped off the tailgate, unsteady on his feet. I reached for him as he half fell into me.

"Brett! My man Brett! Occifer Cinnamon—" he slurred "—this is my man Brett." He patted my chest. "He's a good guy." Then he pointed toward Kelly. "That's his lady. Hi, Kelly." He grinned sloppily. "That's Occifer Cinnamon. She was keeping me company." He hiccupped. "I was working up my nerve to ask her out." Then he placed a finger on his lips. "Shh. That's a secret."

"Sure, buddy," I said.

"It's Officer Gallagher, actually," the police officer stated. "Not cinnamon."

He ignored her. "Brett," he said, sounding indignant. "My key wouldn't work." He held up his key ring, the light catching the silver. "It wouldn't go in the hole."

"That's your house key, you moron," I replied, taking it and tossing it to Kelly. "And the only hole around here is the one where your brain used to be." I felt in his pocket and found the key fob for the truck, flipping that to her as well.

"Thank you, Officer—" I began.

"Cinnamon," Chase inserted. "Occifer Cinnamon.

"*Officer* Gallagher," she said again, sounding far too patient. She was obviously used to dealing with drunkards.

"Nope," Chase insisted. "You're so pretty with all those freckles. Like cinnamon sprinkled on your skin. I like them. I could write a poem about them." He winked lewdly, half leaning toward her. "I'd like to lick them with—"

"Okay," I interrupted him before the officer decided to lock him up for being an ass. "It's time to go home. You need to sleep this off. Say good night and thank you, Chase."

Chase frowned, confused. "Why am I saying thanks to myself?"

I shook my head, dragging him to the truck.

"We're going?" he asked.

"Yep."

"But I didn't get her number. Did you see those eyes? Those freckles? Man, what I want—"

"Shut up," I hissed. "Just shut up before she arrests you for propositioning a police officer or something."

He made a noise of dissatisfaction but stayed quiet.

I helped him into the front seat, not surprised when he immediately shut his eyes and passed out. I grabbed the trash can from the back and a bottle of water I had there and put them in his lap. I hoped we'd make it home before he needed either item.

I returned to where Kelly was talking to Officer Gallagher. "I'm sorry," I said. "That was very kind of you not simply hauling him to the drunk tank."

She smiled. "He was rather cute, muttering about someone moving the keyhole and all he wanted to do was lie down in the back seat. He assured me it was very comfortable for naps."

I laughed. "He does a lot of driving for the garage. He pulls over for naps when he has to."

"I've heard of the garage. I just transferred here," she said. "I need a tune-up, and someone mentioned that name. That's what caught my eye as I was driving by. The logo on the side of the truck. Then I saw Mr. Donner stumbling around, and I came to check it out." She sighed. "Thank God he wasn't attempting to drive. When I asked him, he got quite indignant and informed me he couldn't possibly drive since he was drunk, but he needed to lie down and the back seat was the best place." She paused, a smile tugging at her mouth. "If only he could find the hole the key was supposed to go in."

I pulled a card from my wallet. "Bring your car in. You'll get great service."

"Thanks." She frowned. "From what I gathered from his mumblings, your friend is upset about a fight with his brother."

I sighed. "A bit more complex than that, I'm afraid."

She smiled sadly. The parking lot light overhead caught her face. I could see the freckles Chase was waxing on about. They were all over her face. And her eyes were stunning. A light caramel brown that glittered under the lights. Thank God he hadn't started a sonnet about those too. I couldn't tell what color her hair was since it was tucked under her hat, but her eyebrows were light, so I assumed her hair was too. There was an air of sweetness around her. She didn't seem like your usual sort of cop. She was too young and innocent.

Or maybe not. I had no idea.

I stuck out my hand. "Thank you. I'll get him home and sobered up. I have never known him to have more than a couple of beers, so today is the exception, I assure you."

She nodded, looking over my shoulder toward my truck. "I get that. Everyone has one of those days they need to forget."

Kelly spoke up. "Come by the garage whenever you want. Your car will get great service."

The officer looked at the card. "I will. You guys be safe."

She got into her car and drove off.

I turned to Kelly. "You'll follow?"

"Yes."

I sighed. "Okay, let's get the boy home."

CHAPTER THIRTEEN

Brett

Chase stumbled, muttered, and groaned but never really woke up as I dragged him into the house. I deposited him on top of his bed, shaking my head as I looked down at him.

"He is gonna hurt in the morning," I muttered. "Big-time."

Kelly disappeared, returning with a bottle of Tylenol and some water. She put it beside him and pulled up a blanket as I tugged off his shoes. "Poor kid," she whispered, stroking his hair in a tender gesture.

I left his light on and pulled his door shut. Outside my room, I paused. "You staying?"

"Oh, ah—"

"I'll drive you home in the morning." I ran a hand through my hair. "To be honest, I'm exhausted, Kelly. I just want to go to bed."

"I don't have—"

Again, I interrupted her. "I'll give you a shirt and a toothbrush." I took her hand and lifted it to my mouth. "Just sleep. No bear noises."

That made her laugh. She covered her mouth, giggling. "That was embarrassing."

"It was, but it was also damn funny. The whole leg hitch thing was too. I never know what that kid is gonna say."

I tugged her hand. "Yes?"

She nodded.

A short while later, she crawled in beside me, looking cute and sleepy. My shirt was way too long on her, but I liked how she looked in it. I pulled her close, pressing a kiss to her head. "Thanks, Kelly."

"For what?"

"Coming with me and helping me with Chase. Staying."

She snuggled closer, her head on my chest. "You're welcome." She yawned. "I'm tired too."

"Wore you out today, did I?"

"And last night," she murmured.

I felt a wave of tenderness wash over me. I liked her like this— warm, quiet, and cuddly. It was different for her. "Go to sleep, then."

In a minute, she was out. I enjoyed holding her, having her close. It was the first time she'd ever stayed here with me. The first time we'd ever shared a bed simply to sleep. There seemed to be a lot of firsts in my life lately. What they all meant, I had no idea, and

I was too tired to think too deeply about it. I closed my eyes and, surrounded by the soft fragrance of Kelly, fell asleep.

She was awake early, no doubt used to her schedule of being up and taking pictures at dawn. I didn't object but drove her home, trying not to laugh when she asked me to drop her off at the driveway.

"I'll walk up to the house."

"Charly will still see you."

"She'll think I was out taking pictures."

"You are an adult, Kelly, and after last night, everyone is aware we're sleeping together."

She rolled her eyes and got out of the truck. "I am not giving her more to quiz me about." Then she sighed. "She's probably already on my sofa, waiting to pounce. She'll know I wasn't there all night."

I chuckled. "Sounds like Charly. I'll go in your place, and you go handle Chase."

She shook her head, turning serious. "Be patient with him, Brett. I think he's hiding a lot of pain."

"I know. I will. I just want him to know he doesn't have to hide it. We're here for him."

Her eyes were soft. "I know you are. You're amazing."

Then she turned and hurried up the driveway. As I turned the truck back around to head home, I saw Charly in the yard and laughed.

We were busted, and now Kelly had to face her alone.

That left me with Chase.

When I pulled into the driveway, Stefano was already there. He climbed out of his truck, holding a tray of coffee. "Morning."

I got out, holding a tray as well. "Great minds," I said.

He chuckled. "Figured it would be needed."

We went into the house and found Chase on the sofa. He'd obviously showered, his hair damp and fresh clothes on. He had his head in his hands, his shoulders slumped. We sat down, and Stefano nudged him. "Hey. How you feeling?"

Chase looked up, his eyes bloodshot. "Like shit."

Stefano handed him a coffee. "This will help. So will Tylenol."

"Already took some but wasn't coordinated enough to try the coffee machine," Chase admitted, taking the lid off the to-go cup and drinking the hot beverage. He shut his eyes. "Jesus, did you hear that hit the bottom?"

I chuckled. "We'll fill the tank in a bit when you feel more human. In the meantime, what was that about? Taking off on your own and not talking to us?"

He was quiet for a moment. "This is a hard time for me. Yesterday was the anniversary of when Wes died. Next week is my dad's. A year apart. It brings back a lot of memories. Bad ones."

"And why are you trying to deal with them on your own?" Stefano asked.

Chase looked up. "My brother caused so many problems. My dad was an arrogant ass. That's how everyone knows them. Remembers them." His voice caught. "But I remember them before my mom died. When my dad played with us, carried us on his shoulder, read to us. When Wes was my hero. My big brother who protected me. Let me play with his favorite Matchbox car. Showed me how to tie my shoes. Everything changed when my mom died. My whole world exploded. All this town remembers is the bad that happened afterward. I have no one to share the good with. That's what I mourn."

"You can share with us," I corrected him. "We're your friends, so we would understand."

"Wes hurt Charly. I was part of that. I can't expect them to understand."

Stefano barked a laugh. "Then you're forgetting who Charly is. I know for a fact that she'll be over here today, giving you shit about this, worried and upset. Smothering you in hugs and berating you at the same time. She forgave you. So did Maxx. We all did, Chase. But it seems to me, you haven't forgiven yourself."

Chase blinked at him, then looked at me. I nodded in agreement. "He's right. You were involved, but you changed. You made up for your mistakes."

Tears filled Chase's eyes, and my heart went out to him. "Wes never had the chance. He was too bitter. He hated me when he died. My dad refused to see me. I lost my whole family."

"Wes didn't hate you. He was angry. I think he would have changed his mind had he lived. And your dad was stubborn but stupid. He loved you. He left you millions, kid. That was his way. It all sucks, but you can't heap this guilt on your head every year," Stefano said patiently.

"And you can't deal with it by getting drunk and hiding from us," I added. "We wanted you with us last night. You missed a thoroughly embarrassing dinner."

A glimmer of a smile crossed his face. "Sorry I missed that." He ran a hand over the back of his neck. "I went to a bar and got shit-faced. I sort of recall you showing up, Brett, but not much else."

I sat back with a grin. "Does *Occifer Cinnamon* ring a bell?"

He frowned then suddenly stood. "Holy shit. I hit on a cop, didn't I?"

I chuckled. "Sit down."

He did, and I regaled him and Stefano with the story. Stefano laughed, Chase looked equally amused and horrified. He buried his face in his hands. "I'm never fucking living this down." Then he lifted his head. "She was really fucking pretty, wasn't she?"

"Yeah, she was. And you're lucky. She could have hauled your ass to jail for even attempting to get in your vehicle."

"Shit."

"She just moved here, and she needs a tune-up on her car. I told her to bring it into the shop. I'll make sure she gets looked after." I paused. "You were certainly interested in tuning her up yourself last night."

"Oh God," he muttered. "It was the freckles. I have a thing for freckles."

"Well, you're gonna have a field day when you see her sober. She's covered in them."

"Shit," he repeated.

I leaned forward, serious. "No more, Chase. No more guilt. No more hiding. You're hurting? You tell us. If you're not comfortable with us, then Charly. Gabby. Mary. All three of them. We all care."

Stefano reached over and one-arm hugged Chase. "I know your family is gone, Chase, but we consider you part of ours now. And family takes care of one another, okay? I agree with Brett. No more hiding."

Chase looked down, then nodded. "Got it," he replied, his voice thick.

Hearing the sound of a car door, I looked out the window.

"Hurricane Charly has just arrived. Brace yourself." I stood. "Maybe we should go get breakfast for everyone, Stefano."

He joined me. "Good plan."

We met Charly at the door. "He's in the living room."

"Is he okay?"

"Bad hangover and he's struggling."

"I'm going to hug him until he figures his shit out," she muttered. "Then I have a thing or two to say."

I waved my hand. "He's all yours."

Later that afternoon, I took a drive, enjoying the sunshine and quiet. Charly had been and gone. Chase was asleep, passed out in his bed, exhausted. I planned on dropping by my dad's later, surprising him again, but for now, I was good to be on my own.

Until a flash of sunlight caught something and I slowed down, recognizing Charly's old bike propped against a tree. And in the distance, I saw her.

Kelly.

Armed with her camera, standing in the middle of a field, taking pictures, her dark hair gleaming in the sun.

The need to be alone vanished. I pulled over, parked the truck, and slid out, heading in Kelly's direction. She was so absorbed in her endeavors, she didn't notice me at first. I watched her for a moment, caught in her spell. She was graceful as she moved, catching the light and her subject in the frame of her lens. She bent and swooped. Arched her back to get the right shot. Then, as if satisfied, she lifted her arms and twirled in the light. I was mesmerized, unable to tear my gaze from her. She looked carefree and happy. Surrounded by beauty, she became the focal point of it all to me.

And then she saw me. She stopped, then did something unexpected. Instead of frowning or calling my name and asking what I was doing there, she broke into a run, heading my way. I braced myself, and when she flung herself into my arms, I caught her easily. Laughing, I swung her around, much like she had been doing on her own. I set her on her feet, smiling down at her.

"Hey, Shutterbug. Fancy meeting you here."

She shocked me when she pulled my head down to hers, kissing me passionately. With a groan, I yanked her close and returned her ardent kiss. I released her as she stepped back.

"Not for nothing, but what did I do to deserve that?" I asked.

"You're here," she said. "Oh Brett, I'm so excited."

"Tell me."

"I don't start my assignments with the paper until this week, but last week, I sent them some pictures I'd taken around town and while I was out walking. I called them Forgotten Beauty." She flipped through her viewfinder, showing me some examples. "That little waterfall on the edge of Lomand. The baseball fields at night as the sun goes down. Look how it turns the metal bleachers into a blaze of color," she explained. "The lilac tree a few blocks from your house on that empty corner. Nothing around it, but its beauty is vivid."

"Those are amazing," I praised. "I take it they liked them?"

"Bob loved them. He wants to add them to the paper. He asked for more." She gripped my arm. "There is so much beauty here people forget, Brett. I want them to remember what it was they loved about this place. Why they chose to live here. To rediscover this town."

I had no choice. I dragged her back into my arms and kissed her until she was breathless. The way she saw the world around her, read people, understood them. She was amazing.

She grinned up at me. "Stay?" she asked. "Walk with me and see what I see." She winked. "You can play my assistant and carry my bag."

"Absolutely."

I followed her, stopping to pick up the bag and sling it over my shoulder, unable to halt the thoughts racing through my head.

Could I help her discover enough beauty that she would want to stay?

I was too afraid to hope, yet too overcome not to.

I shadowed her the rest of the afternoon. We didn't talk much, aside from what lens she wanted or her showing me a picture she was enthralled with. I liked watching her in action—the way she lost herself in capturing just the right angle, trying to see what it was she had discovered that made her stop and lift her camera. What I saw as mundane or inconsequential, she saw as beauty, form, and the need to lift it higher for others to experience. It was a perfect afternoon. I loaded the bike into the back of the truck and drove her wherever she wanted. Once she was done, I headed to Littleburn, pulling up in front of the store. "I think a cold soda is in order."

"Awesome," she agreed.

We headed inside, my dad sitting on the stool, pen in hand, doing the crossword puzzle. He looked up as we came in, offering us a smile. "Well, there's a sight for sore eyes."

Kelly walked over and kissed his cheek, making him beam in happiness.

"We need cold drinks. Kelly's been taking pictures for the paper."

"Can I see?" he asked.

Kelly showed him as I grabbed some cold sodas, taking a long drink of the orange one I favored. The icy liquid felt good on my throat, and I handed a Coke to Kelly and a ginger ale to my dad. We clinked bottles, and Kelly tilted her head back, drinking in long pulls.

"Whew, I needed that," she said, then burped. Loudly.

For a second, I stared at her, then winked. "Impressive."

"I'm so embarrassed. Excuse me," she muttered, her cheeks going pink.

I tilted back my head and drained my bottle, then let out a loud belch. "Impressive but nowhere near as good as mine."

My dad laughed. "We used to have belching contests. Your mother would get so annoyed."

"Betcha I can still win." I egged him on.

He shook his head, taking only one sip and letting out the loudest one of them all. "Amateur," he sniffed. "I'm old, but still got it."

We all laughed, and Kelly forgot her embarrassment. I liked seeing her like this. I liked teasing her. I also liked the fact that my dad was in a good mood.

"Does Rosa agree with you on that?" I asked slyly.

He grinned. "I don't kiss and tell."

Kelly lifted her hand, and he high-fived it.

Then she set down her bottle. "I should go. I was gone longer than I planned, and I promised Charly to help her with a project she has on the go."

"Charly always has a project on the go," I replied.

"She does."

"I'll take you."

"No." She waved her hand. "I'll get my bike and go. You stay with your dad."

I followed her outside and lifted the bike out. She put her bag in the basket and swung her leg over the seat. "Thanks for today, Brett."

I leaned down and pressed a kiss to her cheek. "Thanks for letting me tag along, Shutterbug."

I stood and watched her pedal away until she disappeared around the corner.

I turned and found my dad sitting in one of the rockers, his drink in his hand, a fresh bottle of soda beside him waiting for me. I sat down, accepting the bottle.

"So, *Charly's* friend, eh?"

"Say another word, old man, and I'm telling Stefano you kissed his mother."

He chuckled. "I got meatloaf in the oven for supper. You want to join me?"

His voice held a hopeful note, yet it was resigned. He expected me to say no.

I leaned back. "You making mashed potatoes with it?"

"Yep."

"Then count me in."

He leaned back, rocking slowly.

"Great."

I matched his position, pushing off the old wooden deck in the rocker.

"Yep. Great."

The next few days were busy and productive. We met with the contractor, finalized the plans, and agreed on a start date. Kelly started her job with the paper, so she was in and out. She and Charly worked out a schedule, and Gabby came in one day a week, so the office was always staffed. I enjoyed working with Charly and Gabby, but I missed seeing Kelly every day. I told myself to get used to it since she wouldn't be around forever, but the days she was there, I know I smiled more and found reasons to go to the office.

I was surprised to see her on Thursday. I took an invoice in, asking her to check if it had been paid. Standing behind her, I studied the back of her neck, noticing the fading mark behind her ear.

Unable to stop myself, I traced a finger over the skin of her neck, fighting back my smile as she shivered.

"I didn't know you were here today," I said.

"It's going to storm. I can't be out in the rain."

I nodded. "I miss you around here," I murmured so only she could hear me.

"That invoice was paid on Monday," she replied, a slight tremor in her voice.

I leaned on the desk, peering over her shoulder at the screen. To anyone looking, I was simply checking out the information on the computer. But I was close enough to smell her light fragrance. Feel the heat of her skin. I braced my hand on the top of the chair, teasing the skin on her back. "There haven't been any bear sightings recently."

She gasped, a quick intake of air. "Brett," she protested.

"Raccoons either," I added. "No wildlife."

"Stop it."

I straightened, dragging my hand up her back and through her hair. "Just keeping you informed."

I headed to my office.

"I'm going to do inventory later. In the barn. Charly wants a count of the tires," she informed me.

"I'll be sure to check in on you."

"You do that."

Smirking, I headed to my desk. I dropped the invoice on it and walked out to the garage. At the sound of a raised voice, I looked over to where Ward was talking to a customer. Ward looked frustrated and the customer unhappy. He was a tall guy, broad shoulders, and a bald head that gleamed under the light. He wore a dress shirt and looked uncomfortable in his own skin. He was in Ward's space, obviously trying to intimidate him. I walked over, forcing a smile to my face.

"Problem, gentlemen?"

"Yeah, your guy is trying to rip me off."

I crossed my arms. "I find that hard to believe. What seems to be the problem?"

"Damn car took a nail to the tire."

"I can put a plug in," Ward explained. "But his oil light is on, and it's way past its service date. I told him we should do an oil change while it's here so he doesn't burn out his engine." He paused, looking at me meaningfully and offering me the clipboard with the work order. "Way past due."

I glanced at the information. I was shocked his car hadn't seized. For the owner of a newer vehicle, he wasn't taking care of the car.

"I told him to do it, but I just want a regular damn oil change. I'm on the road, and I need it. He's jacked up the price."

I looked at the estimate. It was fair and accurate.

"As I tried to explain to Mr. Dane here, the price is for synthetic oil, which is necessary for his car. He wants regular oil."

I nodded. "Regular oil won't work with your engine. We have to use synthetic. In fact, this car requires a certain brand. It is expensive, but necessary. Your manual tells you all this. So does your warranty."

"Bunch of damn BS. Just give me regular."

"We can't do that." I crossed my arms. "We either fix the car properly, or you can arrange to have it towed elsewhere."

"The damn tow guy said this was the best place in town and brought me here."

I held in my sigh. As much as I appreciated the business, we didn't need jobs like this. We were already too busy. I'd ask Charly to get the word out to send people to Finn's Auto Repair. They could handle jobs like this easily.

I met his angry gaze. "There is a reason we're the best. We don't cut corners, and we don't do shoddy work. If I did an oil change without the proper oil, I risk damaging your engine. I refuse to do that. Any mechanic worth his salt would refuse to do that."

"Then forget it. Plug the tire."

"You're putting your—"

He cut me off. "Just the damn tire."

I shook my head, marking on the form that the customer refused our advice. "You heard him, Ward. Plug the tire, make sure it's okay, and send him on his way."

I returned to the office, where Kelly had been watching. "He's been a pain since he came in. I moved appointments around to get his car done and get him out of here."

"No more accepting tows. Booked appointments only."

"I think Charly said yes because Finn's was closed today. His wife had a baby last night."

"Ah. Makes sense. Okay, we'll get him done and out of here before he causes any more trouble."

"He's drunk his weight in coffee already."

"Great. No wonder he's so antsy and ready for a fight."

Chase appeared in the door. "Brett, Stefano needs you out back."

"Shit," I swore. "Is it Monday? It feels like a Monday."

Kelly laughed. "Go help Stefano. I've got this covered."

Twenty minutes later, I walked back into the garage. Two things struck me. The pain in the ass's car was no longer on the hoist. The second was that the pain in the ass was now in the office with Kelly, and as I watched in horror, he gripped her arms, pinned her to the wall, and began to yell.

One second, I was in the bay area; the next, I was in her office, dragging him away, my fist connecting with his jaw with a satisfying crunch.

"You fucking dare to touch her?" I raged. "What the hell is the matter with you?"

He glared at me from the floor, pushing up, ready to throw down. "Motherfucker," he swore. "You are going to pay for that."

I fell into my stance. "Bring it on."

But before he could move, Maxx rushed in. Stefano followed him, along with Chase. They stood beside me.

"Explain," Maxx barked, looking at me.

I straightened. "He was hassling Kelly. Touching her!" I yelled. "He had her pinned against the damn wall!"

Maxx faced him. "Get the hell out of my garage."

"I'm going to press charges," Mr. Dane sneered.

Stefano moved quickly, getting behind him and bending his arm. "You press anything you like. We have witnesses who can verify you attacked a defenseless woman unprovoked. If anyone should press charges, it's her."

Kelly spoke. "I'm fine. Just get him out of here."

Stefano frog-marched him outside, Maxx following.

I spun around, facing Kelly. She was pale, but calm.

"Are you okay?" I asked.

"Yes. You arrived before he could do anything."

"What set him off?"

"His credit card was declined. He said it was my fault. That I had done it incorrectly. I tried it again and got the same result. He wasn't happy."

"That doesn't give the fucker the right to touch you," I seethed. "I want to go out there and beat the shit out of him."

She placed her hand on my arm. "I'm okay."

I took her hand and tugged her into my office. The blinds were down, and it was more private. I shut the door behind her and pulled her into my arms.

"Kelly," I murmured. "Seeing him grab you. Jesus, I wanted to kill him."

She linked her arms around my waist, leaning into me. "I'm okay," she replied. "You got there so fast."

"Not fast enough. He still touched you. Are you hurt?"

She paused, then sighed. "Just shaken up."

Maxx walked in, shutting the door behind him. I didn't release my hold on Kelly, and he didn't ask me to. "He's gone. I got his license plate, and Stefano is calling the cops to tell them. Are you okay, Kelly?"

"Yes." Her voice was muffled, her face still buried in my shirt.

"That has never happened before. Never fucking happening again."

I explained how he'd ended up here. "I don't understand the chip on his shoulder."

Maxx shook his head. "Over an oil change."

Kelly eased back. "Maybe there is something else going on in his life and that was the icing on the cake."

"He still—"

"I know," she interrupted me.

"You're too good," I rasped.

She leaned back into me. "No, I'm not."

I met Maxx's concerned gaze. "We'll be out in a minute."

He shook his head. "Charly is going to freak out over this."

"Don't tell her," Kelly said, easing back. I let her out of my arms but slid my hand over hers, holding it tight. I felt her spread her fingers, entwining them with mine. I liked feeling our palms melded together.

"Pretty sure she'll find out. I don't keep things from her, and if I don't tell her, she is gonna be riled. And not in a good way."

Kelly chuckled, some of her tension easing away. "Fine. But make sure she knows I'm fine, Brett was right there, and it's over. I don't want to make a big deal about this."

He lifted his shoulders. "I'll try, Kelly. It's Charly. I have zero control over that woman."

He left, and I glanced down at Kelly.

"Okay, Shutterbug?"

"Yeah." She straightened her shoulders. "Let's get back to work."

"Okay."

KELLY

I wasn't surprised to find Brett at my door not long after the garage closed for the night. Charly had already been and gone, upset over what had occurred.

"Brett's right. No more tows. I was just doing them a favor," she fretted. *"I'm sorry. Are you sure you're okay?"*

"I'm fine."

"Are you coming for supper?"

"No, I'm tired, and I have to get some prep done for the next couple days. I have lots of pictures to take."

"Okay. I'll send something over."

"I have food. It's fine." I hugged her. *"Please stop fussing."*

The next knock was Brett, and I was happy to see him. He held a bag in one hand, a pizza box in another.

"Dinner," he said, handing me the box.

"And the bag?" I asked as I walked to the table, sliding the pizza on top.

"I'm staying."

I turned. "Staying?"

He opened the kitchen cupboard and grabbed two plates. "After today, I'm not taking any chances."

"Brett, he was an asshole having a bad day. He left."

He sat down. "Well, I'm not leaving."

I sat down, watching him open the pizza box and slide two pieces onto my plate. He met my gaze. "You wanna challenge me on that?"

I hid my smile. "Nope."

He took a bite of pizza, chewing it, and swallowing. He got up and went to the refrigerator, returning with a couple of sodas. He slid his hand around my neck, tugging back my head and kissing me hard. "Good," he grunted and sat back down. "Wouldn't listen anyway."

I tried not to stare. When I'd first heard about Brett from Charly, she'd described him as the "sweetest, nicest man." Kind and quiet.

The Brett I knew was all that. He was also a dirty-talking, crazy-good-at-sex alpha who liked to give orgasms as much as he liked having them. He was an incredible kisser. Charming and funny. And now add caring and overprotective to the list?

He was the whole package.

"What?" he said, taking a sip of his soda. "Why aren't you eating?"

"Oh." I picked up my slice and took a bite. "You have layers, Mr. Conner."

He snorted. "Whatever."

"Sexy. Sweet. Funny. Smart. Charming. A great friend. A good son. An incredible lover. Bossy. Caring. Protective."

He frowned. "That's how you see me?"

"Add in amazing and a great belcher, pretty much."

He chuckled. "Not as good a belcher as my dad."

"We can't all be that good. But the rest, you ace."

He studied me. "I didn't know."

"Didn't know what?

"You saw me that way."

"How did you think I saw you?"

He bit and chewed, looking thoughtful. "I don't know. I wasn't sure you ever saw me past our hookups."

I dropped my slice, reaching over to grab his hand. "I'm sorry I made you feel that way. I always saw you." I swallowed. "I always thought you were incredible. I thought you knew that. It's me, Brett. I'm the fucked-up one."

"I don't think you're fucked up. Misguided and confused but not fucked up."

"I'm sorry," I offered.

"For what?"

I shrugged. "So many things. I leave because it's all I know. I can't stay too long anywhere."

"Are you searching for something, Shutterbug?" he asked quietly.

"I don't know."

"Maybe you need to figure that out so you can stop running. You may have found what you need already and don't even know it."

I knew what he was implying. I had no idea how to respond, except I knew that, right now, I was exactly where I wanted to be.

I squeezed his hand and he smiled.

"So exactly how sexy do you think I am?" he asked.

The evening was quiet. I worked on the schedule, Brett on the sofa beside me, studying a manual. "What is that?" I asked.

"Chilton's Auto Repair. I like them. Chase prefers Hilton." He winked. "More pictures."

I laughed. "You give him such a hard time. Is he okay?"

"Yeah, way better. He knows we have his back. All of us. Next year will be different for him."

"Why are you reading an auto repair manual?"

"You see something different with every car. We have one right now I am at a loss to figure out. So I'm seeing if I can find an idea to explore."

"Ah."

"How's your schedule coming?"

"It's going to be a busy couple of days. Tomorrow is more town and business pictures. Saturday, I have three fairs to attend."

He stretched out his legs. "You want some company on Saturday? I can offer my services as an assistant. Maxx is covering the garage."

"Really?"

He ran his finger down my cheek. "Yeah, really. We can spend the day together. You can take your pictures. I'll stuff myself with fair grub and be at your beck and call."

"That would be awesome. I didn't want to ask—"

He interrupted me. "Always ask, Shutterbug."

I smiled and leaned over, kissing him. "Okay."

He grinned. "Okay."

I yawned and covered my mouth. "Tired?" he asked.

"Yeah." I stood and shrugged off my sweater, draping it over the sofa. "I'm going to head—"

I stopped speaking at the furious look on Brett's face. "What?"

He stood, tracing his fingers over my arms. I was shocked to see bruises on my flesh. "He left marks on you."

"They don't hurt," I assured him. "I didn't even know." I grabbed his hand. "Please don't get upset."

His face was like thunder. Stormy and angry. Even his eyes darkened. Our gazes clashed, and I caught my breath. He was angry because someone *touched* me. Because someone *hurt* me. Because he cared enough for that to never happen. It was in that very moment, I knew I had failed. I had guarded my heart, run from him every time I felt myself growing attached. But it hadn't worked.

I was in love with Brett.

But I wasn't sure he would ever love me again.

With a low cry, I flung myself at him, letting him yank me close. We kissed, our mouths moving together in a symphony of unsaid words. Broken promises. Unfilled wishes and daring dreams. He lifted me, carrying me to the bedroom.

And for tonight, I pretended I would be safe like this with him —always.

CHAPTER FOURTEEN

Brett

The next day, Stefano and I were bent over the plans, discussing an added change. Simple, but highly effective for the business. I tapped the back wall. "Right here. An extra roll-up door. If we need to expand again, easy. We have a bigger job, we can open the door for more room."

"Great idea," he mused.

Theo walked in, squirming between us. Stefano ruffled his hair. "Hey, little man. You done hanging with the girls?"

Theo huffed. "They're just looking at Kelly's pictures. They're kinda boring."

I chuckled. "So, Kelly's with them?" I asked casually. I was still worried over that asshole yesterday and her sudden emotion last night. Our lovemaking, while still passionate, had an air of sadness to it, and I was confused. She'd been gone all morning taking her pictures for the magazine, and it had required all my control not to check on her constantly via text. I was glad she was back. Gabby had worked in the office all day and had gone to feed the baby and have a break.

"Yeah. She said she was done for the day. She's tired."

I glanced at my watch. She'd been gone all day—I wasn't surprised to hear she was tired.

"You don't like the pictures?" Stefano asked, surprised. "You usually like to see them."

"They aren't of the jungle or the beach." Theo shrugged, looking at the plans in front of him. "Just people." He rubbed his nose. "Old people."

I laughed again. Anyone older than twenty was old at his age.

"What is that?" He pointed to the line I had added.

"Another garage door—a big one so we can get trucks in."

"Like semis?"

"Yep. Extra-high roof too."

"Neat."

He glanced up, looking between Stefano and me with a confused frown.

"What?" Stefano asked, his tone indulgent. Theo always had questions, and Stefano adored the kid he considered his own son and loved answering them.

"If Nonna Rosa and Brett's dad get married, will you be brothers? Does that make Brett's dad my grandpa?" he asked, scratching his nose.

I met Stefano's confused gaze.

"Why would you ask that?" I replied, curious.

Theo huffed a sigh. "Dad says I can only kiss a girl I want to marry. That's why he kissed my mom so much. I don't want to kiss any girls, so I must not want to get married," he added. "Dad still kisses Mom so much they hafta lie down all the time." He shook his head. "Boring."

I had to look away for a minute to hide my amusement. Theo was the king of overshare on everyone else's behalf. Stefano's voice was amused. "So why would you ask about Nonna?"

"'Cause of Kelly's pictures of Nonna and Brett's dad kissing."

Our gazes clashed, and we both pushed off the table, heading outside. Theo trailed behind us, running to keep up. "Hey, Dad, wait!"

Stefano swung him up into his arms as we rushed toward the house. Charly, Gabby, and Kelly were on the porch, looking at Kelly's laptop. Charly looked up, grinning.

"Incoming."

I skidded to a stop in front of Kelly. "May I have your laptop for a moment?"

"No," she replied, suspicious.

"Please."

"It's valuable."

"I won't break it."

"He wants to see the kissing picture," Theo said.

With a sigh, Kelly swiped the screen and handed it to me. Stefano and I peered at the images, slowly going through the photos. Kelly had taken a lot around town today. Little alleys, storefronts, people milling about. I stopped at the shot of the general store. The rockers. Rosa and my dad grinning at the camera. Him leaning over, pressing a kiss to her cheek, her laughing.

I relaxed. "It's fine," I muttered.

Then I swiped again. The next shot, my dad's hat was off, covering their faces. His hand was on Rosa's knee, her hand on his arm. I had a feeling what was going on behind the hat didn't involve her cheek. Another swipe confirmed it. The hat was chin-level now, and they had their foreheads pressed together, smiling at each other.

"My mother's hair is down. I haven't seen it down since I was a kid," Stefano said, shocked. "She always wore it down for my dad."

"She looks lovely," Kelly said. "They were adorable."

"Yes, they are," Gabby said. "Stay out of it, Stefano," she warned.

I looked at Stefano; he looked at me.

"So, *will* you be brothers?" Theo asked again.

That did it.

I pulled up in the front of the store. Dad and Rosa were still in the rockers. A plate of cookies sat between them. They were holding hands.

Stefano cursed under his breath.

"Just stay calm," I hissed. My words had no effect as Stefano climbed out of the truck, closing the door with more force than necessary.

"I think we need to talk," he said, walking up the steps.

Dad stood, offering Rosa his hand to help her from the rocker. Inside, he asked Lyle to mind the store, and we went upstairs.

Stefano didn't waste any time. "What's going on with you two?"

"We're friends," Dad stated.

"Friends?" Stefano repeated. "From the pictures I just saw, I would say more than friends."

"Friends wiz benefits," Rosa said, crossing her arms.

Stefano made a funny choking noise, and I was pretty certain he just swallowed his tongue. I grabbed his arm.

"Rosa," I said calmly. "Are you sure you know what that means?"

"Yes." She stuck out her chin. "Mack and I go to supper. We hold hands. He kisses me. Tell me I'm beautiful. He make me happy."

"And that's all?" Stefano growled out.

She frowned and stood. "Why you no happy for me, Stefano? I let you live your life. You let me live mine. It's nice to have friend. I like the benefits. I didn't raise you to be so mean. You be happy."

"Mama," he said, all the anger going out of his voice. He took her arm and quietly explained what friends with benefits meant. Her eyes grew round, and she shook off his hand.

"No!" she said, horrified. "We no do that. You think I do? You think that of your mama?"

Stefano shook his head. "You said it."

Dad stood. "Let's all calm down. Yes, Rosa and I are friends. More than friends. We hold hands. And yes, I kiss her. But, boys," he sighed, shaking his head. "I'm sixty-six. Your mama is sixty-two. I can barely get out of the bed in the morning with my arthritis. Your mama needs help to get out of a chair at times. You really think we're having some sort of passionate free-for-all sex thing on the side?" He chuckled. "Our benefits include sharing a meal. Talking about our deceased spouses, our kids. How the world has changed. We understand each other."

He met our gazes. "We aren't so lonely when we're together."

Stefano and I looked at each other.

"I think your mother is amazing. She likes me. We enjoy each other's company. We hammed it up a little for the photos. Good God, the two of you are overreacting."

Rosa sniffed. "You butt out. I like Mack. He make me happy."

The look on Stefano's face did it. I began to laugh. The whole thing was ridiculous. But the shock and horror of Rosa telling Stefano to butt out was priceless.

"Theo wondered if Stefano and I were going to be brothers," I offered. "I was wondering if that meant I got to boss him around since I'm older and all."

My dad's lips twitched. "You're both acting like adolescents."

Rosa nodded. "You go home. Go to bed with no supper. I am staying with Mack. We're having spaghetti. He like my spaghetti."

"I can drive you home later," Stefano offered, trying to make peace. "It will be too late for Mack to drive at night."

"No, I stay over like usual."

"Like usual?" he asked, his voice once again choked.

"Your mother stays in Brett's old room. We have breakfast, and I drive her back in around lunch, or sometimes she stays for the day and helps me in the store. It's nice to have her around. I take her out to dinner and drop her at home."

"Oh."

"I think we need to go now," I said. I wasn't sure I could handle any more facts about Rosa and Dad's relationship.

"Probably for the best," Dad agreed. "We're playing cards with Angus and Fred after dinner. We have quite the competition going."

"We beat them tonight," Rosa said, rubbing her hands in glee. "I bring cookies Fred likes. And wine. Distracts him—he no count his cards right."

We walked downstairs and out to the truck. Inside, we were silent for a minute.

"Your dad kisses my mom."

"Your mom stays over, and they play cards."

"My mom snookers their opponents with wine and cookies so they can win." He rested his head in his hands. "I don't wanna know how they celebrate her victory."

I had to laugh.

"Friends with benefits," Stefano scoffed. "I can't believe my mama said that."

"Yeah, ziti benefits," I replied. "The look on your face, though…" I trailed off, chuckling. "Priceless."

We looked at each other, smirking. "We're idiots."

I backed up the truck and headed toward the garage. Stefano stared out the window, not speaking for a moment.

"Are they playing us?"

"Yep," I sighed.

"We're fucking going to be stepbrothers, you know that? Those two are in deep."

"Yep."

"You so do not get to play the older brother card."

"Whatever."

Stefano slapped his knee. "I need backup." He pulled his phone from his pocket, dialing a number and hitting speaker. His eldest brother Vince answered the phone. "Hey."

Stefano got right to the point. "I hope you're sitting down. Mama is dating Mack Conner."

"And?"

"Mack Conner," he repeated. "Brett's dad. He and Mama are *dating*."

"Hardly a news flash, little bro."

Stefano gaped at me then shook his head. "*You knew?*"

"Who the hell do you think drives her to Littleburn when she wants to see Mack?"

"And you're okay with this? With our mother dating?"

"Jesus, you *stupido*. She's happy. Leave it alone. You are such a mama's boy." He let off a string of curse words in Italian even I recognized. "I'm hanging up on you now. Leave it alone, you big baby."

Stefano looked at his silent phone. "I am not a mama's boy."

"Um, yeah, you are, you idiot. Your brother is right."

"Fuck," Stefano sighed. "I didn't expect this."

I had to agree with him.

"What do we do?" he asked.

"What your mama said. Butt out. What Vince just told you. Leave it. They're happy. Let's let them be happy. What happens later, happens. Life is too fucking short."

"Dammit, I hate when you make sense."

"I'm channeling my inner Charly."

"Well, tell her to shut up."

Then we both sighed.

"He better not hurt her, *capisce?*"

"She better not get knocked up," I replied, joking.

I began laughing at the horrified expression on Stefano's face. Then he joined me.

"God help us both."

I could only nod in agreement.

"You're off tomorrow?" he asked, changing the subject. I knew he'd moan to Gabby, and she'd make him see sense. He listened to her.

"Yeah. Going with Kelly to some fairs to take pictures. I'm her assistant."

"You're spending a lot of time together. Is this going somewhere this time?"

"I don't know. It feels different. She seeks me out at times. We spend more time together as people, not just…"

"Fucking?" Stefano asked dryly.

"Yes." I paused, thinking. "I feel as if we're building something."

"Have you had that conversation?"

"No."

"Why?"

"I'm a coward," I replied honestly. "We will. And soon. But for now, I'm letting us happen the way we're happening."

I pulled up in front of the garage.

Stefano patted my shoulder. "For what it's worth, Gabby and I think you're a great couple. You suit each other. She likes Kelly a lot, and she gets her."

"I think we're pretty great too." I looked over his shoulder. "Uh-oh, here comes your little man."

He chuckled. "He'll be full of questions."

I swung out of the truck. "Always is. Information and observations, too. The personal kind. Far too personal," I drawled.

Stefano laughed.

"You got that right."

I nudged him as we walked toward the house.

"Mama's boy," I snickered.

"Coward," he hissed.

On the porch, Charly stood and faced us, her hands on her hips. "The two of you knuckleheads better not have upset Mama Rosa and Daddy Mack. You'll answer to all of us." She indicated Kelly and Gabby standing beside her.

"Shit," we both muttered, our footsteps faltering. It was too late to run.

We were doomed.

CHAPTER FIFTEEN

Brett

Kelly held her stomach, shaking her head. "Stop!" She had been laughing too hard. "Oh my God, Stefano, Mr. Big and Strong Macho Man is *such* a mama's boy."

I smirked. "Yeah, he is. I admit, I'm still struggling a little, but they're happy, and we have to leave them alone and let them figure it out."

She turned to me. "Why are you struggling?"

I shrugged. "Just changes, I suppose. Worry it won't work and he'll be hurt and lonelier than ever."

"You have to take that chance sometimes."

I glanced at her, but she had turned back to the front and was looking at the road. "Yeah, you do," I said softly.

I opened my mouth to ask her if she was wanting to take that chance with me when she spoke.

"Okay, first up is the Bronx Fair. It's only about twenty minutes from here. They have that great dinosaur display kids love."

"Next?" I asked, knowing this wasn't the time for any more personal conversation.

"The Applewood carnival. Then is the Rib Fest at Bankhead."

"I am looking forward to that one. I plan on eating a lot of ribs once you're done with pictures."

"I hear the Bronx Fair has an entire candy tent. All the contestants vie for top prize."

"Good thing my shorts have a drawstring. Between the candy and the ribs, I am gonna need the room."

She laughed. "You'll work it off traipsing behind me, helping. I remember there were times I didn't get to eat for a whole day when I was helping Carl. We'd be so busy and caught up..." She trailed off.

"You miss it?" I asked, turning onto a gravel road that would lead to the first stop.

"I miss seeing new things. I don't miss being treated badly," she replied, not looking at me.

"You'll see lots of new things today."

She relaxed. "I'm looking forward to it."

"Not as exotic as some of the locales you're used to."

She shook her head. "It's not the sand and water that make the shoot. It's the people and the small things you can elevate with a picture." She sighed. "Carl and I always disagreed on that. To him, it wasn't worth taking a shot unless everything was perfect.

Life isn't perfect, and sometimes that is the beauty we have to show."

I pulled into the large field and found a parking spot. The place was already busy. I lifted her hand and kissed it. "Then let's go find some beauty, Shutterbug."

She nodded. "Let's go."

I was in awe of Kelly the entire day. She was warm and gracious, often stopping people, asking if she could take their picture, explaining it might be in the newspaper or on her web page. It was my job to get them to sign a waiver. Not a single person refused. Many asked if they could purchase copies. Already anticipating that, Charly had had business cards printed up, which I handed out like cash. Kelly took pictures of babies, kids, adults, families, couples, people on their own. Old people.

She found art in places I would never think to look. A half-eaten bowl of ice cream melting in the heat of the day. The way candy floss looked held up in the sunlight. A rusted tin can sitting on a fence post. A flag flying at sunset, the colors vivid in the fading light. She lay on the ground, taking pictures looking up at the dinosaur collection and the kids playing on them. Beautiful images of a mother holding her new baby, watching her toddler on the carousel with her father.

She snapped pictures of the arts and crafts, the rides, the candy tent. Me sampling treats in the candy tent. I sampled a lot. She had pictures of me with rib sauce all over my face. Holding a massive, caramelized beef rib, dripping with sauce, that we shared. We walked for miles, drank overpriced lemonade, ate more candy. Ribs. We devoured a brisket sandwich the size of my head. And everywhere we went, she captured moments in time.

We held hands. I stole kisses. Sweet ones. Sloppy ones. A few deep and passionate ones behind the Tilt-A-Whirl in the growing darkness.

Finally, we made our way back to the truck.

"My feet are sore," I mused. "Yours must be killing you. I stood a lot of the time while you were running around."

"A bit," she admitted. "Your shoulder must be tired, carrying that bag all day."

"It's fine."

She nudged me with her elbow. "I'd give you a shoulder rub if you played your cards right."

"I'd rub your feet." I winked at her. "Anything else that was sore too."

I reached the truck and put the camera bag in the back. I turned to her, smiling and tapping the end of her nose. "Anything come to mind, Shutterbug?"

She tilted her head. "Nothing one of your infamous leg hitches couldn't fix. I hear they make a girl feel better."

Laughing, I drew her into my arms, holding her close. I wrapped my leg around her hip, pressing her into my pelvis, letting her feel me. "I can make you feel good," I murmured into her ear, kissing her neck and enjoying the shiver that raced through her body. "I brought blankets. You, me, the flat bed of the truck under the stars, Shutterbug? You want that?"

She moaned low in her throat. "Yes."

"I saw a deserted farmhouse about five miles back. Lots of empty fields for stargazing."

She gripped my shirt, bringing me to her mouth. "Take me there, Brett. Show me the stars."

I grinned against the softness of her lips. "My pleasure."

The sky was an endless sea of inky blackness above us. The stars shone, their glow bright in the ebony. Lying on the blankets, I pointed out some constellations, tracing them with my finger for Kelly to see.

"The Big Dipper." I moved my finger. "The Little Dipper." I traced another in the air. "Orion."

"I didn't know you liked stars too."

"My dad and I used to look at them together."

"Have you ever seen a comet? Or a falling star?"

"Yes. Years before my mom died, we went on a family trip to Northern BC. I saw the northern lights. And the stars. My God, they were so clear, it was as if you could touch them. My mom could barely get us to come into the cabin at night. I saw several shooting stars and a comet. It was incredible."

"Have you ever been to Iceland? I hear the lights are spectacular. And the stars."

"No, I have always wanted to, though."

Kelly lifted her head from my chest. "You have? You want to leave Littleburn?"

I smiled, tucking a strand of hair off her forehead. "Just because I love small-town living doesn't mean I never want to travel."

"I didn't know that."

"You never asked. It's like taking the bike out for a drive. I enjoy cruising along, but sometimes I like to change things up. I start shifting gears. Going faster and enjoying the rush. Then when I'm ready, I shift back, going slower again. You can't stay at the same speed all the time."

"I like that analogy."

I chuckled. "It's what I do. Mechanical analogies."

She hummed. "Where would you like to go?"

I tucked my arm behind my head. "I would like to see parts of the world. Greece, Scotland, Iceland. More of Canada. The ruins in Mexico. The heat of Africa. There are lots of places I would like to go."

"What's stopping you?"

"Someone to share it with," I said quietly.

She stiffened, and I remained silent for a moment.

"Don't you ever want a place to call home, Kelly?"

"I don't really know what home means," she admitted. "Growing up the way I did, I wouldn't call my parents' house a home. It was like a prison."

I chose my words carefully. "Home is where you can be yourself. Find rest and sanctuary. Reconnect to a life that sustains you.

Recharge so you can go out and have adventures again, knowing you have a place to return to."

"That sounds nice."

"I think, with the right person, it can be."

She was silent. When she lifted her head, our eyes met. Hers contained questions, worries. Mine sent reassurance, silent promises.

I don't want to be trapped.

I'll never clip your wings.

I'm afraid to love.

I can't live without you again.

I don't want to lose you.

Tell me how to keep you.

I bowed my head, our mouths meeting in a soft kiss. Our lips moved, molding, fusing together. With a low groan, I gathered her closer, pulling her up my body until our chests pressed together, our thundering heartbeats echoing off each other. I tugged the extra blanket over her, wanting her safe and warm. Protected from the night air. We kissed endlessly. Differently from in the past. There was no frenzy, no dominance. There was passion, desire, and need. I explored every inch of her hot, sweet mouth. She did the same, our tongues seeking and stroking. I slid my hands under her shirt, running them over her softness. She straddled me, pulling her shirt over her head, her creamy skin standing out in the dark. I cupped her breasts, teasing the nipples, sat up and yanked my shirt over my head, then pulled her back to my mouth. We rocked slowly, her legs wrapped around my waist. We tugged and pulled until we were bare to each other, refusing to break our connection even for a moment. I knew her curves. My hands knew how her soft skin felt under their touch. My ears attuned to her whimpers and moans. My torso molded to hers, the roughness of my skin melding to her tender suppleness. I knew how she would feel wrapped around me, the heat and grip of her around my cock.

Yet it felt like the first time. I felt nuances I hadn't noticed until now. How her breathing hitched when I rolled my hips into hers. The soft gasp as I nuzzled her neck, swirling my tongue on her skin. Her low moan as I cupped the back of her head, kissing her harder, needing her more than I needed my next breath. The way she gripped my shoulders, dug her blunt nails into my skin as I lifted her, easing my cock into her slowly, listening as she sighed when we were flush.

I let her take her lead, groaning as she moved. Rolling her hips, lifting and dragging herself over me. I felt the night air kiss my cock as she rose, then sheathed me back in her warmth. Over and again, going faster as the minutes slipped by. She let her head fall back, offering me her breasts as she chased her release. I licked and sucked. Whispered her name. Praised her movements. Begged her for more. Slid my fingers between us, stroking her clit as she began to tighten. Took her mouth again as she came around me, my orgasm like the snap of a whip tearing through my body. Hot, fast, unexpected. I buried my face in her neck, riding it out. Holding her close as she burrowed into my chest, limp and exhausted. I lay back, taking her with me, being sure the blanket covered her.

We stayed silent, her body so still I thought she'd fallen asleep.

"That didn't feel like fucking," she whispered.

I stroked over her head, the silky texture of her hair rubbing on my hand. "You want to know a secret, Shutterbug?"

She looked up, and I met her gaze, our eyes locking.

I bent and kissed her lips. "It's never just fucking with us. It's more," I said against her mouth.

I felt her smile, then she snuggled back to my chest.

Her reply was so quiet, I almost missed it.

"I know."

There was a subtle shift in our dynamic over the next week. The garage was busy, and although the office was always occupied, I missed her when it wasn't Kelly behind the desk. She'd had to spend a lot of time sorting, choosing, and streamlining her pictures for the paper. She and Charly spent hours with their heads together, adding additional pictures to her website. She sought me out often, asking my thoughts. I knew nothing about photography, but I knew good work when I saw it, and I praised Kelly effusively.

"Shutterbug, these are amazing," I said, looking at the layout and the photos. "They evoke—" I paused, searching for the right word "—feelings. Memories relived, if that makes sense."

She hugged my arm, then leaned up on her toes and kissed me. "Perfect sense. Thank you."

On Friday, Kelly came to me with her eyes glowing, showing me the paper and excited that she'd had several inquiries already for private photo shoots. The paper was thicker than normal, and even the grainy newspaper images showed her talent. She'd captured joy and happiness. Family. Simple beauty. Her photos told a story.

I pulled her close, kissing her head. "Congratulations, Kelly. These are awesome."

She smiled, cupping my face. "Can we go out and celebrate?"

I couldn't hide my delight. "Yeah? I'd love that. Dinner?"

She nodded. "I'd love a good steak. Zeke's?"

"I could take you into Toronto for something fancier."

"No, I like Zeke's."

"Okay."

"I have some errands to run and calls to make. How about I meet you there?" she asked.

"What time?"

She mulled it over. "Seven?"

I kissed her nose. "Perfect. We'll celebrate twice."

"Twice?"

I leaned down, capturing her mouth in a scorching kiss. "Dinner out, then a private celebration."

She blinked as I pulled back. "Okay, then," she breathed out and walked away. I tried not to smile as she stumbled a little, catching the doorframe to steady herself.

I failed.

I was running late, and I texted Kelly to tell her. When I arrived at Zeke's, I stepped inside, scanning the room. Kelly was at the bar, sitting in the seat beside the wall. She looked uncomfortable, her shoulders back, her glass in her hand. I watched as a guy sidled up to her, leaning close. She jerked back, covering her glass in a defensive gesture and shaking her head. He leaned nearer, and I saw the panic on her face. With a low curse, I hurried in her direction, calling her name as I got closer. She glanced up, seeing me, the relief on her face obvious.

The guy stood, glancing my way with a scowl. I pushed past him, leaning down and kissing her on the mouth. She grabbed the lapel of my jacket, fisting it in her hand. "Hey, baby," I crooned. "Sorry I'm late." I turned to the stranger. "Can I help you with something?"

He narrowed his eyes but shook his head as he looked between us. "Nope, my mistake." He turned and walked away.

"That's right, jackass," I muttered. "Keep walking."

I glanced down, surprised to see how tightly Kelly's hand gripped my coat. I covered her knuckles, stroking gently. "Okay, Shutterbug?"

She sighed, leaning into me in one of her rare displays of vulnerability. "I am now you're here."

I wrapped my arm around her, holding her tight until I felt her relax. I pressed a kiss to her head. "Want to get a table?" I asked. "Or go home?"

"Table," she replied, sliding off her barstool. I took her hand, heading toward the booths on the other side. "You don't want to take your drink?"

"No," she replied.

We were lucky, and the end booth was open. She slid in the side facing the wall, and I slid across from her.

"Are you sure you're okay?" I asked.

She blew out a long breath. "That's the first time I've been out on my own since it happened," she admitted. "I've never felt so exposed before. I was afraid to take my eyes off my drink. And because I didn't know the bartender, I was afraid to drink it." She shook her head. "I never thought about it so much before. Then when that guy came over, all I could think about was making sure I kept my eyes on my glass. It can happen so fast." She lifted her shoulders. "The stats. The stories. It happens so often, Brett. It's frightening."

I took her hands. "I'm sorry I was late. I'm sorry you were so nervous on your own."

She squeezed my fingers. "That's all new for me. A year ago, I would have been careful but not paranoid. Especially here."

I shook my head. "You're not paranoid. You have to be aware."

The waitress came over, and Kelly straightened. "Let's talk about something else and enjoy the evening."

We spent some time talking about what to order for dinner and decided on a bottle of wine. When it arrived, Kelly took a sip and hummed in satisfaction. "Delicious."

Over appetizers, she told me the editor asked her for more photos. "Rob said the phone was ringing off the hook at the paper this afternoon. He wants another picture spread of the town, plus another weekend fun one."

"That's great. You'll be busy."

"Theo goes to school soon. Gabby found a great day care that will take them both right now, so she is happy to do two or three days a week in the garage," Kelly said. "Charly is the same, and I can pick up the slack until you find the right permanent replacement," she finished. "I know neither of them wants full time."

I schooled my features not to show my reaction. It was a punch in the gut. A reminder that this wasn't forever. I concentrated on the actions of eating my salad, chewing the hot bread that came with it. Sipping my wine to stop myself from reacting.

Kelly was still talking, but I was only half listening. She was going to leave. I knew that. I had known it all along, but hearing her voice did something to my chest. It ached, knowing we'd say goodbye again. Knowing she'd leave and be somewhere in the world without me. Without my protection. Without my love.

And I'd be here. Without her.

"Brett?"

I looked up, meeting her worried gaze. "Sorry, I was lost in my thoughts."

"You're crying," she whispered in shock.

"What?" I lifted my hand, feeling the dampness on my cheek. I wiped it away, forcing a smile. "No, my eyes are tired and sore. I got some stuff in them earlier, and they keep watering. I'm fine." I shoved a large piece of bread into my mouth, chewing and swallowing. "I'm good."

She looked at me suspiciously. "Are you sure?"

I wanted her in that office beside me where I could see her, even if it was only once a week. I wanted dinners like this where we celebrated simple things. I wanted every night with her alone, wrapped around her in a bed we shared.

But I couldn't say any of that. She would only leave sooner.

So I did what I did best when it came to Kelly. I smiled and lied.

"I'm good, Shutterbug. I'm good."

CHAPTER SIXTEEN

Kelly

I blew out a sigh, stealing a glance at Brett. He was talking with Maxx, Stefano, and the contractor, making the final tweaks to the design. He stood with his back to the wall, his arms crossed, concentrating, listening, and nodding on occasion.

It was odd how my gaze was drawn to him all the time. Wherever he was in the garage, I would find him, watching him, studying him.

Since our dinner the other night, he had been different. We'd gone back to my place afterward, and we'd had another drink and ended up in bed. Not a surprise, but it was his lovemaking that struck me as different. I was used to Brett being in control. His low curses and dirty promises. How he touched me, always gentle, yet with intent.

He'd been quieter. No demands. His words had been few and uttered in a tone so low, I couldn't understand what he was saying. His kisses were deep and passionate, his touch bringing only pleasure, yet I had a feeling he was holding back. As if part of him had stepped away.

I missed that part.

His tears at dinner had shaken me. Although he denied it, he couldn't hide his sorrow. He refused to discuss it, brushing it off as having had problems all day with dust and watery eyes, but I knew he wasn't telling me the truth. I didn't know how to get him to confide in me.

The bottom line was I didn't offer him that honesty, so I had no right to expect it of him.

It frightened me how much I wanted him to.

And since that night, we'd had a disconnect I couldn't explain. I had worked again on Saturday, going to two festivals to take pictures. Brett had to work in the garage, and Charly had come with me for the day. We had a lot of fun, but it wasn't the same as with him. There were no stolen kisses, no teasing and banter. Charly was great at cajoling people into signing the waivers, pointing out things that would make interesting shots, but somehow the day was dimmer. I was tired at the end of the day, and there was no Brett to rub my feet. No strong neck muscles for me to massage. No stars to share the night with. I knew he was spending some time with his dad, but still, I missed him. I wanted to text him and tell him, but I stopped myself, unsure if I should. Ours wasn't a texting "Where are you?" sort of relationship.

Anyone looking at us wouldn't see anything different. He was friendly, affectionate even. But he was holding himself back. I could feel it.

Last night was one of their monthly classes. The garage felt as if it was filled with women, although I knew the classes topped out at thirty people. Even after two years of running them, they still had a wait list.

I watched it from the office, trying not to scoff at some of the women. They were dressed to the nines, their hair and makeup perfect, and I doubted they cared about what happened under the hood. They were only interested in the men up front. Tonight, it was Brett and Stefano with Chase. All dressed in their coveralls, looking handsome and sexy. One blond woman was so focused on Brett, she was practically attached to him. She followed him between the cars they were giving hands-on demon-strations with, constantly interrupting other women, trying to monopolize his attention. She laughed too loudly, waved her hands often, playing the damsel. At one point, she cornered him, pouting and telling Brett she didn't want to break her nails or get dirty. Then she winked. *"At least not with a car."*

Overhearing that remark, I marched into the garage, grabbing a clipboard for a prop.

She moved in closer and then had the audacity to touch him. Place her fake-nailed fingers on his chest, touching the buttons of his coveralls playfully. *"Besides,"* she purred. *"If I can fix it, I won't have an excuse to visit you, Mr. Conner. I bet you know how to tune me up well. I mean, my engine."* Then she laughed, the sound grating on my nerves.

Brett glanced up, seeing my glare.

"Is that the confirmation on that job order?" he asked, sidestepping her, relief evident in his voice.

"Yes, I need your signature right away."

He nodded. *"Excuse me,"* he said to the woman. *"You should go join the rest of the class. I need to handle this."*

"Maybe you'd like to handle me later," she replied.

I barreled right between them. "I don't think so. Page two clearly states no fraternizing with class attendees."

"And you are?" she snapped.

"His boss. Excuse me." I grabbed his hand and pulled him away. In the hallway, he grinned down at me.

"Thanks. She was getting a little handsy."

"I noticed."

"My boss?" he asked with a grin. "You came to save me, Shutterbug?" he whispered, sliding his hand up my neck, cradling my head. "Claim your territory?"

I groaned as he covered my mouth with his, kissing me. I wrapped my arms around his neck, holding him close. He yanked me tight to his torso, devouring my mouth like a starving man.

Behind us, I heard Stefano's voice ring out. "Okay, ladies, we're moving on to tires. Everyone grab a pressure gauge."

Brett dropped his head to my shoulder. "Dammit, I have to go. I need to avoid Michelle if I can. She'll want to grab my pressure gauge."

I began to laugh, and he kissed me again. His eyes were warm and soft. "Thanks for saving me, Shutterbug. I like you all possessive."

I smiled up at him, sensing our connection growing again. Loving his teasing. His touch. He returned to the group, leaving me restless without him. Our eyes met several times the rest of the night, but I was alone again when I returned to the apartment.

I missed him. Oddly enough, I realized I missed *us*.

The meeting wrapped up, and they all shook hands. Maxx followed the contractor out, and Stefano and Brett spoke for a few moments, Brett rubbing his eyes more than once.

When Stefano left, waving to me as he headed down the hallway, I stepped into Brett's office.

"You, ah, need anything?"

He rummaged in his drawer and pulled out a bottle of Tylenol. "Just for this headache to go away."

I grabbed a bottle of cold water from the small fridge he had in his office and handed it to him. He accepted it and took the pills, swallowing them down with the water. I pulled the ice pack from the freezer and wrapped it in a rag, then pressed it to his neck. He startled at the cold, then relaxed. "Thanks."

"How bad is it?"

"Bad enough. It started last night. I can't seem to shake it."

"Did running away from Michelle aggravate it?" I teased.

"She aggravated *me* to no end," he replied. "I told Charly to put her way down on the list—I don't want to see her back here for a long time, if ever. We're not running these classes for that nonsense. The other women actually want to learn about their cars. They're not here for a random hookup."

"I'm sorry."

"Thanks for rescuing me." He searched for my free hand, squeezing it. "I was going to come see you after, but this headache did me in."

I felt relief at his words. "I missed you," I confessed.

He tilted up his head. "Yeah?"

"Yeah." I swallowed. "All weekend, actually. Are you upset with me?"

He was quiet before he replied. "No. Just a busy time—for both of us."

"Okay."

"Any feedback on your pictures?"

"Lots of good stuff. They'll run in this week's edition, plus another Local Heroes piece. And I picked up a couple more private gigs."

"I guess soon enough you'll be able to move back to Toronto," he said, his voice flat. "Out of this small town."

I moved the ice pack to the front, pulling his head back to my stomach as I pressed the ice pack to his skin. "No," I replied. "I'm staying here for the time being."

"Oh?" he asked after a moment. "I thought you were anxious to get back to Toronto. Any reason why?" His voice was mild, his eyes shut while he let the ice do its job.

"I still want to help Charly. And I have the work at the paper. I like the apartment. I have way more room there than I would get in Toronto."

"Hmm," he replied.

The phone rang, and I lifted his hand to hold the ice in place as I hurried to my office to answer it. In the doorway, I paused. "And one other reason," I said.

"What is that?" he asked.

"You're here," I confessed and returned to my desk.

He stood, walking through my office on his way to the garage. He stopped behind me, bent and kissed my neck, then kept walking.

I smiled, feeling something ease inside me.

BRETT

I frowned at the engine Maxx had been working on. He was frustrated and confused.

"We have to be missing something," I agreed. "This is the third time she's brought it back in for the same thing."

Maxx crossed his arms, looking deep in thought. "We've done everything by the book. Everything the manufacturer told us to do. The diagnostics show it's fine. But it keeps stalling." He rubbed the back of his neck. "I'm going to call her and tell her to keep the loaner until we figure this out."

I nodded then grimaced, the movement causing my aching head to hurt more.

Maxx looked at me with concern. "Go home, Brett. You look like you're going to pass out or hurl any given second. I don't want to deal with either."

Chase looked up from the motor. "I'll drive you. I have to go pick up some parts anyway. Leave your truck, and I'll take you."

I pushed off the car. "I think I have to."

Maxx clapped me on the shoulder carefully. "We'll get through. Red can come help Kelly if needed."

I paused before turning to go. "Could this be as simple as a bad solenoid?"

"We checked it."

"But it's intermittent. Maybe it's working fine at times, not at others. We get it to work, it fails on her."

Maxx stroked his chin. "Could be." He chuckled. "We're looking for something big, and meanwhile, a ten-dollar part is causing all the trouble. I'll try it, then go after the manufacturer to get some of the money back if that's the cause of all this trouble. They were the ones who told us what to replace yesterday."

"Okay."

I followed Chase outside. "Take my truck," I said, tossing him the keys. "It's more comfortable."

He put the vehicle in drive, but we hadn't even made it down the driveway when I held up my hand. "Stop."

He looked at me in concern. "What?"

"I can't take the motion. I'm gonna be sick." I climbed out of the truck. "Take this and do your errands. I'll go lie down somewhere until this passes, and I'll go home with you later."

"Okay."

I trudged up the driveway, pausing. I didn't really want to go to Maxx's place. The barn wasn't exactly conducive to sleep. And I couldn't take the sun, so lying on the grass wasn't an option. I skirted the garage and headed up to the apartment, knowing Kelly would be fine with me resting there for a while. I opened the door, using the extra key over the light, and went inside. It was dim and cool with the shades drawn. Grateful, I headed to her bedroom, toeing off my boots, and taking another couple of Tylenol. I got the ice pack from her freezer and lay down on her bed, sighing in relief at the cool and quiet.

I drew in a deep breath, relaxing into the softness of the pillows. The linens smelled like Kelly. Soft, light, and unique.

Since our dinner, I had been more conflicted than ever. The thought of her leaving had cut me so deep, I had cried unknowingly. I hadn't cried since the day my mom died. There was no point—tears never solved a situation. But the tears and the pain I felt went even deeper than losing my mom. I refused to admit it to Kelly, denying the tears and what I was feeling, but both were real.

I tried to avoid her, but the bottom line was, I couldn't stay away from Kelly. I attempted to remain distant, step back, but my resolve melted every single time. Against my better judgment, against all my instincts, I was drawn to her, and I couldn't control my reactions. When she was close, I wanted to be closer. When she wasn't around, I missed her. When we were together, I felt whole. As if she filled in that missing part of me. I knew it wasn't forever. Even if she decided to stay for now, one day, she'd be gone. I told myself over and over to stop hoping, yet the smallest of flickers refused to die.

I sighed as I felt the drugs and ice begin to work, the pounding easing off to a dull throb. The muted noises from the garage below were like a slow, steady beat that helped lull me into sleep. I gave up fighting it, and I drifted.

Sometime later, I woke with a start, hearing voices. Charly and Kelly were in the living room, Kelly sounding anxious and Charly triumphant. I lifted my head, pleased the headache had settled into a manageable throb in the back of my head. I sat up, swinging my legs over the mattress, planning on going to the living room to alert them to my presence.

Until I heard Charly.

"After what that fucker Carl did to you, Kelly? He deserves this and more."

I was shocked to hear the loathing dripping from Charly's voice. And her swearing. She rarely ever did. She used funny, made-up expressions to express her displeasure. Her hatred of Carl was obvious.

"Then it makes me no better than him."

"No, this is different," Charly insisted. "We're taking back your files and destroying the shit he was trying to blackmail you with."

I frowned.

Blackmail?

What the hell was Charly talking about?

"I've got a new account all ready, Kelly. We're going to transfer all the stuff he stole into it, plus the other photos. In and out. Then we'll destroy those pictures."

"He will still have them on an SD card. He keeps everything on SD cards. Hundreds of them in a case he had built that he takes everywhere. Sorted in date order," Kelly replied. "He's terrible with passwords and always worried he would be somewhere and not be able to get to his remote storage, although I told him it was far safer than carrying a case of SD cards around."

"Well, his forgetfulness is working in our favor since you got the notice he was trying to sign in somewhere. We've blocked him, but we have to hurry."

"Okay."

I didn't know what they were talking about. Pictures. Blackmail. But I felt my anger beginning to grow. I knew there was more to this story than Kelly had let on.

I could hear furious typing, Charly's mumbled questions, and Kelly's equally low responses. I knew they were probably bent over a laptop, doing whatever they were doing. There were some silences and mutterings as they worked. About ten minutes passed, and Charly made a low grunt of satisfaction.

"Done. I got all your photos back. You'll have to fix the metadata he changed on the ones he stole."

Kelly sighed. "That is awesome."

"You really want to change the password back to something he'll recognize?"

"I don't want access to his work. I just wanted my stuff back. Give him his account."

"We could make him work for it a little, though," Charly said.

Kelly was quiet, and I could picture her looking indecisive and worried. "No, leave it."

"Okay."

"What about the, ah, other?"

Charly sighed. "I sorted the files date-wise. There were four folders from that time, and I downloaded them all. We have to look at them to figure out which one it might be. They only had the date and a letter."

"Move, and I'll look." Kelly sounded odd. "I don't want you to see them."

"I know they aren't real."

"Please," Kelly begged.

I heard movement, and Charly spoke. "Okay. Be quick."

A moment later, Kelly made an odd noise. "May 3, B file. That's the one."

There was more movement, and I heard the rapid tapping of keys.

After another few moments, Charly exhaled. "Okay. I uploaded the files to the new Dropbox. I deleted the ones in Carl's Dropbox and replaced them with duplicates from another file so he doesn't know they're missing. You can delete them from the files if you want to. But I think you should keep them for evidence if you ever decide to go after him."

"It's his word against mine."

"You should still face him. Let him know he didn't win."

"I don't want anyone to see those pictures. Staged or not, they look real. They make me look—" There was a beat of silence. "I feel ashamed."

I was burning with curiosity, my blood rushing through my head. Whatever was happening out there was big. And bad. And I wanted the whole damn story.

I waited patiently, not at all prepared for Charly's next statement.

"Carl stole your work, Kelly. He drugged you and took those pictures to blackmail you. You're lucky you didn't die from the reaction to those drugs. He violated your trust, your health, and your mental well-being."

The world around me disappeared, Charly's words exploding in my head.

He drugged you.

Took those pictures.

Blackmail.

Lucky you didn't die.

Over and over, they spun, overlapping one another, becoming one long sentence.

Images of Kelly when she first returned hit me.

Thin.

Pale.

Ill.

It wasn't an accident.

It wasn't a random stranger.

Carl had done that. The man she trusted, idolized. She considered a mentor and friend.

He had done those things to her.

And she had been suffering in silence because of feeling shame.

I was off the bed and in the living room in fast, furious strides. Kelly and Charly looked up, startled. Kelly's eyes went wide, and she stood.

"Brett," she breathed out. "I didn't know—"

I cut her off.

"I am going to kill him," I snarled.

Charly stood, shaking her head. "No, you're not."

Kelly was frozen, staring at me as if she'd seen a ghost.

Charly began to talk, and I held up my hand. "You need to go now, Charly. I need to be alone with Kelly." I indicated the computer. "Are you done there with whatever you were doing?"

"Yes."

"Then leave."

She looked at Kelly, reaching for her hand and squeezing it. "You okay with being alone with Brett?" she asked.

Kelly nodded, still not speaking. Charly headed my way, stopping in front of me.

"She's already been hurt by this. Do not add to it because as much as I love you, I'm not sure I could forgive you for that."

I tore my gaze away from Kelly's pale face and met Charly's green eyes. "I have no desire to hurt her. I simply want the truth so we can move forward. And I want to help."

Charly gazed up at me, her voice so low I had to bend to hear it. "You love her," she whispered.

I only acknowledged her words with the tilt of my chin.

"She needs you," she added.

"Leave, Charly."

She walked out, shutting the door behind her.

Kelly and I stared in silence. Then she cleared her throat, straightening her shoulders. "I thought Chase drove you home."

"I was nauseated in the truck. I decided to stay and rest a bit. I didn't think you'd mind if I borrowed your place for a bit."

"And you heard. Everything."

"I heard, but the only thing I understand is Carl needs to be held responsible for far more than stealing a photograph of yours."

I narrowed my gaze. "And you're going to tell me the entire story. I'm not leaving until you do. So, start talking, Kelly."

I crossed my arms. "Now."

CHAPTER SEVENTEEN

Brett

Our gazes remained locked as the silence stretched between us. Kelly's light-blue gaze was rife with anxiety. Mine was furious. I clenched my fists, shutting my eyes and inhaling deeply. I rolled my head on my shoulders and loosened my muscles. When I opened my eyes, Kelly was still frozen to the spot, and her apprehension was obvious.

I held out my hand. "Come here, Shutterbug."

She looked at my hand, then at me, not moving.

I waggled my fingers. "Please."

She stepped forward, and with a groan, I met her halfway, encasing her in my arms.

"I need you to tell me. Stop hiding this. Stop hiding from me."

She nodded against my chest, and I tugged her to the sofa, sitting beside her.

"Tell me. Tell me everything."

She drew in a deep breath, seemingly gathering her courage.

"After I left last time, something was different," she began.

"With Carl?"

She shrugged. "With both of us, I think. Usually when I would get to the locale, I was excited. Ready for the next adventure. Happy to be traveling again. My, ah, usual enthusiasm wasn't there."

"I see."

"I did my work, I smiled, everything seemed normal, but I was more withdrawn than usual. Carl was off. Constantly snapping, impatient with me and his other assistant. So much so, in fact, she quit after a couple of months, and it was just him and me again."

"Extra work for you."

She shrugged, looking over my shoulder to the window. "We hired people in the different places."

"You were gone a long time, Kelly."

"Carl has a place in the Caribbean. When Sal sold his house and my apartment was gone, there didn't seem to be much reason to come back here. It was winter and blah in Canada, and lovely and sunny in the islands. A far better place to spend the winter months. Carl had lots of jobs lined up, so I stayed busy." She sighed, plucking at a loose thread on the hem of her T-shirt. "After how I left, I wasn't sure I'd be welcome here, and I thought the distance was the best thing."

I didn't want to get into our personal history right now. I wanted to know what had happened to her.

"Let's stick to Carl and why he needs to be in prison," I growled.

She met my eyes briefly, then once again looked away.

"Like I said, we had lots of jobs. Magazine spreads, private shoots, it seemed endless. We traveled and took pictures. I lost myself in work. For the first while, it was okay. I was busy, constantly on the move, still learning and growing. I took different kinds of pictures from Carl. He was all about perfection. The right model against the background. Or the pristine, idyllic beach. I liked nature. Odd objects that caught my attention."

"I always said you had a better eye than he did."

She smiled, rubbing her hands on her legs in a nervous gesture. I hated seeing her this way—unsure, vulnerable. I stilled her movements.

"Kelly, just say the words."

"After a few months, Carl decided it was time for a break. I went to his place in the Caribbean, and he went God knows where. I stayed busy, exploring the island, taking more pictures, sorting through his library of photos and organizing them. When Carl returned, he was different somehow. Even edgier and almost angry. I wasn't sure why. His demands increased, and I was run off my feet. Although his calendar was full, he refused to hire another assistant, and at times, I had no help on shoots. It was difficult, but I pushed through." She laughed without humor. "It wasn't as if I had somewhere else to go."

"You should have come back here," I snapped.

She met my gaze with a lift of her shoulders. "I didn't think I'd be wanted."

I wasn't sure how to respond.

She stood and walked around the room, straightening a picture on the wall, staring out the window.

"Carl became more erratic. He was always a perfectionist. Time was money. I always arrived early and got everything ready, so when he got there, he went right to work. I always had everything prepped. That was my job. But he began showing up late. Throwing a fit over something trivial. Yelling at models, calling me names." She sighed, leaning her head on the window for a moment, then she turned and leaned on the frame, her hands behind her. "His work suffered."

"In what way?"

"Carl's images were always so precise and inspirational. He always understood what the client wanted. That's why he was so sought-after. I know you thought he was a pain, but he could see something on a bare stretch of beach. A way to use the light on the sand to highlight the picture. How a splash of color could make a photo change. How to coax a model into just the perfect mood to get the picture." She shook her head. "But he was different. He yelled more, snapped and insulted more than cajoled. He was demanding, throwing tantrums on the sets. Angering people. And his photos reflected that—it was as if he'd stopped caring. They became almost ordinary. We fought constantly, and he told me everything happening was my fault. I wasn't a good assistant anymore. He blamed everyone around him for all the problems. Including me. More than once, I had to step in and smooth ruffled feathers. I was getting tired, and the breaks between shoots were getting longer. I was offered a couple of small jobs that I accepted, and they were well received. Carl told me my work was inferior."

"Fucking bastard."

Kelly came back to the sofa and sat down. "We had a job in South America. A big one. Different for Carl. There were very few model shots. It was mostly nature. He struggled with it." She shook her head. "His work was uninspired. Common. Like a snapshot a tourist would take on holiday. He wasn't happy. He was short-tempered and nasty. We broke for a couple days so he could relax and clear his head. I traveled around taking pictures on my own, and when I got back, it was as if a switch had been turned on. Carl was relaxed and happy. At ease. We finished the shoot and headed back to his place. The client was thrilled with the end result. Carl had insisted on handling all of it. It surprised me, but at least he was showing an interest again, and I didn't think much about it. I was used to his whims. We did a couple of other jobs, then we headed to Costa Rica." She stopped, her sudden silence showing me her tension.

I nodded, knowing we were getting to the crux of the story now. "Keep going, Shutterbug. Get the words out."

"This time, I was allowed to hire a couple of locals. One of them I liked, the other I was leery of, but he took off some of the burden, and it wasn't forever. Carl and he got along well." She stood again, wandering the room, fixing the blanket on the back of the sofa, adjusting the fringe on a pillow. "Carl let me share his Dropbox account. I was the one who organized it, kept it updated, deleted shots he didn't like, sent files to clients, all that sort of thing. He knew how, but it was a grunt job, so I handled it. He had an unlimited storage account, and I stored my stuff under my name. He was fine with it, and it saved me money—in fact, it was his suggestion. I was also the one who kept up with the emails and social media. He hated all that, and I was good at it. It was a nice way to wind down sometimes, returning emails, posting pictures he took but wasn't using. He got a lot of work and sales from those posts."

"I never doubted how effective you were at your job. My objection was with the way he treated you."

She stopped wandering aimlessly and met my gaze. "You were right."

"That doesn't make me happy."

"I know."

I held out my hand, and she let me pull her beside me.

"What happened in Costa Rica?"

"He was having lunch with the client, and I saw an email about the last job in South America. They were praising the photos, especially a series of shots of a beach. I was confused because Carl had never gone to that particular beach. It was where I had spent my time while he was on his break. I did some digging and found the files he had sent without my seeing them. There were five pictures—all mine. I was shocked. I did even more digging and found he had changed the metadata on the pictures, making them his property. In fact, he had changed the entire file of that shoot. He walked in and found me at the computer. He knew right away that I'd discovered what he had done, and we had a huge fight." She sighed, rubbing her eyes. "It was awful, the things he said. Accusing me of stifling him, not being cooperative, sapping his creative energy. When I told him he was full of it and the bottom line was that he stole my photos, he told me he had to. I gave him no choice. The client wasn't happy with his work, and since it was my fault he couldn't do his job, he took mine."

I barked out a laugh. "Typical narcissistic behavior. Blame everyone else."

She swallowed. "He let it slip he'd been doing drugs and was hooked. I shouldn't have been surprised, but I was. He was always such a health nut and ate clean. It explained his erratic behavior too. He told me he could quit anytime."

I snorted. "The famous words used by all addicts."

She nodded. "It got ugly. At least on his part. I was in such shock, I couldn't believe what was happening. I told him I quit and I was going to the client to tell them the truth. He laughed and told me no one would believe me since the photos were in his Dropbox, and the information on them showed his watermark. He told me he'd give me a commission for 'my effort.' I was so angry, I stormed out."

"But that wasn't the last of it."

"No. He called me the next day and apologized. He said he knew what he did was wrong, but he'd been desperate. He begged me to meet him for a drink so we could talk and clear the air. I went, hoping we could figure it out. I still admired him, and everyone makes mistakes."

I shook my head. She was far too trusting.

"We met, and he told me he'd been crippled with anxiety for a while. Depending on the drugs to help him. Fighting it and too ashamed to admit it. He said his work suffered and he was desperate. He was skimming his photos while I was gone and saw a new upload to Dropbox. He looked at the pictures and knew they were exactly what the client wanted. He admitted to stealing them, plus a few others. I was traveling and hadn't noticed." She sighed. "He begged me to forgive him. Promised me it wouldn't happen again. Assured me he would compensate me. Said we'd finish the job and head back home, and he'd get help. Go into rehab. I believed him—he seemed so contrite. Upset. More like the Carl I had first met than the man he had been. He asked if I'd reconsider working for him. I told him I had to think about it. He said he understood, then he went and got us a drink."

"That was when he drugged you?"

Kelly nodded, the pain of the memories showing on her face. "Yes. A few sips and I started to feel odd. Hot. Dizzy. Carl acted concerned. I passed out. When I woke up, I was in his hotel room, and it was the next day. He was waiting for me. I was confused and sick. Unsure what happened." She was silent, not meeting my gaze, tears filling her eyes. "He was a different man that morning. Evil. Uncaring. His eyes so black I was frightened. I was so sick I could barely function, and he pulled me out of the bed and showed me what he'd done."

I took her hand. "Tell me."

"He's taken a set of pictures of me and the guy I'd hired but didn't like. The way he shot them, they looked like stills from a porn movie. Like we were having some wild, kinky sex."

"Jesus Christ," I spat out. "Kelly, you said you weren't—"

She shook her head. "I wasn't. I was checked."

"But you were fucking violated. Assaulted."

"Yes," she whispered. "He told me if I said anything to anyone, he'd release the pictures. Destroy my reputation. He assured me in a pious tone of voice he'd made sure I wasn't hurt, but he needed insurance. His reputation was too valuable. As if that explained it or made it okay." She looked down. "Then he left. He just walked out, and I was alone. I was so ill, a maid found me, and when I woke up, I was in the hospital. I'd had an extreme reaction to the drugs, and I was sick for a while. When I finally began to recover, I knew I had to come back. I needed Charly. I needed the safety of this place." Her voice became choked. "I needed you."

"Why didn't you tell me?"

"I was terrified you would look at me differently. That you would never touch me again."

I groaned, thinking of how I had handled her at times. "I would have been more careful with you," I admitted.

"No," she whispered fiercely. "I needed to be Kelly with you. *Your Kelly*. The woman you lost yourself with. I was afraid, if you knew, you'd be disgusted and not ever think of me that way again." She hung her head as the emotion began to sweep over her, pulling her under. "I had already lost so much, I couldn't bear to think of losing that too. Even if all it was for us was memories. I didn't want them tainted with this. Your touch erased it all, Brett. You made me feel like Kelly. Wanted and adored. Strong and capable. Still able to be what you needed."

I slid to the floor in front of her, using my fingers to lift her chin. I met her gaze, the shame, worry, and tears that filled the blue orbs making my chest ache.

"Nothing will ever change how I see you, Kelly. I think you're brave. Beautiful. Amazing. That you went through what you did and didn't break is astonishing. That you let me touch you is a miracle. What happened doesn't make you less. It makes you more in my eyes. You are what I need. You always have been."

She gripped my hand. "I was so scared." She let out a shaky breath. "At times, I still am."

"You don't have to be scared, Kelly. I'm here. You're surrounded by people who care."

"Do you?" she whispered.

"I never stopped," I admitted. "I know we want different things from life, but it doesn't stop how I feel about you. God knows I've tried."

"I hate that I hurt you."

"I hate what you went through."

Our eyes locked, her pain dripping from hers. "You were right, Brett."

"About?"

"Why I left last time. I was feeling so much for you. It over-whelmed me. Scared me. I could see a forever with you, and I had no idea how to handle it. What that meant. So I hurt you, and I ran. I stayed away, certain if I gave it enough time and distance, how I felt would go away."

"And by staying away, he hurt you." I shook my head. "I would rather you hurt me a hundred times over than for you to have experienced what he did to you, Kelly."

"I don't want to hurt you anymore."

"Then don't."

She looked away and nodded.

I stepped closer and pressed my forehead to hers. Her breath drifted over my skin.

"Did staying away work for you?" I asked quietly.

I felt the movement of her head against mine. Barely discernible but it was there. It didn't work. She was still feeling something for me. I tucked that information away for later and readdressed the issue at hand.

"I really want to kill him."

She eased back with a small sigh. "I'll never see him or work with him again."

"Good. But he should be punished."

She sniffled, and I grabbed her a tissue. "What were you and Charly doing earlier?"

"He signed in to Dropbox, or attempted to from a different location, and forgot the password. My personal email was the secondary recovery one, and they sent me a notice. Every time I had tried, he beat me to it. I assume he was traveling, or was high and careless, and this time, Charly and I jumped in, and she helped me take back my photos. He had all my work locked in that account, but now I have it back. Charly took the other photos out of the files he had them in, and I have those too. He still has them on SD cards, but at least I have something. And all my work. He can't steal any more of my pictures and take credit. I never have to see him again, and that makes me feel better."

"There needs to be more in the way of punishment."

"I've heard some gossip. He isn't getting as much work. He can't keep an assistant. His drug use is becoming an issue." She lifted her shoulders. "Knowing Carl the way I do, he'll implode soon enough. Self-destruct." She shook her head. "I know you didn't like him, but it's so sad. Such talent and an incredible flair gone to waste."

"How can you feel sorry for him after what he did?"

"Because I remember the man I first knew before fame went to his head. The man who taught me and gave me a chance."

"And almost killed you in the end."

"I'm still here," she protested.

I cupped her face, holding it between my palms. "Thank God."

"When I woke up in the hospital, all I could think of was seeing you again," she whispered. "I had missed you so much."

"I would have come to you. Helped you."

"Would you?" she whispered, tears filling her eyes again.

"I'll always come to you, Shutterbug."

She broke. A wild sob escaped her mouth, and tears poured down her cheeks. I gathered her in my arms, sitting on the sofa, holding her close. I let her cry. I didn't tell her everything was all right. I didn't lie and say I was okay, because I wasn't. I was angrier than I had ever been in my life. If Carl appeared in front of me right now, he would be dead for what he did to her. For some photographs. Because his overinflated ego couldn't handle the fact that he failed. He stole from her to cover up his own inadequacies. He lied. He covered it up, and then instead of admitting what he did, he hurt her. Blackmailed her. Even worse was the fact that he could have easily killed her with his callousness.

I held her a little closer, letting her cry and thanking God she was here. Safe. With me. Now that I knew what happened, I could help her. Be the man she needed me to be and show her nothing had changed.

Except perhaps the fact that I was deeper in love with her than ever. And this time, I wasn't letting her go.

I wasn't sure how she would take that news. Except, given her confession, I felt that spark of hope light up again. I only prayed that, this time, I wasn't wrong.

CHAPTER EIGHTEEN

Brett

K elly cried herself out in my arms. I let her go when she pushed away, knowing she wasn't going far. She slipped to the bathroom, and after she left, I went to the kitchen, opening the cupboards and fridge. There was little, but I knew where to find supplies.

I hurried over to Maxx's house, walking in the side door. Charly was in the kitchen, talking to Maxx. He held Vivvy in his arms and was listening to Charly intently. They both looked upset.

"How is she?" Charly asked.

"She'll be fine. I'll make sure of it. I can't guarantee the same for that asshole."

Maxx nodded. "I'm with you on that."

"Charly just told you?"

He nodded.

I looked at Charly in surprise. She shrugged.

"Kelly made me promise. I don't break my promises. But since she told you, I decided to tell Maxx the whole story. He only knew the basics."

"She needs all the support she can get," I replied. "She's been carrying this too long." I scrubbed my face. "You got all her pictures?"

"Yes. I deleted them from his Dropbox. I wish I could get my hands on his computer and erase anything he has there. Plus those damn SD cards."

"Did you see the pictures?" I asked, knowing she would understand which images I was referring to.

"Quickly, to make sure I had the right files."

"They're bad?"

"They are to Kelly. The way he staged them, he knew how to get the best effect."

"In other words, the worst one."

"Yes."

"Will he know you took her work?"

"He'll know it's gone. He may figure it out. I'm watching her website and emails. I know she blocked his number and him on every social media outlet she could." She shook her head. "I am going to help her fix all the metadata he changed. Luckily, he was lazy and only changed the ones he sold. Kelly had way more pictures of the same shoot plus similar ones, so hopefully if it ever came down to proving ownership, she has the upper hand."

"Okay, good."

"What do you need?"

"I need to feed her, and I need a fucking drink," I admitted. "There's hardly anything in her fridge."

"She often comes here." Charly turned and pulled a casserole out of the oven. "I made this for you to eat. Take whatever liquor you want."

I took the still-hot dish and tucked a half bottle of scotch from the cupboard under my arm. "Thanks."

"You need us, we're here," Maxx offered. "Don't drink and drive."

"I'm not going anywhere tonight."

Charly nodded, looking relieved. I headed back to the apartment, climbing the stairs and letting myself back in. Kelly was on the sofa, her head in her hands, and I hurried to her side.

"Shutterbug? What is it?"

She looked up, wiping her face. "I thought——" she swallowed "——I thought you left."

"No, I went to scrounge food from Charly and liquor from Maxx. I need both." I traced my finger over her cheek. "I told you I'm not leaving you."

She captured my hand, pressing a kiss to the palm. "Thank you."

I smiled at her gesture. She wasn't given to overtly sweet displays of affection. At least she hadn't been before.

"Can you eat?" I asked. "Charly sent a casserole. It smells great."

She hesitated.

"Please. You need to eat. Just a little. I need you strong."

"I can't believe…"

"What?" I asked. "You can't believe what?"

"That you're still here. I was sure…" Again, she trailed off.

"Sure I'd walk? Why? Why would I blame you for something that wasn't your fault?"

She didn't answer for a minute. "My mother blamed me all my life. Carl blamed me."

"And they were both wrong. I'm not them. And none of this—those pictures, him drugging you—was your fault. It's all on him. He is the guilty party here. All I'm concerned about is getting you stronger and helping you move past it."

"I hope I can."

"If he makes trouble, you have backup now. Me. Maxx. All of us."

"Charly told Maxx?"

"Yes. He is almost as angry as I am."

"She didn't—she didn't show him the pictures, did she?"

"No. And no one will see them. God knows I don't want to."

"I don't want you to either. They make me feel ill."

"My reaction would be slightly different."

"What?"

I leaned over, cupping her face. "I would be furious that someone touched you without permission. Jealous as hell that a stranger knew how soft your skin was. I would want to rip him limb from limb for being part of such a despicable act."

"I don't remember any of it."

I stood, pulling her up with me. "Good. I don't want those memories in your head. Only good thoughts, Shutterbug. Me. You. Us together. That's it." I tugged her to the table. "Now, let's eat."

Her appetite was off, but I got her to eat a little. Drink some water and a cup of tea. She looked weary, and after we ate, I coaxed her back to the sofa, and she curled up with her head on my lap. I stroked her short hair, feeling her begin to lose the tension and relax.

"I love your hair," I murmured.

"Really?"

"I like how sexy it looks on you. How soft it is when I touch it."

"Carl once told me I looked like a boy."

I snorted. "Carl's an incompetent imbecile. His opinion means nothing."

"My mom kept it short when I was a kid. She didn't have much time for me, so it was easier. And I got used to it." She laughed, the sound sad. "I mean, really short. Like a crew cut. I keep it a little longer now."

I pictured her as a kid. Cropped hair, big, wistful blue eyes, scrawny, and sad. I hated that image as much as I hated the thought of seeing a picture of her with another man.

"I love it," I repeated, running my fingers through the silky tresses repeatedly. She sighed, and her eyes drifted shut. She let out a long sigh as she slipped into sleep. I didn't stop caressing her, wanting her to stay sleeping.

After a while, she shifted, rolling so she was tucked tight to me, her face buried into my stomach. I touched her cheek, and her hand fluttered up, grasping mine and holding it as she slumbered. I smiled in amusement at her. My phone vibrated, and I used my free hand to swipe up the message from Stefano.

Stefano: I heard. Are we hunting?

I typed back my reply.

Me: No. Protecting.

His reply was swift.

Stefano: Anything you need. Anything. You don't even have to ask.

I didn't have to reply. I knew what he meant. He understood what it meant when the woman you loved was in trouble or hurting. He would help in any way he could. He and Maxx, even Chase, would stand beside me.

I looked down at Kelly, nestled into me, trusting me. She had no idea how to ask for help. She expected nothing from anyone because that was how she had been treated all her life. The only person she could ever rely on besides herself was Charly.

That had changed now. And tomorrow would be the start of a new way of life for her.

And I planned on being part of that life.

I stood carefully, taking her with me. She didn't stir as I carried her to her bed and tucked her in. I slipped off my jeans then reached for the light. Her eyes fluttered open, and she looked panicked to find herself in bed.

"Brett?" she gasped. "No—please don't go."

"I'm not," I assured her, sliding in beside her and tugging her to my chest. "I'm right here, Shutterbug."

"Oh," she sighed, patting me, already drifting back to sleep. "Good. Stay."

"Not going anywhere," I replied.

I pressed a kiss to her head. "And neither are you."

"Okay," she mumbled. "Okay."

KELLY

The sun was barely rising when I woke up. I was warm and content. Wrapped in a pair of strong arms, the heat of Brett's skin soaking into me. Carefully, I tilted up my head, peering at him. Asleep, he was relaxed, the tension he often carried in his jaw gone. He had a dimple in the middle of his chin you only saw when he smiled or when he slept. As if it knew only to come out during those times. His hair was a mess, the curls he tamed so ruthlessly appearing like his dimple in secrecy. The scruff on his jaw was lighter than his hair color, glinting gold in the early morning light.

I had never shared a bed with another person until Brett. I didn't do overnight guests. The few times Charly and I'd had sleepovers, one of us slept on the floor or the sofa. I wasn't used to waking beside someone, although I had to admit, I liked waking up with Brett. I felt safe and protected. Even before I realized I needed to feel that way, he did it for me.

I gazed up at him, studying his face, his broad chest, the muscles in his neck. Even in rest, they showed. He was strong. Powerful. Yet with me, even in passion, always gentle.

"I feel your eyes on me, Shutterbug," he murmured, his voice rough with sleep. "You know what happens when you eyeball me."

I cupped his face, loving the feel of his scruff and the skin stretched over his cheekbones. "You stayed," I whispered.

He opened his eyes, the clear blue of his irises holding my gaze. "I told you I would."

"Brett…" I began, then stopped.

He lifted his hand, running it over my cheek, and smiled. "What?" he asked.

"I never meant… That is, I should have said—" I huffed out a sigh of frustration.

"Just say it, Shutterbug. We need to stop keeping the words to ourselves."

The words poured out before I could stop them. "I didn't mean to hurt you when I left. I didn't mean to make you think I didn't care. I did. So much. So much so it scared me. How I felt about you made me question everything I thought I wanted. How I saw myself. How I saw my future."

"Why didn't you talk to me?"

"Because I was afraid."

"Of me?" he asked, sounding incredulous.

"No. I'm terrified if I allow myself to feel, to become attached, I'll wind up being my mother. Clingy, needy, focused only on someone else and ignoring the world around her—even her own child."

He shook his head. "Do you think I would allow that? I love your independence. Your free spirit. I have no desire to crush that side of you. And you couldn't be that way. You're too much your own person. And I like you that way."

"Even if I can't stay in one place?"

He grimaced then sighed. "As long as you come back, Shutterbug. I need to know you'll come back."

"That doesn't seem fair to you."

"Let me decide what is fair to me. Just come back to me. That's all I ask."

I had no idea what to say. How to tell him I thought one day I would return and not want to leave because he was there.

"I will," I promised.

He lowered his head, kissing me. I wrapped my arms around his neck, returning his passion. Kissing him back. Moaning in satisfaction as he slid over me, pressing me into the mattress, the feel of his erection trapped between us.

"I want you," he groaned.

"Then have me," I replied.

"Slowly." He drifted his lips over my neck, sucking my lobe into his mouth and biting down. "I want to savor you this morning."

"Yes," I replied. I didn't care how he wanted it as long as he took me along for the ride.

He lavished me with attention. His mouth rarely left my skin as he stripped me then explored every inch of me. His lips, his tongue, his fingers, left trails of heat, whispers of adoration, his touch branding me as if he was imprinting himself on my body. I felt cherished. Adored. Worshipped. When he finally slid inside me, I was sobbing with need, with desire for him. Everything about him. I clutched at his shoulders as he moved inside me—long, leisurely thrusts of his hips, drawing almost completely out then sinking back in, making me gasp. I begged for more, for faster, harder, but he refused.

"Slowly, Shutterbug," he whispered. "Feel me loving you. Feel what you mean to me."

He moved and rocked. I wrapped my legs around his hips, in sync with his body. I never wanted it to end. I never wanted to leave this bed and the circle of his arms. I cried out, whimpering his name as my orgasm hit me, building low and branching outward, gaining momentum, gathering its strength like a sudden summer storm. I felt it in every part of my body as I spasmed around him. He dropped his head to my shoulder, lifting me to his thighs, moving fast now, grunting and cursing until he was spent, his body tightening, my name a whispered breath on his lips.

"Mine," he sighed. "You're mine."

I knew he was right. I had to stop fighting it. Fighting him.

I pressed a kiss to his head, and his arms tightened.

"I have you, Shutterbug. Even if you're not here, I have you."

Tears filled my eyes, and for the first time in my life, I had a glimpse of real love.

Its name was Brett.

CHAPTER NINETEEN

Kelly

I had never known myself to be so aware of another person before now. I felt Brett all day. I could hear his voice, trace his laughter, even from the farthest corner of the building. Every time I caught sight of him, I felt a thrill deep inside. And most of the time when I looked at him, I caught him looking back, his gaze as intense as my own.

As I was talking to a customer in the office, he strolled in, standing behind me, joining in on the conversation. He leaned over me, tapping the screen as he answered a question about a part. His breath drifted past me, his unique scent enveloping me. I wanted to lean back into his warmth, but I had to resist. I did feel the press of his hand as it flexed on my shoulder. I swore I felt the brief pressure of his lips on my head as he stood, but I must have imagined it.

A short while later, I felt him behind me again.

"You need something?" I asked, not looking up from the file I was working on. I was afraid to meet his eyes, afraid he would see the desire and need in them.

He leaned over me again, and I shivered. His voice was low and amused. "Yeah, I do. I need to touch you."

And he did, wrapping his hand around the back of my neck and tugging my head back. He kissed my forehead, his lips lingering.

"We're in the office," I protested weakly.

"And everyone is busy," he replied, then kissed my mouth. Once. Twice. A third time.

"I feel you watching me," he murmured. "It's as if you're touching me."

"I feel you too," I whispered.

A customer walked into the garage, and Brett released me, leaning on my desk. He picked up an invoice, pretending to study it. I tried not to notice how his coveralls were stretched over his erection.

"You, ah, seem to have a problem there."

"The *problem* presents itself every time I get close," he said, not looking up from the invoice. "When I feel you look at me. When I see you. It's constant."

"How unfortunate," I replied. "Can I, ah, help?"

He jerked as I slid my hand over his thigh, cupping him through the denim. "Jesus, Kelly," he hissed. "Keep doing that, and we're gonna have a far bigger problem on our hands."

"Well, right now, my hands are full," I teased. "But I have to go check out a set of tires in the barn. Behind the tarp. In five minutes. If you're there, I could assist with your, ah, situation." I reached for my lip balm and sat back, smoothing it on my lips. He watched me, his problem becoming clearer with every passing second. I pursed my lips teasingly. "Only if you were interested."

Narrowing his eyes, he stared down at me, then wordlessly pushed off the desk and headed down the hall. I heard the back door slam shut, and I had to cover my mouth to stop my giggles. I had no tires to check in the barn. I had no business in the barn.

Until now.

I waited a few moments, then headed over to Chase. "Can you watch the phone for me? I have to help with a problem."

"Everything okay?" he asked.

"Yep. I won't be gone long."

"Sure."

"Thanks."

I headed for the barn with a grin on my face. I had a feeling it wouldn't take long to help alleviate Brett's situation. I rubbed my lips together. They felt soft and smooth.

Brett was going to enjoy the feeling of them on his cock.

Problem solved.

Later that afternoon, Brett appeared beside me again. "Sorry, my friend," I quipped. "One barn blow job a day."

He chuckled. "I still owe you."

I met his gaze with a smile and a wink. "You know it."

He lifted his hand, tracing over my mouth. "I love how you smile at me. The way your lips form my name." He dropped his voice. "How they feel wrapped around my cock."

I grinned. Earlier, in the darkness of the barn, I had surprised him by dispensing with any sort of foreplay, instead dropping to my knees and taking him in my mouth. I had worked him fast, using my lips, tongue, and hands, feeling satisfaction as he groaned my name and slid his hands into my hair, his hold on my head gentle. He came quickly, gasping as I swallowed around him, then stood, brushing off my knees and kissing him. He reached for me, but I evaded his hands.

"Later," I promised. "I just wanted to take the edge off for you."

"I want to return the favor," he growled.

"Live with it," I teased. "That was just for you." Then I winked and headed back to the garage.

When he reappeared, he was relaxed and happy, although his gaze was still intense, and I shivered every time he got close.

"What are you doing after work?" he asked.

"No plans."

"My dad called. Rose Cottage is in full bloom, and he thought you might want to take some pictures."

"Rose Cottage?" I asked.

"It's a house in town. The woman who lived there loved roses. She planted, like, hundreds of them. She died last year, but some of the townspeople cleaned up the garden in the spring, and everything is in bloom."

"Sounds great. I'd love to take some pictures."

"Okay. Dad invited us for dinner. It's meatloaf. Dad makes great meatloaf."

I was thrilled that Brett and his dad were mending fences. Making the effort to spend time together.

"I would love to join you and your dad for dinner."

He paused, staring at me. A wide grin broke out on his face, and he bent, sliding his hand around the back of my neck and pulling me to him. He kissed me hard, deep, and with passion. Then he pulled back.

"Goddammit," he muttered. "The shit you do to me without even knowing it."

But he was smiling as he walked away.

I waited for Brett to finish on the last car. I sat outside, checking my camera bag to make sure I had everything. Charly sat beside me, Thomas playing not far from us, and Vivvy dozing in her mother's arms.

"So, dinner with the family," Charly drawled.

"Dinner with Brett and his dad," I corrected.

"That is Brett's family."

I frowned at her. "Whatever."

"I'm going to assume everything went okay with you two last night after I left?"

I sat back with a sigh. "I told him everything. He wants to kill Carl."

"Actually, he, Maxx, and Stefano want to form a gang and go after him. Then provide one another with an alibi," she retorted. "The *Car-liminators.*"

I couldn't help my laughter. "That's pretty lame."

"I thought it was funny. Cars, Carl… They want to—"

I waved my hand. "I get it. That has you written all over it."

She shrugged. "I wouldn't stop them."

I shook my head. "Not happening. No one is getting in trouble because of me. It's done. Thanks to you, I got my work back, and I can move forward. I want to leave it alone."

"What does moving forward entail?" she asked, gazing across the lawn. "Does it involve a certain mechanic who is crazy about you?"

I followed her line of vision. Maxx and Brett were standing outside the garage, talking. I watched him for a moment, once again caught in the pull of his presence.

"Charly?" I asked softly.

"Hmm?"

"How do you know if you really love someone?"

"I think if you are wondering, then you may already know."

"He scares me. What he makes me feel scares me."

"Do you trust him?"

"Yes," I replied.

"Then know he's there for you. I think if you try, Kelly, you would find Brett is exactly what you need in your life."

"He told me he doesn't mind if I have to go for a while, as long as I come back."

"Because he understands you."

She turned and faced me fully. "But I will say this. Brett is an amazing man. He knows he can't pin you down. But don't leave him without something. And I don't mean hope. Commit to him. Show him you are as serious as he is. Admit your feelings, so he knows. He deserves that."

"Am I enough? Is that enough? Is that fair?" I asked.

"Let me ask you a question."

"Sure."

"Is this forever? The wandering? The refusal to settle down?"

"I always thought so. Until…"

"We all need a place, Kelly. Somewhere safe to call home. Someone to call our own. Can you see Brett as that place? That person?"

"I think maybe I can."

She shook her head. "You have to be sure. You have to know. You can't string him along. He deserves better. You deserve better." She grasped my hand. "I know your childhood was rough. I know you are frightened of what love means. But when it's right, when it's real and strong, it is amazing. What I have with Maxx. What Gabby has with Stefano. It's a gift, Kelly. Your parents aren't a good example. How you were treated as a child was wrong. On every level. But you can move past that and find your place." She drew in a deep breath. "Because I think that's what you're looking for. Why you keep searching. But I think if you are honest with yourself, you would know you don't have to search anymore. Go and take your pictures. But know where your home is." She nodded toward Brett, who was walking over. "He is your home. You need to figure that out before it's too late." She looked sad as she stood. "Because if you lose him, I fear you'll search for the rest of your life."

Brett's dad was pleased to see me—and even happier to see the cake we had picked up at the bakery on our way over. Mack Conner had the same sweet tooth his son possessed, so watching them discuss who got a bigger piece was entertaining. With Mack's blessing, I wandered the large apartment, seeing where Brett grew up. The big windows made the rooms bright. The building was older, and the apartment retained all the charms of that era. Wood trim and baseboards, chair and picture rails. Hardwood floors with a beautiful patina to their dull sheen. I studied some pictures on the walls, watching Brett grow up in front of my eyes. I saw him as part of a family, his mom and dad smiling at the camera, Brett with them, often with his mother's arm holding him close. I recalled the house I grew up in—everything in its place and nothing out of order. No pictures of a laughing, happy family. I tried to remember one instance of being held. One happy memory. I had none.

I noticed the pictures ended when Brett was a teenager. His graduation picture showed a solemn face, his eyes sad. There were none of him and his dad except what I assumed was taken around the same time at his actual graduation. They stood side by side, not touching, smiling for the camera, but their stance showed their separation. Their sadness reflected in their expressions, their distance already present.

I decided right then that I needed to add to that wall. Brett and his dad needed some new memories. I found my bag and took out my camera, snapping some photos before they noticed. Them arguing over the cake. Mack, mashing potatoes while Brett stole a broken piece of meatloaf and grinned. The two of them staring at me aghast, their expressions and posture so alike it made me smile.

"What are you doing?" Mack asked.

"Taking pictures. It's what I do."

"Why are you taking them now? I thought you were going to look at Rose Cottage."

"Warming up," I lied.

We ate the best meatloaf and mashed potatoes I'd ever tasted at the round table in the dining room. Mack shared some stories of Brett growing up, shaking his head at the memories.

"He once snuck downstairs, and I found him the next day, asleep on the floor, surrounded by empty potato chip bags and candy wrappers," he chuckled. "I'd just added both to the store inventory, and he made a pig of himself."

"Oh no," I laughed. "Was he grounded?"

"His mother was furious. I thought it was funny. I couldn't bring myself to punish him. His sore tummy did it for me. He didn't look at either of those things for months. His mother took away his baseball mitt and ball for a week. That was enough."

Brett got back at him by teasing him about Rosa. Mack chuckled at him.

"Stefano is a regular customer now. Drops by at least three times a week. Not sure why the boy needs so much butter."

Brett laughed over that.

"That explains the abundance in the fridge in the garage. Charly took some to the house to make cookies yesterday."

"I told him last night to just drop in. He doesn't have to buy anything, but he insists he needs it. Who am I to argue with a customer?"

After dinner, we took a walk, Mack pointing out some different spots I had never noticed. Littleburn was a charming town. Tiny. Filled with older homes and wide streets. Downtown consisted of a four-block radius. It was a throwback.

We turned down one street and stopped at the end. My breath caught in my throat. The Rose Cottage was aptly named. The structure resembled something you'd see on an English postcard, with a swooping roof and curved walls. Ivy grew along the fence, and the garden was a mass of color. Roses of every shade grew in the beds, wrapped around trellises, cascading over railings. Reds, pinks, whites, and yellows exploded everywhere I looked. Huge blossoms that filled the air with fragrance. Tiny blooms that clustered together to form their own bouquets hung from heavy branches.

"Oh my God," I murmured. "This is incredible."

Mack smiled. "It is."

My fingers itched. "Can I go closer?"

He smiled. "I am one of the caregivers of the garden, so yes, you can."

Brett followed me as I walked around, discovering all the wonders of the yard. It was a feast for the eyes and the nose. In the back were beautifully cultured vegetable gardens, their bountiful crops growing in the raised beds. I gasped at the scene

242

beyond the back fence. The trees that surrounded Littleburn were thick and tall, leading into the forest. A small stream ran along between them. The late evening summer sun cast a burnished glow around it all. I snapped photo after photo, catching the changing light.

Finally, I turned to Brett. "What will happen to the house?"

"Dad says her daughter is going to sell it. She worries whoever buys it will tear out the garden, but she knows it's beyond her control. She was so pleased when the townsfolk offered to care for it this year, but she knows the house will fall into disrepair if she leaves it." He shook his head. "Dad worries someone will buy it for the land since it backs on to the forest and tear it all down."

"Oh no," I murmured. "It's too beautiful."

Brett chuckled. "I'm shocked, Shutterbug. I had no idea you liked this style of house."

"I find them romantic and beautiful. All that wood and the nooks and crannies," I admitted. "I would love to see inside."

He held out his hand. "Come on, then."

"Really?"

"Yeah, Dad has a key."

I took his hand eagerly. Inside, I fell in love. The bay windows, the woodwork, the curved room off the living room that overlooked the garden. Even the kitchen that needed updating was perfect in its imperfection.

"I hope whoever buys this house loves it and takes care of it," I murmured, running my hand along the staircase rail that was smooth from years of wear.

He looked at me, a small smile on his lips. "I hope you get your wish."

I followed him out, feeling strange. As if I had left a small piece of my heart behind me. I shook my head at my silly thoughts. I'd never felt that way about anything. Especially a house in a little town. Or the man who walked around it with me. Both seemed to have wormed their way into my heart.

I wasn't sure what to do about that.

CHAPTER TWENTY

Kelly

A few days later, my phone rang in the morning, and I frowned at the unknown number. I answered it warily.

"Kelly Ryerson."

"Kelly, this is Garner Holmes, editor of *Toronto Now*."

"Um, hello."

"I saw your photos in *Littleburn News*. My mother lives there," he added by way of an explanation. "I was impressed. You have quite the eye."

"Thank you. What can I do for you, Mr. Holmes?"

"Garner, please. Come into the office and see me. I'd like to discuss an offer with you."

"An offer?"

He chuckled. "I don't like to do business over the phone. If you can't come here, I'll come to you." He offered.

"No, I can come in tomorrow."

"Perfect." He gave me the address, and we agreed to meet at eleven.

"How did you get my number?"

"I sent an email to your website. Your assistant—Charly, I think —called me and gave me your info." He chuckled again. "I think she was verifying my identity. She asked a lot of questions."

"Ah, yeah, sounds like Charly."

"Bring in some more samples of your work with you," he requested.

I hung up and stared at my phone. Charly was excited when I told her, agreeing to be in the office so I could go.

"More work, Kelly! He wants to hire you for his magazine."

"I hear you gave him my number."

"I wanted to vet him," she said primly.

I snorted. "Detective now, Charly?"

She laughed. "I just wanted to make sure he was on the up-and-up. And he is. I mean, look!" She tapped on her keyboard, bringing up the website. "They are big!"

"Who's big?" Brett asked, walking in.

Charly showed him what she was looking at. "The editor just called, wanting to meet with Kelly," she explained. "I think he is going to offer her a job!"

He blinked, then looked at me. "Really?"

"Let's not get ahead of ourselves," I cautioned.

He shook his head, offering me a wide smile. "I'm sure Charly is right. They saw your work and got in touch. That's great," he said, sounding enthused.

He grabbed a part he'd left on the desk earlier. "I need this." He picked it up. "When are you going in?"

"Tomorrow morning."

"I'll be in the office," Charly said.

"Okay." Brent squeezed my shoulder. "You need a ride?"

"No, I'll catch the bus."

"All right," he agreed. "If you change your mind, I'll take you in."

"No, I'm good."

He bent and brushed a kiss to my crown. "This is awesome, Shutterbug."

I went back to work, mentally going through my portfolio. I was grateful I had my photos back that Carl had held hostage from me. As soon as I could, I hurried upstairs and got to work.

I lost track of time, startling when Brett walked in, carrying a pizza. He shook his head at my bewildered look.

"I knew you'd be so busy getting ready, you'd forget about the time or dinner."

I glanced at my phone. "Oh my God, is it really eight o'clock?"

"Yes. Take a break and come eat." He waved his hand. "Please."

I sat beside him on the sofa, suddenly starved. I devoured three slices of pizza and drained a bottle of water.

Brett smiled in satisfaction and indicated my laptop. "Are you almost done?" he asked.

"Yes."

"Good. Then I'm putting you in a tub, and you're going to bed."

"Brett—"

He shook his head, interrupting me. "No arguments. What bus are you catching—the nine a.m.?"

"Yes. Then I can sit and have a cup of coffee before I meet him and gather my thoughts."

"You are going to wow him, Shutterbug. You already have—he must have liked what he saw since he reached out."

"I know. I'm just worried about getting too excited."

He grinned and leaned over, kissing me. "I'm excited enough for both of us."

"Why does this excite you?"

He tilted his head, studying me. "More work keeps you local, Shutterbug. Toronto's not that far down the road."

"Ah," I murmured.

He stood. "Now, you finish. Then bath and bed."

"Are you staying?"

He bent and kissed me again. "As if you had to ask. Pretty sure I still owe you from this morning. I never let a debt go unpaid."

I felt the stirrings of desire. They were always there for him, just waiting for a look or word from his mouth to begin flickering, ready to burst into flames when he touched me.

"Okay," I replied.

He winked. "Okay."

I stared up at the tall building across the street. It felt strange to be in the big city again. I glanced around at the thousands of people hurrying toward the buildings, rushing for the subway, grabbing something in one of the many restaurants.

Were there always this many people?

And when did it get so loud?

I racked my brain. I lived here for years, and the noise never bothered me. Neither did the crowds of people.

What had changed?

I shook my head and headed across the street. I was right on time. Brett had made sure I was at the bus stop early and that I had gotten on board with no issue. He had sent me two texts checking on me. I had dressed with care this morning, and he had whistled when I came out of the bedroom. I wore my favorite dress, a mid-calf wrap-around in midnight blue. Paired with low heels, it was stylish, and I always felt pretty in it. I added a jacket and carried my tablet in a messenger bag. It was loaded with my photos that I had arranged by subject and date. Anything Mr. Holmes asked to see, I could find quickly.

I was ready.

I straightened my shoulders and walked in the door.

Here went nothing.

An hour later, I sat back as Garner offered me a job.

"Your photographs are distinctive. They're unique. You highlight something small and make it stand out."

"What would the job entail exactly?"

"Much the same as what you're doing in Littleburn, but on a bigger scale. I want some different pictures for our Around Town section. We try to highlight local events."

"I'm already committed on most weekends."

He waved his hand. "Toronto has hundreds of events daily and almost every night. I want to feature some of those. And any weekend you aren't committed to Rob." He paused. "He says you're one of the best photographers he's ever worked with."

I blinked. "Oh." Then I frowned. "He knows I'm here?"

"I asked his permission. He said yes, but I wasn't allowed to steal you away completely."

"I don't live in Toronto."

"Smart girl. Crazy place to live," he said with a chuckle. "We'll cover travel costs. Put you on retainer at a set fee per month, plus additional monies for the photos we buy." Then he named a figure that made me swallow a sudden thickening in my throat. I could be independent again.

We discussed timing and deadlines. Equipment and shared desk space for the times I was in the office.

"Well?" he asked when he finished. "Are you interested?"

I drew in a deep breath. "I am, but I have another job as well. I'd like the chance to discuss it with my boss. Give him time to find a replacement."

"What is your other job?" he asked with a frown.

"I work at an auto shop, in the office. Reynolds & Co. Restoration."

"I know that place. Great reputation. You talk to him. I'm sure he'll agree you are wasted there." He tapped my tablet. "This is your passion and what you should be doing."

"I'll call you tomorrow."

He stood and shook my hand. "You do that, or I'll come to Little-burn and talk to him myself."

I smiled and laughed, but I had the feeling he wasn't kidding.

I texted Brett on the way back, and he was waiting at the bus stop for me. I climbed into the truck, and he leaned over and kissed me. "Tell me all about it. How impressed was he?"

I clipped on my seat belt and gave him a brief recap. "He offered me the job."

"When do you start?"

"I told him I had to think about it."

He frowned. "Why?"

"Because of the garage and Charly—and the paper. I have commitments."

He pulled over, turning to face me. "First off, you will figure out the paper. Second, Charly is way ahead of you. She spoke with Mary and Gabby. One of our class regulars is looking for part-time work. Charly thinks she'd be a good fit."

"It better not be Michelle." I scowled.

Brett laughed. "No. Morgan—she's married to Riley, the cop. I'm perfectly safe, Shutterbug. So are all the other men in the garage." He leaned over and kissed me again. "I like you jealous."

"Whatever," I muttered.

"Charly and Maxx are fine with you staying in the apartment. You can drive Charly's car to the bus and park behind Dad's store. Or I can drive you. Or you can drive into Toronto using her car as well. Or one of the garage loaners."

"Anything else you guys decided on while I was gone?" I asked sarcastically.

He wasn't at all worried. "Just a celebratory dinner at Stefano's tomorrow."

"Why were you so certain?"

"Because I know how talented you are. And now, others will too." He squeezed my hand. "And your new boss is right. You are wasted in the garage. As much as I'll miss you in the office next to me, you should be out doing what you love." He paused. "Just come home to me when you're finished."

My throat felt tight, but I nodded.

"So, you'll accept?"

"Yes."

"Then let's celebrate."

The next two weeks were a whirlwind. I was constantly on the go. I spent some days and evenings traipsing around Toronto, attending craft fairs, concerts, art shows. Other times, I was wandering festivals and carnivals. Brett came with me when he could, and those were my favorite days. Otherwise, the magazine had someone who accompanied me if I needed. Mitzi was a small ball of energy, drove like a madwoman, and was stronger than an ox. I enjoyed working with her.

The first assignment I handed in, I had sat across from Garner and waited, nervous and anxious as he perused the photos. He was silent, then sat back, observing me.

"Exactly what I wanted." He tapped his screen. "Look at the lighting here. How it plays on the ceiling. What a brilliant stroke of genius. And this one —with the old couple watching the kids onstage? The way you captured it from both angles and merged them—astounding. The kids watching them, the couple watching the kids." He shook his head. "I knew you were the right fit."

"Thank you."

"It's just the start, Kelly," he assured me.

Brett and I had celebrated hard that night.

Twice.

My phone rang, bringing me out of my thoughts. I frowned at the number.

"Garner?" I asked.

"How is my favorite photographer?"

"Good. Is there a problem?" I had emailed him this week's photos instead of making another trip into the city. I had copies of the first magazine. It was an emotional moment for me to see my work in glossy color, and my name attached to my photos. The magazine had shared a short bio and set me up with an email account, and it was filled daily with requests.

"Nope. Your first set of photos was a hit with our readers. I couldn't be happier. And the latest ones you sent? That one with the drummer and the way you caught the sticks and the water exploding off the drum? Loved it."

"Yeah, that was fun." Brett and I had enjoyed the concert and making out in the dark at the back of the floor after I was done shooting. I still had a love bite on my neck from his teeth when he got carried away.

"I need another meeting. I'm in Littleburn later to see my mother. Can we get together for coffee?"

"Sure."

"Will four work? The diner on Main Street?"

"Yes. Are you sure everything is good?"

"More than good. See you then."

I stared at my phone, wondering what was going on.

I shrugged and went back to editing some photos for Rob. I'd know soon enough.

Garner was on the phone when I arrived at the diner. I slid into the booth, studying him. He was in his early fifties, handsome and rugged. His beard and short hair were a silver-gray. His eyes a deep brown. He had laugh lines around them. A heavy-looking wedding ring sat on his left hand. I had seen the pictures of his wife and family scattered around his office. I liked him.

He hung up and offered me a smile. "Sorry. My wife is renovating the kitchen and just found something she wanted to run by me." He grinned, looking almost mischievous. "Suddenly, she remembered the word budget." He laughed to himself, not looking at all worried. "I don't really care as long as she's happy."

The waitress came and refilled his coffee cup, and I ordered myself one, plus a muffin. I had been on the go all day. Garner got himself one as well. "I'd love one of their Reuben sandwiches," he admitted. "But my mother is making dinner and wouldn't be pleased if I didn't eat."

"You grew up here?"

"In Lomand. But my parents moved to Littleburn when I left home." He chuckled. "They thought Lomand was getting too big."

I laughed. "Really?"

He nodded. "They both grew up on a farm. No one around for miles. Lomand seemed like a bustling city to them. They were horrified when I chose to live in Toronto. It overwhelmed them, and with my dad gone, I come here to see Mom. She comes in for holidays if I pick her up, but she prefers it here."

"I was surprised how much bigger and louder Toronto seemed when I came in to see you," I admitted. "I lived there for years and never noticed."

"That happens."

Our muffins came, and I took a sip of my coffee. "So…"

He chewed and swallowed.

"So, I'm sure you know *Toronto Now* is owned by a larger publication."

"Yes."

"They publish a travel magazine as well." He paused. "They want you to do some work for it."

I blinked. "What?"

"I brought up your name to my boss. Showed him your work. He was impressed. They were looking for a new photographer." He wiped his mouth. "They are interested in you."

The nomad in me sat up, eager and excited. Travel. Photos. Exactly what I had always wanted to do. My life's dream being offered to me.

Yet for the first time ever, a small part of me hesitated. It whispered one word, quiet and wistful.

Brett.

I swallowed the constriction in my throat. "Can you tell me more?"

He grinned. "I can tell you everything."

CHAPTER TWENTY-ONE

Kelly

Charly gazed at me, her eyes wide in her face. "Oh my God, Kelly. Really?"

I nodded.

"You look shell-shocked."

"It doesn't seem real. I mean, it's my dream job. Or at least, it could be. They want me to do this first assignment, and if they're pleased, I could be under contract with them."

"But you're hesitating."

"Everything would change, Charly. I would have to give up the paper here since I would be traveling. They would work out my schedule with *Toronto Now*, so I would still be doing some work there."

"Would you move to Toronto?"

"Garner asked me that. With having to get to the airport more often, it makes sense, but I told him I wasn't sure."

"Something holding you back?" she asked with a knowing grin.

I sighed. "This is just happening so fast. I haven't had time to digest it all."

"It's awesome, though. It's your dream."

I shook my head in disbelief. "Garner showed me the schedule. Mexico. Alaska. Greenland. Places I've always wanted to go."

"Where do you want to go, Shutterbug?" Brett asked, walking in. He'd been out when I got back, and I hadn't had a chance to tell him anything. I'd had to talk to someone, and of course, Charly was always happy to listen and offer an opinion.

"Kelly's boss offered her a promotion!" Charly exclaimed.

Brett grinned. "Wow. That was fast. Told you that you were spectacular. What would you be doing?"

"It is with another one of their publications. The travel magazine. They're looking for a new photographer, and they offered me the chance to go and do the first shoot. If they're happy, I'd be one of their team."

A strange look passed over Brett's face. "So, when does this occur?"

"In two weeks. I'd only be gone for about a week."

"Where to?"

"Mexico."

"I told her it's only the start," Charly insisted.

"Of course it is," Brett agreed easily, but his tone was off.

"I would be under contract with them. I would have to give up the paper here."

He nodded. "You'd be gone a lot."

"Yes." I tried to meet his eyes, but he seemed to be looking anywhere but at me. "But I'll still be around."

"It would only make sense to move closer to town. Since your life will revolve around Toronto, you might as well be there," he said.

"I—"

He cut me off. "I'm not surprised." He squeezed my shoulder, a vacant look on his face. "Congratulations, Kelly. It's what you wanted. Out of this small town and on to bigger and better things." He smiled, although it didn't reach his eyes. "I know it'll be great. I'm happy for you." He turned and walked out, leaving me gaping after him.

Charly frowned. "That was weird."

I stood. "Yeah, it was. Can you cover?"

She chuckled. "Yep. Go get him."

I followed Brett to the barn. He wasn't even aware I was behind him. He was leaning on the workbench, his head hanging down.

"Brett."

He whirled around, startled. I stepped closer, shocked at the glimmer of tears I could see in his eyes.

"What is it?" I asked. "What's wrong?"

He laughed, the sound brittle. "I told myself, I *convinced* myself, this time was different. Things had changed. *You* had changed." He shook his head. "Nothing has fucking changed. I'm right back to square one."

"What are you talking about?"

"Your new job, Kelly. You're gone again."

"But I'll be back."

"For how long? Until the next time? Until you move to Toronto, and the time I get to see you becomes even less? I already know how it will go. Longer spans between time together. Then we'll start calling instead, then texting, then silence."

"You have that little faith in me?" I asked.

He shook his head. "That little faith in us."

I gasped at the sudden onslaught of pain his words caused.

"I was so stupid," he snarled, pacing. "Planning, hoping, thinking you had settled. That taking pictures here and in Toronto was enough. That you'd be happy." He yanked on his hair. "I know you. You need to roam. Nothing is going to change that. I'm not going to change that."

"You said as long as I came back…"

He shook his head. "I saw your face as you were talking about this, Kelly. You were alive. Excited. In a way I can never match. You want that more than you want me. More than you want anything."

I felt my anger build. "I never said that. Stop putting words in my mouth. You haven't let me tell you—"

"But I'm right," he interrupted.

"This has been my dream for as long as I can remember," I admitted, frustrated. "And this time, I can do it on my own merit. No Carl. Not behind the scenes. Because my photos have proven I am good at what I do. I deserve this chance. This time, I'm enough."

He smiled sadly. "You've always been enough. The bottom line is that I'm not."

"Brett—"

"If I asked you not to go, not to do this, what would you say?"

I shook my head. "Don't ask me that."

We stared at each other.

"I want to ask *you* something," I began, stopping when Chase rushed in, interrupting us.

"Brett, Maxx needs you. One of the hoists malfunctioned, and Ward is pinned. We need you. *Now*."

Brett hurried past me.

I grabbed his arm. "We're not done," I insisted. "I'm not running."

"Maybe I am," he replied.

I watched his retreating figure, then sat down on the workout bench, my legs too shaky to hold me. I shut my eyes.

I hadn't expected this reaction from him. I hadn't planned on telling him in front of Charly either. I had so much else to say. So much to tell him. Plans I had come up with. Ideas.

All he saw was me leaving. My life revolving around travel again. I shook my head in frustration. He hadn't let me tell him the whole story, instead simply jumping to conclusions.

I had to admit, I couldn't blame him. My past behavior had given him reason to be skeptical. But I thought he trusted me. That he knew how much he meant to me. And I had changed. Because of him.

I sat for a while, allowing my emotions to calm. I didn't blame him for being upset or worried. I huffed out a long sigh and pushed off the workout bench. I would wait for him in his office. I had to tell him. Clear the air so he understood. Tell him my plans.

Except as I walked out of the barn, I was shocked to see someone standing there.

Carl.

He crossed his arms and glared at me. Already angry and frustrated over Brett's attitude, I became furious. I stalked toward him.

"What the fuck are you doing here?"

"I came to see you." He held up a copy of *Toronto Now.* "Imagine how surprised I was to see your pictures, read your name in this. My little protégée all grown up and working for herself."

I grabbed the magazine and flung it away. "No thanks to you."

He shook his head, drawing attention to his shorn hair. He looked thin and ragged. Not at all the well-put-together, trendy man I was used to seeing. There was no doubt his drug habit was still in play.

He shrugged. "I taught you a lot. I deserve some of the credit."

I laughed. "You took enough credit from me. I owe you nothing."

"Ungrateful." He sniffed. "I expected better of you, Kelly."

"Odd. I never expected you to drug me, steal my work, and leave me stranded. I guess we both learned a lesson." I glared at him. "I have nothing more to say to you. You can leave."

I turned and went back into the barn, stopping just inside when I realized he was following me.

"Get out of here, Carl. You are not welcome. Trust me, if anyone sees you, I won't be held responsible for what they do."

"Oh, been whining to your little friends, have you?"

"I wouldn't call it whining, and yes, they are my friends. Real ones."

"And how is that strapping lover of yours? Perhaps he'd like to see my artwork featuring his lovely girlfriend. Maybe all your friends would."

Carl had shown distaste for Brett since they met. I ignored his insults about him and everyone else.

"They all know already, Carl. I'm warning you—get out."

"Not until you put back what you stole."

I laughed. "You mean took back? Those were *my* photographs, Carl. Not yours. I'm done letting you walk all over me."

He narrowed his eyes. "How would your new employer feel if they saw my photos of you, Kelly? The Burchard Group is known for their high values. I bet they wouldn't like seeing you in all your natural beauty doing—"

"Shut up," I hissed. "I wasn't doing anything, and you know it. I was drugged and unconscious, thanks to you."

"A detail I will be sure to omit when I send them to Mr. Holmes. I'm certain he will share with his boss, and once again, you can go back to taking pictures for the rinky-dink town paper. If they'll even have you." An evil smile crossed his face. "Or come back to work for me."

"Never."

"Then give me back those pictures."

"No."

"You think you're better than me, you little bitch?"

I lifted my chin. "I know it."

His glare became malevolent. "You think I didn't figure out you removed the pictures I took of you from Dropbox?" He sneered at me. "You know I keep a backup, Kelly. I will destroy you unless you give me back those files. I need them."

"So you can make more money off me? No."

"You'll be sorry."

"I think you'll be the sorry one," a voice sang out from behind him.

He turned. "What the hell are you doing?"

I gaped at the sight of Charly holding out her hand. On her palm were three SD cards. They were Carl's preferred brand. Expensive.

How did she get them?

"I don't think these stand up well to pressure." She smirked and dropped to her knees, holding up a rock.

"Don't you fucking dare," he snarled, inching forward.

"Or, what? You'll knock me out and take pictures?" she responded. "You take one more step, and I'll scream. Holy moly, asshole, the man who will appear from that building will resemble hellfire, and all his anger will be directed at you."

She narrowed her gaze. "What you did is reprehensible. And now it's over. You have nothing."

In the blink of an eye, she smashed the SD cards. Hard and fast, she hit them over and over. The sound of the plastic splintering set Carl off. He howled like a man possessed and rushed forward. Charly screamed and fell back on her ass, then sprang to her feet and turned to run. I sprinted from the barn, grabbing Carl's arm, screaming for Brett.

Carl turned, pushing at me. I grabbed his jacket, pulling hard. He lifted his arm, the arc high, and I watched as it came toward me, already feeling the pain before his fist hit me.

Except a roar exploded behind us, and in a blur of motion, Carl was pulled away, his fist glancing off me instead of hitting me directly. I stumbled from the impact, watching in horror as Brett dragged Carl away, his fists flying. Over and again, he hit him, cursing and yelling until Carl was a crumpled mass on the ground. Maxx dragged Brett away, holding him back.

"Enough. You'll kill him."

"That was my intention."

"Charly, are you okay?" Maxx asked.

"Yes," she said, returning to the SD cards. She piled up the plastic bits and ground them down, then dug a hole, burying the little shards. She patted the ground, satisfied. "Job well done, I'd say." She looked at me and winked. "Good thing he's so particular about his SD cards. Easy to find that time period. I took the whole month just in case. And his password on his laptop was super simple. His name. What an idiot. All those pictures are gone from his drive now too."

Then she stood and looked at Carl on the grass. He was moaning and struggling to get up.

"Do we need an ambulance?" she asked dispassionately.

"I-I'm calling the cops," Carl spat out, groaning loudly, then fell back, blood flowing from his nose and mouth. "And I'm going to sue."

Charly shrugged, not at all concerned. "Whatever. Maybe I should let Maxx at you next."

Carl whimpered, curling into a ball.

Maxx shook his head. "Call the ambulance, Red. Kelly, are you okay?"

"I'm fine," I said, my voice shaky.

"Let me go," Brett said. "I won't touch him."

"You better not," Maxx growled. "Murder charges are hard to get out of."

I stared at Carl's balled-up figure. Brett's furious face. Charly was smug, not at all worried about the man lying on the ground. Maxx was confused and upset.

I couldn't wrap my mind around everything that had occurred in such a short span of time.

Meeting Garner and getting another job offer. My initial excitement. Brett's reaction. Our fight. Carl appearing. Charly destroying the SD cards and breaking in to his laptop. Brett beating Carl.

It was too much.

A frantic giggle escaped my mouth. Charly looked at me strangely.

"Kelly?" she asked.

I shook my head, fighting down the hysteria I was feeling.

"Oh no, she is losing it," Charly muttered, laying her hand on my arm.

"I-I…" A sob burst from my lips, and I shook my head wildly. "I can't——"

I put my head into my hands, and I began to weep.

"Maxx!" Charly gasped, sounding panicked.

"I got this," Brett said, his voice floating over me, surrounding me with its warm tone.

I felt Brett's arms around me. Felt him lifting me.

I turned my face into his shoulder and cried.

I sat on Brett's lap in the barn, his arms tight around me. I had no idea how long we had been there. Outside, there were voices and sounds I couldn't identify. I didn't care. All I needed was right here. I breathed him in, gulping down big lungfuls of his scent, greedy for it. He smelled so good. Like safety. Like home.

The only home I had ever known.

Gasping, I sat up. He cupped my face, stroking the wetness on my cheeks with his thumbs. "Calm, Kelly. I need you to calm down."

My words were rushed and garbled. "You didn't give me a chance to finish—to say what I needed to say."

"I'm sorry. I was angry. Upset. Let's get through this, and then we can talk."

I shook my head wildly. This was too important. I had to tell him. But I couldn't stop crying.

He enfolded me in his arms again. "Calm," he repeated. "Please calm down."

I realized one of the strange noises I could hear was me. Gasping for breath and still crying. I dropped my head to his shoulder, and he pressed his hand to my neck, rubbing the tight muscles, his touch soothing and gentle.

I began to relax. My breathing smoothed out. I was still leaking tears, but they were slowly stopping. I sniffled and wiped at my nose. Brett offered me a rag.

"It's pretty clean," he said. "It's all I've got."

I wiped my face and blew my nose, still resting on his chest.

I heard the sound of footsteps, and Brett looked up, his voice rumbling in his chest.

"Well, well, if it isn't my old friend. How are you, Officer Gallagher?"

I lifted my head, meeting the shocked gaze of the police officer who had helped Chase. Maxx was beside her, frowning. Her amber-colored eyes took us in. "You," she said, her lips quirking. "I thought it was your friend who caused trouble."

"We're all equally guilty," Brett said dryly.

"The, ah, man, Carl Enders, who is being loaded into the ambulance, says you attacked him with no provocation."

I pushed off Brett, trying to stand. My legs felt wobbly, and I had to sit back down.

"He was defending me. Charly can vouch for it."

"He's accusing her of stealing his property."

Maxx snorted. "My wife isn't a thief. She took back what belonged to Kelly in the first place."

Officer Gallagher shook her head. "I need to take you to headquarters, Mr. Conner. I'll need your statement. Mrs. Reynolds too."

"My wife isn't going anywhere," Maxx growled. "That ass came onto my property, tried to attack my wife and her friend. Brett was defending them."

"I'm only doing my job."

Brett pressed a kiss to my head, sat me on the bench, and stood. "I'll go. Can't you take Charly's statement here?"

She wavered, and I stood as well. "Maxx is telling the truth."

"Fine. I'll take her statement, but she has to come down if I need her."

Maxx crossed his arms, but Brett stepped in. "Fine."

"I want to make a statement too."

"Okay. Give me a minute."

Maxx followed her out of the barn, and Brett turned to me. "Stay out of this, Kelly."

"No. This is my fault."

"I'll go make my statement and answer their questions. You stay with Charly."

"No," I snapped. "I was there. You weren't."

"You are always so stubborn."

He took my arm.

"So are you," I muttered.

I sat in the waiting room of police headquarters. I wanted to laugh at the absurdity of that grandiose-sounding name for this small building in Lomand. I could hear Brett's voice in the back as he spoke to the officers. I waited for my turn, holding a cup of cold coffee.

When Officer Gallagher came in and escorted me to the back, I sat down, looking around the tiny room. Sparse and barren, it held a table, two chairs, and a camera.

"You aren't facing any charges," she informed me. "So I'll just take your statement."

"Brett shouldn't be either."

"Mr. Enders has a broken nose, black eye, and a lacerated cheek. His ribs are bruised and his hands injured, which, as I was informed, are essential to his line of work. He is insisting on charges."

I scrubbed my face, wanting to cry again.

"Tell me what happened," she said.

I made a decision.

"Maybe I need to start a while back for you to understand the whole story."

"Okay."

I shut my eyes, and I started to talk.

Eventually, I stopped. She hadn't interrupted me once. Didn't ask me a single question. When I opened my eyes again, she hadn't written anything down. She was studying me.

"So he drugged you, stole your work, and is essentially black-mailing you. And he showed up today, demanding that you return the work he stole so he could use it for his own gain. Mrs. Reynolds fully admits to opening his trunk, removing some SD cards, and destroying them in front of him. She didn't say what they contained, but I assume it was the pictures he took to compromise you."

"Yes."

"And when she screamed and you tried to stop him from getting to her, that was when he tried to hit you, and Mr. Conner came to your defense."

"Yes."

She tapped the pen on the notepad. "All your stories line up without the extra detail."

"So, you can drop the charges?"

She shook her head. "It's not up to me. Mr. Enders tells a different side of the story. He's lying in a hospital bed. It's up to a judge."

"He deserves what he got."

"I'm not allowed to express my opinion on that."

"Can Brett go home?"

"No. He'll be held overnight."

"That isn't fair."

Her eyes softened. "I know. But he refuses a lawyer, and Mr. Enders is insisting on the charges."

My mind whirled. I knew Carl. He was furious. I had witnessed it once, and I knew his temper was lethal. Not only had I refused him today, Charly had destroyed the evidence he'd possessed to hurt me. And Brett had physically humiliated him. He would dig in his heels, and even if he couldn't make the charges stick, he was going to do everything he could to destroy Brett, Maxx, and Charly.

And me.

I drew in a deep breath. "Officer Gallagher, could I ask you for a favor?"

"Um, sure."

"Would you drive me to the hospital?"

"Are you feeling unwell?"

"No, I want to visit an old friend."

"I don't advise that."

I leaned over the table. "I have to try. I have the one thing he wants, which means nothing to me. But the people he is threatening do."

"You would give him your photos?"

"They're just pictures. I can take more."

She pursed her lips. "Off the record, he deserved what he got and more. He should be in jail, not Mr. Conner. And I think you're a brave, incredible woman."

"So, you'll drive me?"

She stood. "Yes, I'll drive you."

CHAPTER TWENTY-TWO

Brett

I crossed my legs, leaning my head back on the cold cement wall. The throbbing behind my eyes was constant, and my hand ached like a bitch. The holding cells were all full, and I had a feeling I wouldn't be getting any sleep tonight. The last spot was the vacant bench across from me, and I had a feeling I'd have company soon.

I flexed my sore fingers, remembering how it had felt to hit Carl. The satisfaction of driving my fist into his face and gut, hearing his pain-filled gasps. He deserved every drop of agony for what he did to Kelly.

I wasn't worried about the charges. I had lots of witnesses. I was worried about Kelly, though. How she was handling all of this. What would happen after tonight. I regretted my earlier anger. I should have done a better job of dealing with it. She was right—I never let her explain. I assumed it was the same situation as last time. She was going to leave me behind.

I had been making so many plans. Moving ahead with what I thought was a future for us. It all came crashing down when I saw the excitement and hunger on her face as she talked about this new opportunity.

I had to face reality. Kelly needed to be free. She was never going to be happy tied down for long. I couldn't give her what she needed. I had to let her go once and for all.

I sighed as I heard footsteps approaching. I opened my eyes, meeting the sympathetic gaze of Officer Gallagher. I glanced behind to see if she had another person with her who would be joining me in the holding cell. I was shocked to see Maxx.

"What are you doing here?"

"Springing you."

"What?"

Officer Gallagher opened the door. "The charges have been dropped. You're free to go."

"Dropped?" I repeated. "How?"

"Does it matter?" Maxx asked. "I'm taking you home."

"Where's Kelly?"

"With Charly."

"Take me there."

Officer Gallagher smiled. "You have quite the lady on your side."

"She isn't mine," I denied, the words almost painful to get out.

She laughed. "I think you need to rethink that."

I followed her and Maxx, mystified.

What the hell had happened?

We pulled up to Maxx's house. Charly was on the porch, and she bounded down the steps, flinging her arms around me. "Holy moly, Brett. Are you okay? Did you get roughed up in the slammer? Become anyone's bitch?"

I had to laugh. Only Charly. I set her on her feet. "No, I'm good. I was only there a few hours." I glanced behind her.

"Where's Kelly?"

"She went to her place a while ago. She was tired."

"I need to talk to her."

Charly grabbed my arm. "Are you going to listen this time?"

"Yes."

"She has a lot to say."

"So do I."

"Don't make me wish you were back in the big house, Brett."

I pressed a kiss to her head. "Thank you for being brave and resourceful today."

She shrugged. "You park your car in my driveway and leave the keys in it, I am going to look around. Not my fault a few SD cards fell out of the trunk and I stepped on them. It was an accident. And all I did was shut his laptop. I have no idea how the files were erased." Then she lifted up on her toes. "As soon as the coppers left, I dug up the pieces and burned them. They are gone. Completely gone."

I pressed another kiss to her head and walked across the yard. I knocked on Kelly's door, waiting until she opened it. She was wan and tired-looking, but she seemed pleased to see me. Relieved.

"You're out."

"I am."

For a moment, we stared. "Did you want to come in?"

"As long as you're up to it."

She stepped back, waving me inside.

I stopped as I went past her. "I'm ready to listen."

Her smile was tremulous. "Okay."

I sat on the sofa, listening to Kelly move around. She sat beside me. "Here."

I opened my eyes and took the plate she offered me, piled with sandwiches.

"Charly sent this home with me so when you got out of the clink you'd have something in your stomach."

"Has she spent all evening googling prison slang?"

"That and destroying evidence."

I chewed and swallowed. I'd already taken some Tylenol, and hopefully, with the food, my headache would go away. I reached over and tilted Kelly's head, studying the bruise I could see on her cheek. "He still got you."

"Not too bad. You gave him much worse." She indicated the plate. "Eat. I'm going to make coffee."

When she returned, I set down the empty plate and accepted the coffee gratefully. I took a few sips of the bracing, hot liquid and sighed in satisfaction. I could already feel the food and caffeine smoothing the raw edges. I set down the cup and turned to her.

"Why were the charges dropped?" I asked directly.

She met my gaze. "I made a trade with Carl."

"For what?"

"The photos from that one shoot."

"The same ones he stole?"

"Yes. There were ten more. I gave them all to him."

I shut my eyes. "Why, Kelly?"

"I know Carl. He's vindictive, especially now. He would press this. Go after you. Maxx and Charly. I couldn't risk it." She stood and came back with the coffeepot, filling our cups. "He was desperate. The client who bought the original pictures wanted more and had seen those. Carl couldn't get to them." She sighed. "His work has gone downhill. He needed the money."

"So you let him win."

"No, I gave them to him. They're pictures, Brett. Pretty images. But they're not my best work. When I went through all my photos after I got them back, you know what I discovered?"

"Tell me."

"My best work has happened since I got here. Felt inspired. Loved what I did. The imperfect perfect images I captured. The people in them who are real. I've captured love, happiness, joy. Sadness. Amazement. Life." She huffed out a long breath. "I don't care that he got those pictures. He can have them. I have my peace of mind back. He got what he wanted, and he'll leave me alone. He won't dare come back."

"How can you be so sure?"

"Officer Gallagher drove me to the hospital. I, ah, I told her what he did. Without him knowing, I taped the whole conversation. He agreed to leave me alone. I agreed to not file charges against him, if he dropped the ones against you and left us alone."

"And you believe him?"

"Hannah—that's Officer Gallagher's name—had a little chat with him. Told him I wrote out a complaint against him. If it gets filed, it will stop him from traveling. Needless to say, he agreed."

"And how did the pictures come into play?"

"I gave him the pictures as a thank-you for what he taught me."

I shook my head. "He doesn't deserve them."

"No, he doesn't. But the bottom line is, they're another level of insurance. I know the truth. So do other people. I had others from the same shoot in a different file that he'd never gotten around to touching. It shows my watermark. My work. I could prove it, and he knows it." I shook my head. "He told me he plans on leaving in a few days for his place in the Caribbean. He is selling his place here, and I'm not sure he'll be back. I just want him gone and out of my life."

"I hate that you gave up your work. That he gets credit for it."

"It doesn't matter anymore."

"It does to me."

She studied me for a moment, not speaking. Then she dropped a bombshell.

"That's what you do for the people you love, Brett. You make sacrifices."

KELLY

It took a moment for my words to sink in. I saw when understanding dawned in his eyes. His expression changed, his weary shoulders drawing back as if suddenly energized. The frown between his eyes lifted.

"Charly, you mean."

"And Maxx."

His shoulders drooped again. "Ah."

"And you," I said softly.

Our eyes locked and held. "But you're leaving," he said.

"For a *job*. I plan on coming back."

"But it's only temporary." He swallowed. "You need to be free. I can't keep you."

I sighed. "If you would stop jumping to conclusions and give me a chance to explain, you would understand something."

He dropped his head. "Sorry."

I couldn't resist sliding closer, covering his hand with mine. "It's okay. I know I hurt you before, Brett. I don't want to hurt you anymore."

He lifted my hand and kissed it. His voice was rough-sounding when he spoke. "Then talk."

"When Garner offered me the job, I was excited, yes. Thrilled. And all I could think of was the places I could go. The images I could capture and share." I squeezed his hand. "And how much I hoped you would come with me."

"What?"

"You said you wanted to see the world. We can do both, Brett. Have a life here and see all the wonderful places you've dreamed about. I can have my base here—with you. I told Garner I was only interested in three or four trips a year, and he said that was fine. I can plan them around us." I drew in a deep breath. "If there is an us."

"But you said—"

I stopped him. "Forget what I said. I am free with you, Brett. You give me that and so much more. You don't trap me. You let me breathe and live. You offer me support and love. Comfort. All the things I've never had before. The excitement you saw was because I could hardly wait to share all of it with you. And you were right. It wasn't the small town I hated. It was the life I was forced to lead. I love it here, but not because of the town. Because of the people. Because of *you*."

"I can't believe what I'm hearing."

"Believe it. Charly was right. She always said I was searching. But I had no idea what I was searching for until I almost lost it. I was looking for you. You give me everything I need. I was just too afraid to admit it." I hesitated. "I don't want to be afraid anymore. I want to live this life—with you." I swallowed. "If you still want that."

He turned, his knees pressing into mine. He clasped my hands, his larger ones shaking. "You said something earlier. I need to hear you say it again."

"I love you, Brett Conner. I love you more than anything."

He yanked me into his arms, his mouth covering mine. He kissed me, pulling me onto his lap. "Say it again."

"I love you."

He buried his face into my neck. "And I can keep you?"

"Yes."

"And we'll build a life together. Some of yours, some of mine?"

"Ours."

"I still hate you gave up your work."

"They're pictures. I can take more. There's only one you. You're worth more than anything else to me."

"Kelly," he whispered.

"Please say it," I whispered back.

"I love you, Kelly. I would follow you to the ends of the earth if that's what it took."

"How about just to Mexico?"

He kissed me. "That's a good place to start."

I woke up, wrapped in Brett. We had talked late into the night, then collapsed into bed, exhausted and worn, falling asleep fast. I had texted Charly, telling her all was good and Brett needed to come in late. Her response was fast.

Charly: He is covered for the week. Make your plans.

I cupped Brett's cheek, stroking his skin. He had a couple marks from where Carl had defended himself, but nothing major. Carl had looked a lot worse last night.

I was barely able to contain my hatred as I looked at him in his hospital bed. At first, he was smug, certain he had won. Until he noticed Officer Gallagher behind me and I informed him I had completed a report against him.

Then he shook his head. "Didn't happen here, if it happened at all."

"I have the hospital reports. It happened. I can file a report here. It will certainly make your career harder since you can't travel with a criminal record." I was totally bluffing, but he had no idea.

"What do you want?"

"Drop the charges against Brett, and I'll drop mine."

"What else?"

"I never want to see you, hear from you, about you, ever again." I pursed my lips. "And if I hear one thing about me, catch one piece of gossip, I am going to go public with the fact that you stole my work and claimed it as your own."

He peered behind me. "I need those other pictures."

I lifted my shoulders. I had already resigned myself to that fact. I didn't care anymore. "I might be persuaded. Drop the charges."

He picked up his phone and called his lawyer. A moment later, he nodded. "Done."

I pulled out my phone and tapped on the keys. "I emailed you the pictures."

He nodded.

"I have the email as proof, Carl. Stay the hell away from me and anyone I care about, and leave. I never want to see you again." I paused at the door. "Get some help, Carl. Stop wasting your life."

Then I walked out.

A touch on my cheek brought me out of my thoughts. Brett's eyes were warm and happy as he gazed at me. "Hi," he murmured.

"Hi."

"You were thinking pretty hard there."

I shook my head. "Just thoughts. Nothing major." I didn't want to talk about Carl anymore.

He yawned and stretched. "It's late. I slept in." The blanket fell away, exposing his torso. The morning light played on his muscles, highlighting them. I blinked and looked away.

"The garage is covered. Charly thought you might need some extra sleep to recover from your ordeal of being thrown in the slammer."

He chuckled. "She is getting too much enjoyment from this."

"I know."

"Would you go somewhere with me today, Shutterbug?"

"Yes."

"Okay. I need a shower, then I'm taking you to breakfast. I'm starving."

I let my gaze roam over him. He was relaxed, happy. He grinned as he met my eyes, and I couldn't help but notice the way the blanket was tenting over his growing erection.

"Anything I can help, ah, feed before we leave?" I asked, sliding my hand under the covers and wrapping it around him. He was thick and heavy in my hand. Steel encased in velvet. I swiped my thumb over the head, and he groaned, rolling on top of me.

"I thought you'd never ask."

A while later, we headed down the stairs toward his truck. We were both smiling, our hands linked together.

"Hey!"

We turned to see Chase jogging toward us. He wore a pair of coveralls with one of the garage hats on his head turned backward. He had a streak of grease on his cheek, and he was wiping his hands.

"Hey," Brett greeted him. "What's up?"

"I hear I missed all the excitement yesterday while I took Ward to be checked out at the hospital."

"How is he?" I asked.

"Fine. Some bruises and a scare, but he's good. Maxx is having the hoist fixed." He grinned. "So I missed the ass-kicking, you being hauled off to jail, Charly and her light fingers. All of it. You okay?"

Brett smirked. "I'm fine. In fact, I'm great." He wrapped his arm around my waist, tugging me close. "We're great."

Chase looked between us. "That is terrific. Everything, ah, settled?"

"Yep."

"So, what we talked about, Brett. It's a go?"

"I hope so."

I looked between them. "What is 'a go'?"

Brett winked. "You'll see."

Chase grinned. "Seriously. I'm glad you're both okay." He looked over past my shoulder. "Are you sure everything is settled?"

I looked back, seeing the police cruiser pulling up. I relaxed when I saw who stepped from the driver's side and turned back to Chase with a grin. This should be interesting. "Yep, everything is fine."

I nudged Brett, and we turned to watch as Officer Gallagher walked toward us. I heard Chase's fast intake of air, and I looked at him. He was watching her, a frown on his face as he tried to place her. I saw the recognition hit him, and he cursed under his breath.

"Hot damn."

She stopped as she got close to us. "Morning."

"Hey," Brett and I said at the same time.

"I just wanted to drop in and check on you. See how you are." Her gaze drifted to Chase, who was staring at her as if he'd seen a ghost.

"We're fine, Officer Gallagher," I assured her.

She smiled. "I told you, it's Hannah. At least when I'm off duty. And this is a personal visit."

Chase exhaled hard. *"Han-nah."*

She focused her attention on him. "Mr. Donner. You are far more alert than the last time we met. I trust you're not as tired." She paused. "Or intoxicated."

"It *is* you," he said, awestruck. "I thought you were a dream."

"I'm sorry?" she responded.

"I knew I'd spoken with a police officer, but I…" He trailed off. "Not you," he muttered. "Officer Cinnamon."

Brett and I watched the two of them with amusement. Chase was dumb struck, and she was sweet.

Brett cleared his throat. "Your car still in need of a tune-up, Hannah?"

She nodded, her eyes never leaving Chase's face.

"I can do it," Chase said, stepping forward. "I'll tune you up. I mean—your car. I can tune up your car."

"Awesome. I'll make an appointment."

"I can do that too." He held out his hand. "Come with me, and I'll arrange it. All of it."

She looked at his hand, and he grimaced. "Sorry. I, ah, I just didn't want you to trip on the uneven ground." He wiped his hand on his coveralls. "I'm dirty."

Her eyebrows flew up. "Pardon?"

"*My hand.* I mean my hand is dirty. I was working on an engine," he rambled.

She smiled at him. "I don't mind." Then she stepped forward, sliding her hand into his. "Really."

They walked away, neither of them acknowledging us aside from a quick wave from Hannah.

"Well, *that* is going to be interesting," I said.

"Yep. Fun to watch. His turn now," Brett replied with a chuckle. "Come on, woman. I'm dying of hunger."

I let him tug me to the truck. I was pretty damn hungry myself. Two orgasms in a row did that to a girl.

Not that I was complaining.

Later at breakfast, Brett kept grinning at me, then looking nervous.

"What are you up to?" I asked.

He shook his head. "Just enjoying my freedom. Life on the outside is sweet."

I burst out laughing.

He chuckled. "I love sitting across from you, Kelly. Having breakfast. Knowing I get to do that the rest of my life."

"There will be times you can't come with me."

"I know. But I also know you'll be back."

I entwined our fingers. "Always."

"Then I'm good. I'll miss you like hell, but I look forward to celebrating your return."

He finished his coffee. "Ready?"

"Yep."

He tugged me from the booth. "Then let's go."

We drove to his dad's store and went inside. Mack was working on his crossword puzzle and looked up with a smirk.

"I heard you were sprung."

Brett laughed and hugged his dad. "Charly's already been here?"

"Yep. Full of gossip." He eyed the way Brett's arm snaked around my waist. "I hear the two of you are finally communicating."

"Yes."

"Good. I like you two together. You're good for my son."

"We're going to Mexico," I said.

He nodded, stroking his chin. "Sounds great. You should see the world. Enjoy life."

I wandered over to the soda machine, unable to resist. I grabbed a bottle of orange to split with Brett, and as I turned, I saw his dad hand him something and wink.

Brett came over, taking the bottle and tipping it up, almost emptying it.

"Hey!" I protested.

"I'll buy you another when we come back. I need you to take a walk with me. I have to do something for Dad."

"Okay." I downed the last sip, still cold and somehow sweeter knowing Brett's mouth had been there before mine. I let him tug me from the store, and we walked in silence.

"I should have brought my camera," I mused.

He chuckled. "Next time."

A few moments later, we arrived at Rose Cottage.

"Oh," I breathed, once again caught in its charm. "Your dad needs something here?"

"Yep."

I followed him inside, once again smiling at the quirkiness. I trailed him into the living room. "Oh, some of the furniture is gone."

"The family sold the house. They're removing some things."

"Oh," I breathed out, a feeling of sadness tugging at my chest.

Brett smiled. "To me."

I gaped at him. "What?"

"You loved this place, Kelly. I saw it. I thought we could share it. Make it our home base."

"You bought it before…" I trailed off.

"I bought it when I hoped you loved me. When I hoped I was enough to stop your running. Your searching. I bought it because I loved you enough to hope that I was what you had been searching for."

I flung my arms around his neck, laughing and crying at the same time.

"I love you," I murmured. "I love you, I love you, I love you."

He held me tight. "I will never get tired of hearing you say those words." He kissed me. "You want to look around our new house?"

I cupped his face. "It's not just a house."

He smiled. "You're right. It's our home."

I nodded.

Home.

I had finally found it.

EPILOGUE

Two Weeks Later

BRETT

I shut my eyes as I chewed the last bite of ziti. Rosa Borelli could cook for the gods as far as I was concerned. I sighed, laying down my fork, full. I looked around the room filled with people. Laughing, talking, eating, and enjoying themselves. Rosa's table grew bigger all the time. Beside me, Kelly shifted, and I found her hand under the table and squeezed. She turned her head, meeting my eyes, smiling. Unable to resist, I leaned over and pressed a kiss to her cheek.

"Hey, Shutterbug."

She blushed, the sight amusing me. She was still getting used to being us in front of people. I loved this slightly shyer side I had discovered. I was also eagerly awaiting the day she was comfortable enough to return my caresses.

It would come. I had every faith now.

I cleared my throat. "So, I have a little news to share."

Everyone stopped talking and eating, staring in my direction.

"Kelly and I are leaving in two weeks. She's going on assignment, and I'm going with her."

"As her helper?" Theo asked. "Do you get to boss him around, Kelly, like Charly does Maxx?" He paused, rubbing his nose. "Or Mom does Dad?"

Everyone began to laugh, including Maxx. Neither he nor Stefano denied Theo's words, though.

"I am going to help her, but I'm going as her boyfriend. Her partner."

"How long you be gone?" Rosa asked.

"A month. Then when we get back, we're moving in to Rose Cottage. We get possession the day after we get back. And I'll be traveling with her a lot for the next while."

There was a chorus of congratulations. Some backslaps and lots of questions. Theo, of course, had his own queries.

"Are you getting married?"

Kelly and I had talked about that. Neither one of us wanted or needed a piece of paper to say we were together. Not now anyway. Maybe one day. We were both certain our future contained the other person, but we were happy to see where life led us.

"Not yet, bud."

Theo pursed his lips. "Is that legal?"

"Yeah, we're good."

"Okay, but if you get married, you'll have cake, right? And Nonna can make the supper."

I nodded, chuckling. "Both excellent ideas."

I lifted my plate and accepted some more ziti from Rosa. She sat beside my dad, looking happy and excited today. I assumed she was thrilled about having so many people over.

"What about the garage?" Vince asked. "Won't that leave a void?"

Maxx leaned back in his chair. "I have some news too. With Brett being gone so much for the foreseeable future, I hired a new mechanic. He'll be stepping in both in the front and the office to help Chase."

Vince nodded. "Makes sense. Where'd you find him?"

Stefano spoke up. "He hired Dom Salvatore. I worked with him in Toronto. He happened to drop by the garage one day—his car was acting up, and he pulled in. He was as surprised to see me as I was to see him. I'd heard he'd gone out west. We were talking, and then Maxx came over and I introduced them. One thing led to another…" He lifted his hands. "We got a new man on board."

"You bring him to lunch once, I think," Rosa said. "He was polite. Nice. Even with ink on his arms."

Stefano chuckled. "Tattoos don't make you a bad person, Mama. If they did, Gabby never would have fallen in love with me."

"I remember him. A little older than you, right? Really knowledgeable." his brother, Michael, asked.

"Yep, that's him. He'll be a great asset to the shop."

"I worked with him last week," Chase offered. "He was like a walking encyclopedia. I'm looking forward to learning from him."

"You bring him to eat again," Rosa commanded.

"Sure, Mama," Stefano agreed.

Then my father cleared his throat. "Since today seems to be the day for announcements, I have one."

All eyes were on him as he stood and placed his hand on Rosa's shoulder.

"It's my great honor to announce that Rosa has agreed to marry me."

For a moment, there was stunned silence. I cleared my throat. "Say what now?"

Stefano rose to his feet. "Did I just hear you right? Mama? You're getting married? You never said——"

She cut him off, standing beside my dad. She quelled everyone with one look.

"We are happy. We love each other. We no know how much time we have, so we are taking the happiness and hitting the road."

"You mean grabbing it," Charly corrected. "Brett is hitting the road."

"Ah—whatever." Rosa waved her off. "I make sure all my bambinos happy. It's my turn. Mack make me happy. And if you not happy, you leave." She nodded firmly and sat down, picking up her utensils. My dad sat down beside her, grinning.

I looked at Stefano's shocked face, then at the rest of his family. Gianna spoke up.

"Way to go, Mama. Congratulations to you and Mack."

Vince grinned. "You crazy kids. Enjoy it!"

Stefano and I shared a glance, and I began to laugh. "Welcome to the family, bro."

Theo clapped. "I knew it!"

Stefano dropped his head, his chest heaving in laughter. He met my gaze, shaking his head. "I can't fight love," he muttered.

"Nope," I agreed.

He stood and lifted his glass.

"To Mama and Mack. *Tanti auguri per una vita felice insieme.*"

I joined him. *"Salute,"* I said simply.

There were lots of well-wishes, and I knew at some point we'd be sitting down with them to discuss their plans for the future. But for now, they were enjoying their moment. I caught my dad's eye and winked. He beamed, and I had to admit I was thrilled, knowing he'd be happy while I was gone. No longer alone.

Theo bit into his bread, chewing thoughtfully. "Do I get to call you Grandpa?"

"I'd like that."

He turned to Stefano. "What will you call him, Dad?"

Stefano frowned, but before he could answer, Theo kept talking. "Mom and Charly call him *Daddy Mack.* Is that what you'll call him?"

The entire table burst into laughter, even Theo, who had no idea what he was laughing about.

Stefano wiped his eyes. "Probably just Mack, little man."

Theo wrinkled his nose. "Boring."

I was still laughing as I dug into my food again.

Nothing was ever boring around here. I highly doubted with Theo around it ever would be.

A YEAR LATER

BRETT

I glanced at my wife, napping with her head on my shoulder. I stretched in the warm, late-afternoon sun of Greece. The sheer beauty of the place was still astounding. The blue of the water. The white sands. The people. It was incredible.

The past year had been astonishing. Nothing prepared me for life with Kelly. The vistas I would see. The beauty I would discover. How different sunsets were in each place. The food, the people. Each trip made me long for the next one.

But then we would return to Littleburn and the life we had made there. Rose Cottage had become our haven. It was filled with mementos of our travels. The curved room that had fascinated Kelly so much was now her studio, the walls of our home covered in her photographs. She was sought-after and successful. She went on some assignments without me but said her favorites were when I was there with her. I hated seeing her leave, but I looked forward to her coming home. Because I knew she always would. She loved our life.

And she was happiest when we were tucked away in our own little slice of heaven. She was content and at peace. She loved the town, visiting my dad and Rosa, and taking pictures for the local paper. She did most of her work with Garner via email, only going into Toronto when she had to. So many things had changed in our lives, and all for the better.

I recalled the day I'd sat down with Maxx and Stefano.

"I need time away."

"How much?" Maxx asked.

"I'll be coming and going for the next year—at least."

His eyebrows shot up. "A year?"

"I'm going with Kelly on each of her assignments. I want to be with her. To see the world with her. None of them will be longer than a few weeks. But there could be others."

Maxx rubbed his chin.

"I have an idea," I said.

"I'm all ears."

"Chase could do the job. He knows the business. The contacts. The protocols, as well as I do. Make him assistant manager. When I'm here, great. When I'm gone, he steps in."

"He has no management experience," Stefano pointed out.

"Neither did I. I learned. So will he."

Charly strolled in and perched on Maxx's lap. He slipped an arm around her waist, tucking her close. "I think Brett is right. He's learned so much from all of you. We can hire another gofer," she offered.

"I wasn't aware you were invited to this meeting," I said dryly, knowing that was BS. Charly always was involved, even if we tried to meet in secret. She always knew.

She only smiled. Then she shifted. "Holy moly, big man. Stop poking that at me."

Maxx chuckled and reached into his pocket. "This time, it is a wrench, Red. Sorry to disappoint."

"Hmmph. I'm losing my touch."

"Okay, back to the issue at hand," I muttered. "Take your foreplay elsewhere later."

Charly laughed and Maxx grunted.

"We'll figure out my salary and all the particulars."

Charly laughed. "You all get a month holiday a year. I put that in the partner agreement. You, Brett, have never taken a day. None of you has used all your time. So we can start with you using that time, and then we'll discuss salary."

"Great."

"What about the house?" Stefano asked.

"Chase is looking for a new roommate. He was going to advertise, I think."

"Wow. New job, new roommate—things are changing for our boy."

"Yep."

"You too." Charly smiled. "I've never known Kelly to be so peaceful and happy."

I winked. "Then my job is done."

"What are you smiling at?" Kelly asked, her voice still thick with sleep.

"Thinking about the last year. All the things we've seen." I pressed a kiss to her head. "About going home and reconnecting to our life there."

She snuggled closer. "Yeah. I'm looking forward to going home."

I loved hearing her refer to Littleburn and our cottage as home. It made my heart beat a little faster.

"Do you think they'll be mad?"

I picked up her hand, kissing the thick band that matched the one on my own finger. "That we got married here? No. Charly will pretend to be pissed, then inform us she's having a party, which we will graciously agree to, and all will be well."

"It was so perfect," Kelly whispered. "Just us and the sand and waves."

I chuckled. "The justice of the peace and the two witnesses helped."

"They were background noise. All I saw was you."

I lowered my head and kissed her. "All I ever see is you. No matter what surrounds us, you always stand out to me, my beautiful wife."

She pushed up on my chest, making the hammock swing. "I love you."

I brushed a lock of her hair behind her ear. She'd let it grow, and I loved how it looked hanging to her shoulders, a sleek, dark ribbon of silk.

"I love you, Kelly Conner."

"Do you want babies now?"

I looked at her, surprised. "I thought we agreed another couple years of travel, then we'd discuss it."

We had agreed we wanted children, but we wanted to explore first. I had been surprised Kelly was interested in being a mom, but she'd admitted seeing Charly and Gabby with their kids made her realize she wanted a child. And she loved watching me with the kids, imagining they were ours. I was thrilled but also happy to wait a while. I wanted her to myself for a bit, then we could expand our family.

Was she ready now?

"I just want you to know if you decided you were ready, I would adjust my plans."

"I want us both to be ready. To go on to that part of our journey with no regrets."

"I would never feel regret having your baby."

"Soon," I promised. "We'll discuss it next year."

She slid her hands up my torso. "Okay. Next year." She nibbled on my neck, flicking her tongue out to tease my skin. "We could still practice."

I was out of the hammock with her in my arms in ten seconds.

"Yeah, we can, Shutterbug. Practice makes perfect."

She hummed into my neck.

"We already are, Brett. We already are."

And she was right.

Are you ready for Chase's story?

Keep reading for a taste of what is to come in UNDER THE RADAR.

Enjoy meeting other readers? Lots of fun, with upcoming book talk and giveaways! Check out Melanie Moreland's Minions on Facebook.

Join my newsletter for up-to-date news, sales, book announcements and excerpts (no spam). Click here to sign up Melanie Moreland's newsletter
or visit https://bit.ly/MMorelandNewsletter

Visit my website www.melaniemoreland.com

Enjoy reading! Melanie

SNEAK PEEK OF UNDER THE RADAR

CHASE

I ran a hand through my hair, sitting on the sofa.

What a clusterfuck.

When I'd advertised for a roommate, I thought it would be easy to find someone.

Some of the people I interviewed today were downright scary. Two of them, I was certain, were only here to case the joint. I made a big point of talking about the state-of-the-art security system and the guns I kept in the house.

I had neither, but I hoped that would deter them.

One woman who showed up asked me for reduced rent. She'd "make it up in other ways," she informed me with a lewd wink. She even offered a sample.

I got rid of her as quickly as I could.

Another woman was searching for someone to look after her. When I explained the shared duties, she pulled on her hair and asked me if I could just "do all that stuff" and she'd stay out of the way. I could barely manage on my own, so I wasn't what she needed.

The obviously high dude who asked about using the basement to grow his necessary "medicine" was a no-go as well.

I was ready to give up.

There had only been one decent possibility, and he had called an hour after he was here to say he'd found another place.

I sighed, looking around. It was a great house. Easily shared, but if I didn't find a roommate, I would have to beg Charly to let me go back to the apartment since I couldn't afford to live here on my own.

I knew if I told her, she would laugh and remind me I had millions in the bank, but I refused to touch that money. It was used to help others because it never did me any good when I needed it. I didn't want to use it now.

The doorbell sounded, and I frowned in confusion. I wasn't expecting anyone else. I opened the door a little faster than I should, startling the person on the other side.

Amber eyes, golden-red hair, and thousands of dots of cinnamon on a heart-shaped face that haunted my dreams met my astonished stare. She smiled, her overwhelming prettiness becoming beautiful. I had to swallow before I could speak.

"Officer Cinn—I mean, Gallagher. Is there a problem?"

She shook her head. "You had an ad up in the general store looking for a roommate. Did you find one?"

I gaped at her.

"You wanna be my roommate?"

"Well, I need a place to live. You need a roommate. Solves two problems, I think." She frowned. "May I come in?"

"Oh, right. Yes, of course, come in."

She walked in, her scent swirling as she squeezed past and headed to the living room. I followed in her wake, greedily inhaling. The urge to reach out and touch was strong, but I resisted.

"So you're looking for a new place?" I asked.

She smiled as she sat down. "Yes, I am." She winked. "So much so I took down your ad. I'm the only one to apply."

"Ah, I had one in the paper." I leaned forward. "The applicants were scary."

"Good. Then I guess you've been waiting for me, right?"

She had no idea.

She crossed her legs. "Ask me anything, Chase."

My throat went dry.

Jesus. My wet dream was sitting across from me, her sexy calves on display. She wanted to live in this house. With me. I'd see her every day. Hear her talk and laugh. Maybe see her in a towel.

Or less.

I dropped my head. If I let her move in her with me, I was in so much trouble. It was a really, really bad idea.

"When can you move in?" I blurted out.

She laughed. "Oh, you are a funny one."

I had to look away. I had been serious.

And my first instinct was right, except I was beyond trouble.

The fact was, I was totally fucked.

ACKNOWLEDGMENTS

As usual, a few thanks.

Lisa, another one done. Another one coming. You aren't getting rid of me. #Sorrynotsorry. I bet that no space thing is driving your cra cra isn't it? Heh heh heh. Love you!

Beth, thank you for your feedback and support. Your comments make the story better—always.

Melissa, Trina, Carol, and Deb—thank you for your keen eyes, laughter, and support.

Kim, your laughter during our meetings as Karen and I trade insults really only encourages our behavior. Just saying.

Karen, I adore you today. Probably tomorrow too. Day after? Looking good. May the odds ever be in your favor. LOL. I love you more than coffee and that is saying something.

Seriously, thank you both. I don't understand 99% of what you do but it is impressive. Love you both.

Nina (Valentine PR). Thank you—Kim and Karen ran me out of words.

To all the bloggers, readers, and my promo team. Thank you for everything you do. Shouting your love of books—of my work, posting, sharing—your recommendations keep my TBR list full, and the support you have shown me is deeply appreciated.

My reader group, Melanie's Minions—love you all.

MLM—for all you do I cannot say thank you enough. I wish I could hug you all.

Matthew—the man, the myth, the legend. You are all that and more. Always.

ALSO AVAILABLE FROM MORELAND BOOKS

Titles published under M. Moreland

Insta-Spark Collection

It Started with a Kiss

Christmas Sugar

An Instant Connection

An Unexpected Gift

Harvest of Love

An Unexpected Chance

Following Maggie (Coming Home series)

Titles published under Melanie Moreland

The Contract Series

The Contract (Contract #1)

The Baby Clause (Contract #2)

The Amendment (Contract #3)

The Addendum Coming to Radish 2022 - Wide Release 2023

Vested Interest Series

BAM - The Beginning (Prequel)

Bentley (Vested Interest #1)

Aiden (Vested Interest #2)

Maddox (Vested Interest #3)

Reid (Vested Interest #4)

Van (Vested Interest #5)

Halton (Vested Interest #6)

Sandy (Vested Interest #7)

Vested Interest Box Set (Books 1-3)

Vested Interest Box Set (Books 4-7)

Vested Interest/ABC Crossover

A Merry Vested Wedding

ABC Corp Series

My Saving Grace (Vested Interest: ABC Corp #1)

Finding Ronan's Heart (Vested Interest: ABC Corp #2)

Loved By Liam (Vested Interest: ABC Corp #3)

Age of Ava (Vested Interest: ABC Corp #4)

Men of Hidden Justice

The Boss

Second-In-Command

The Commander

Reynolds Restorations

Revved to the Maxx

Breaking The Speed Limit

Shifting Gears

Mission Cove

The Summer of Us

Standalones

Into the Storm

Beneath the Scars

Over the Fence

The Image of You (former title My Image of You)

Changing Roles

Happily Ever After Collection

Heart Strings

ABOUT THE AUTHOR

NYT/WSJ/USAT international bestselling author Melanie Moreland, lives a happy and content life in a quiet area of Ontario with her beloved husband of thirty-plus years and their rescue cat, Amber. Nothing means more to her than her friends and family, and she cherishes every moment spent with them.

While seriously addicted to coffee, and highly challenged with all things computer-related and technical, she relishes baking, cooking, and trying new recipes for people to sample. She loves to throw dinner parties, and enjoys traveling, here and abroad, but finds coming home is always the best part of any trip.

Melanie loves stories, especially paired with a good wine, and enjoys skydiving (free falling over a fleck of dust) extreme snowboarding (falling down stairs) and piloting her own helicopter (tripping over her own feet.) She's learned happily ever afters, even bumpy ones, are all in how you tell the story.

Melanie is represented by Flavia Viotti at Bookcase Literary Agency. For any questions regarding subsidiary or translation rights please contact her at flavia@bookcaseagency.com

Made in the USA
Monee, IL
14 July 2022

99711385R00184